[R A G S]

ANDREA ANDERSON

RAGS

©Andrea Anderson

All rights reserved. This book or any portion thereof may not be reproduced or used in any manner whatsoever without the express written permission of the publisher except for the use of brief quotations in a book review.

ISBN: 979-8-35094-161-6

[Preface]

Max sat back in his soft leather office chair with his feet on his desk as he sipped a glass of aged Buffalo Trace bourbon. He was completely relaxed, and as the warm golden-brown liquor slid down his throat it gave him a warm glow of comfort. Max was glorying in the ginormous success his last book had and the sales were off the wall. Now a movie company wanted to buy the rights to the book to make a film. His chest was so puffed up it was about to tear his shirt to pieces.

That feeling lasted for about a day and a half, and then he began wondering what he would do next. How could he top himself? He tried to think but his mind was a blank. Max got up and peered out his office window. As he looked down at the park he had a brainstorm. Why not write about the homeless people I see down there in the park? Why do they live on the street? Its something I have always wondered about. To make it real and authentic I would have to do some research.

Max's brain began to whirl. I probably would have to go and live on the streets to see what really goes on out there in order to be genuine in my writing. How bad could it be? I would just stay on the street until I had enough material collected and then come right back to my penthouse and write the book. Right then and there he decided to do it.

The Oxford English Dictionary describes the word rags as, "a piece of old clothes especially one torn from a larger piece and used typically for cleaning things. Or a newspaper typically one regarded as being of low quality "the local rag." The connotation of the term rags indicates that rags are a worthless thing, they are not much use, things meant to be thrown away because they are no longer of any value. Some people feel this way about people who live on the street.

This story is about homeless people, the unwanted rags of humanity that people don't like or want to see, like old rags. Most of these street people are empty souls that have had something happen in their lives that they couldn't cope with, and it literally changed their lives. Some are mean, evil and ugly, some are mentally ill and still others addicts, and there are those who are plain lazy and want to suck off the system. Still others are lonely, but many of them are just poor, sad victims that can no longer make it in their life situations or cope with what they have witnessed in their life. Beware! It could happen to the best of us. What Max didn't know is how his new project would change his life. He had no idea of the real dangers and the challenges that lurk in every minute of living on the street. In the blink of an eye, life as he knew it was gone and now, he was in grave danger.

[Chapter 1]

It was a huge adjustment but after two weeks Max felt more comfortable than the first day, he hit the street. Things had been going good so far even though being out there was a challenge Max had been able to make it. Soon he would go back to his penthouse, take his time writing his book, and everything would be back to normal, then he would get on with his life. Spending a few more weeks on the street would give him just enough time to collect material for his book. He would get to know some of these people and ask them why they lived like that. Maybe Charlene, his girlfriend, would even come back to him. She thought that his idea to live on the street was crazy. She was so weirded out when he told her what he was going to do, she lost it. Getting home late one night he found the apartment empty and a note from Charlene telling him he was crazy, and she was out of there.

    That was several weeks ago, now Max was sitting in his cardboard house trying to think of anything but food. Though his gut was having none of it, it seemed as if his stomach had a mind of its own, it wanted food and right friggen now. It growled and rumbled and wouldn't stop. He thought maybe he could forget about food for a little while if he were able to go to sleep but as soon as he laid down, it began to rain. Soon strong winds began gusting and swirling around the house. The storm made the temperature drop, and it got cold, now Max was freezing. To make matters worse, the rain got heavier and began battering down on the flimsy, cardboard structure he had called home for the last few weeks. Rain was coming down in buckets with hail that seemed to be as big as golf balls. When the edge of the roof which was made of double cardboard sheets began flapping, he knew he would have to find another place to stay after this downpour was over.

In typical Max fashion he had paid a homeless man to make this cardboard house for him, thinking he would only need it for a short time so why not, It wouldn't matter how sturdy it was. He was totally annoyed by his own lack of judgment and now this deluge seemed to prove it. Shit! I can't stay here through this cloudburst. I'll have to find a new place to sleep because water is pouring in. What a pain in the ass, I'm not sure I still want to put all this effort into this project. I did ok so far but now things are getting much harder and I used up all the money I brought with me, I'm freezing, I'm starving and soon I'll be soaking wet. Right now, I don't know what to do. Maybe my idea was bizarre and not doable. After this storm is over, I should probably get going back to my apartment and my old life. It was easy to walk away from everything when I had a belly full of food and a pocket full of money, but now it has become complicated, so I have to plan on how to get back. My scheme to get here worked well but I should have put more thought into how I would get back. To be honest I'm not sure anybody knew I was gone or really missed me, except for some people at work. Anyway, I can't come up with a plan right now with this monsoon distracting me, trying to stay dry and being hungry are my major problems right now.

For the next hour Max shivered and shook and tried to figure out what he was going to do next. If this storm ever stops, I'll have to go out to find some food somewhere before I starve. It might be time for me to start begging. It's upsetting to think of, and something I never dreamed I would have to do, but it's my last resort. I clearly remember how people walking down the street seeing people going through trash felt repulsed and sort of unconsciously moved away from homeless people not wanting to touch them or get near them and especially not to make eye contact with them.

If I begin begging I will worry that someone might recognize me. I should have stuck to my guns when I protested about having my picture placed on the jacket of my last book, but my editor insisted, and it had to go to press quickly so I gave in. There must be another way rather than me begging, maybe I should consider eating out of dumpsters, YUCK! The very thought of that makes me want to barf, but that would be better than starving and easier than begging and it would keep me secluded by sticking to back alleys. I still have my lucky coin, it might be worth something, but no matter what I can't use that I have to hold on to it because it has brought me this far. Once I get some food then I will have time to settle down and think about whether I should stay out here or not.

The cardboard house swayed and trembled as another gust of wind blew through the thin walls and sheets of rain and hail came down every which way. Max heard a burst of thunder and then a loud ripping noise as the entire top of his little cardboard house was blown off. To make matters worse the rain and hail began pelted down stinging his face and hands. Max knew it was time he got out of there. He gathered up his stuff and made a run for the closest dry spot he could think of which was under the ramp of the abandoned warehouse. It was higher than the street and had some pitch to it so that water didn't pool. Max made a mad dash to the metal ramp and crawled under it. He covered the sides with some old plastic bags he found that had been thrown under the ramp, thinking it would save him from getting completely soaked from the blowing rain.

Now under the ramp, Max was grateful he was out of the storm and protected and he felt better at once. It was dryer, and much roomer than he expected. Temporarily forgetting about his hunger and being cold, he was happy to be protected from the storm and he settled in. Using the few dry clothes, he had safeguarded in plastic bags as a pillow he laid down and tried to doze. As soon as the storm passed, he would go and try to find something to eat.

Just as Max felt himself begin to relax and start to drift into a deep sleep, he heard a sound like a motorcycle. He listened closely, but the noise stopped suddenly, so he paid no more attention to it and tried to go back to sleep. It was only a matter of a few minutes before he heard loud shouting. Why in the world would anybody be out in this nasty weather, especially on a motorcycle, was Max's first thought. Worried that the noisemakers might be looking for a dry place to escape from the storm, he was concerned they might try to get into the warehouse and discover his safe spot.

As a precaution he covered his body as best as he could and stayed as still as possible, hoping the plastic covering would hide him. He laid there quietly and listened wanting to see if the noise makers were gone or still there. He had to know in case they spotted him, and he had to make a fast get-away. But before sticking his head out completely to see what was going on, he listened intently and heard two voices. They were male, loud, and harsh, and it sounded as if they were arguing. The voices didn't seem to come closer, which was a good thing and Max sat as still as a mouse not wanting them to discover his hidey hole. He strained to hear the voices so he could be ready to bolt if these men discovered he was there. Then a male voice shouted, "Why are we stopping here? This is stupid. Tell me why we are out in this God dammed storm anyway?"

Another male voice responded angrily, "We're here to talk. I'm telling you for the last time, you need to let her alone and stop accepting money from her."

The first voice answered, "Just a minute, you bring me out in the rain just to tell me that? You must be simple. You might think you are her guardian but I'm the man, she loves. That's why she buys me expensive things, she wants me to be happy."

To Max it sounded like two very angry dudes, arguing over a woman. Their threats sounded as bad as Muhammad Ali and Joe Frazier just before their fight saying nasty, vile things and threatening each other.

Max dubbed the second voice Ali. He shouted, "She buys you things with my money. I have had enough of your interfering bullshit. If you don't leave her alone, I will do something bad to you, I swear, I can't take this God damn shit much longer."

Joe responded sarcastically, "What the Hell do you mean? What bullshit? It would make her very unhappy if she heard you talk like that or if I got hurt, and of course, you know I would have to tell her who did it and she would make you pay for it in more ways than just monetarily. I'll tell her you were in a jealous rage, and you acted like a wild beast, she would hate that. Why did you ever ask me to come here and introduce her to me anyway? You know I have a way with women, and since when is it your money anyway? It's her money and you are just using it to your own advantage, you fucking parasite."

Ali, ignored the questions, and shouted as if he was telling the world, "I can't stand it when I see her in your arms it makes me crazy. I'm asking you, NO, I'm telling you, not to see her again and to get out of this town for good and I mean it!"

Joe laughed in his face, "Not in your wildest dreams lover boy, that is not going to happen. I like it here and if anything happens to me, she will know you were at the bottom of it, and she will reject you once again. What are you going to do murder me? Right old chum and he gave a horse laugh. One more thing who died and left you boss? You boss! That's a joke. Everybody knows you swooped in after her father passed and began exploiting all of it, her business, her money, and her home. She was in no shape to handle her father's death and you knew it. Anyway, how would you get away with killing me? Everybody knows you hate me, and that you're a jealous monster, and an asshole and they know you wish I was dead."

Ali responded, "Ok I tried to talk to you, but you are now and always will be a stupid, pig-headed bastard so we will do this my way. I tried to do this the civilized way but that was a failure that person let me down, so now I have to do this myself."

Suddenly Joe's voice changed, and he sounded concerned and said, "What are you doing with that thing in your hand, you can't be serious?" Put that down, that whatever you call it, put it up now before you hurt yourself! You know I'm stronger than you, and I Oh! Oh! my God, d, d, d, d!"

Max heard loud zinging and hissing sounds and couldn't stand not seeing what was happening. On instinct and before he could think it through, he crawled out from under the ramp, stepped up to the top and looked over and could see the whole area.

"Here have another little zap from this stun gun. How does that feel? Do you like it? Mr. Fucking Snooky asshole?" Ali cried out in a high-pitched voice. Didn't anyone ever tell you can say too much? You never know when to shut up!"

Max stood mesmerized. From his bird's eye view he saw Ali tasing Joe who was now lying on the ground shaking uncontrollably. The man on the ground tried to talk but his words came out in a rat-a tat tat sound like a machine gun. "S, st top,p,p! Pleass s s e Sto o o o op!

Ali got down on his knees and began screaming obscenities at the man, he zapped Joe several more times than he threw the stun gun aside. He was out of control and began punching Joe's face and body, pommeling him until several cuts opened on Joe's face. Shrieking with angry curses, Ali pulled out a knife and slashed at Joe's chest and abdomen like a madman.

A bright red stain appeared and quickly turned pink as the rain poured down and mixed with the blood from Joe's body. Not stopping, Ali was now in a frenzy and kept on stabbing at Joe mercilessly. As Max watched he thought Ali must have hit Joe's femoral artery because blood came pouring out from his pants leg puddling around his body. Ali looked at the gushing blood and watched as it pooled on the ground. Then he began stabbing Joe again.

When he finally stopped, he looked at Joe's face. His eyes were closed, and he was not moving. Halting for a moment as if thinking what to do Ali pulled Joe's watch and ring off, took his wallet and dragged the body over to the side of the building. He piled trash, old newspapers, garbage, and anything else he could find on the ground, trying to hide the body, as he did this Ali screeched, "No one will find you for days mister fucking wise guy. You couldn't keep your mouth shut, could you? No one will find you in this pile of trash for a long time and it's exactly where you belong with trash. That means no one will report the crime too soon while I set up a perfect alibi for myself."

Max was so awe-struck by what he just saw, he forgot he was holding his metal water bottle and dropped it on the metal ramp which made a very loud clanking sound of metal on metal. The noise caught Ali's attention and made him pause, gathering more trash. He turned and looked in Max's direction. Max stood frozen in place.

Ali screamed out and pointed at Max, "I see you! You over there! Don't move!" And he started running toward Max. Max snapped out of his trance, turned, and ran for his life. He ran as fast as he could and didn't stop until he came to an area with a lot of trees along the roadside. He was exhausted, he stopped for a minute and looked back down the road to see if anyone was following him. He saw no one, that made him felt better and he took a few minutes to rest. He got up and looked down the road again, that's when he saw a figure on a bike in the distance. Shit! Shit! Shit! He hesitated for only a second and then leaped over the guardrail and began running again close to the trees until he couldn't run any more. His legs were shaking, and his head throbbed, he was soaking wet. Turning around again he could see that the figure on the bike was gaining on him. It had to be Ali following him. Max was frantic, scared and physically spent, he slid to the ground and only managed to crawl. He crawled along slowly, knowing he could not go much further, and then he saw a pipe sticking out of the side of the bank of the road. He looked in it and thought he could fit into it, so he stuffed himself inside the storm drainpipe. He lay there straining to catch his breath trying to be as still as his trembling body would allow and he listened for the sound of the motorcycle and as the noise got closer, he was sure he was going to die.

[Chapter 2]

The noise of the motorcycle was whirring alternately between a soft and loud whine as Ali drove up and down the side of the road looking for Max. Ali stopped the bike on the road close to the drainpipe, got off and looked around. He looked over the guard rail and nothing was moving, he scanned the area for a few minutes looking for any sign of activity.

Max knew Ali was close because he could smell the odor of the bike's exhaust. Ali shut off the bike and listened intently. After what seemed like an eternity, he started the bike and road away. Max stayed in his position with his ears attuned to any noise, afraid to even breathe. It got quiet and Max was grateful but vigilant. Soon the rumble of the bike sounded again as Ali rode up again slowly and stopped the bike once more. He got off and went to the side of the road and shouted out as loud as he could, "I know you're out there, and you can hear me. So, hear this! I will hunt you down till I find you and then do what needs to be done. I will never allow a filthy, dirty, scum, street bum like you to ruin my career." He got back on the bike and rode away.

Max stayed in the pipe as long as he could. After a while he couldn't stand it anymore. He had been in the pipe in fetal position for what seemed like an eternity and finally found the courage to come out. He inched out of the pipe, though still petrified. His first thought was that I should have tried to help save Joe, I'm such a coward, but I was so scared my feet were frozen in place. What do they say fight or flight I really couldn't do anything I was dumbfounded. Could I have made a difference? I'm sure Joe was already dead after losing all that blood. Max's body shook as he realized it was true Joe was dead. He knew he needed to get out of there as quickly as he could and never go back to that place again. "

Good God," Max said out loud, as he tried to stand, "I can hardly move my arms and my legs they are so stiff from lying in that stupid pipe. I ache all over. This is not the movies where the guy gets up and runs for miles without an ache or pain. No matter, as sure as God made little green apples, if Ali found me, he would have killed me. What should I do now?" If I go to the police, they will never believe me and probably blame this crime on me, and I don't want any part of jail. I'm not sure he saw my face, but I can't take a chance. Oh God! My Jesus! It just hit me! I almost forgot my IDs are back at my cardboard house or what's left of it. I'll have to go back and get my credentials. I have nothing to prove who I am.

After slowly getting his legs to move again Max cautiously went back to the place where his cardboard house was, he waited a long time to be sure no one was around, and he avoided the spot where the body was. He was nervous that Ali might go back there to try to find him. When he thought the coast was clear, Max went to his old cardboard house and saw what was left of it. It was now nothing but a pile of debris, but he had to search for his info. He needed them to prove who he was if he was confronted by the police. He had to find his driver's license and passport. He desperately needed them. As soon as he found them, he was going to go back to his old life and forget this whole nightmare and this cockamamie idea of writing about people who lived on the street and things that happened to them, he had enough of that bad pipedream.

The roof of the cardboard house had been blown away and the walls were hanging by a thread and would drop very soon so Max searched quickly. He had placed the documents in a waterproof bag underneath the floor, but first put them in a hole he dug and covered it with a layer of dirt and put a piece of red plastic over the area. He covered that whole area with an old tarp. Max began ripping up what was left of the floor looking for the documents, the tarp had been blown away by the storm and there was no sign of the red plastic square. He started having a panic attack as reality began to set in. He stabbed at the floor with an old spoon. With the tarp gone the dirt was wet and soupy. Max scraped away the top layer of dirt with his hands. The documents had to be there, they just had to be there. Max sing songed to himself. I have to find them; I must find them. He searched one half of the floor with no luck. He tried to stay cool. I must have misjudged where I buried the documents, I'll try another place. Again, he dug down and nothing. Now he was in full blown panic mode. He dug frantically into the soil with his hands like a dog digging for a bone, still he found nothing. Desperate now, he dug in other sections with still no reward. Beginning to get hysterical Max began to wonder if somehow Ali had come back and found the documents. I can't think like that, I must stay focused. Again, he dug with great urgency ripping up the rest of floor. He found a button, a penny, and an old battery but no documents. He sat back in a semi-kneeling position and tried to quiet himself. He closed his eyes, his fingertips were raw, and bleeding and tears of frustration came down, making small roads in his mud-stained face, as he tried to regain his composure. Once more he tried digging and found a fragment of what he thought was his plastic driver's license, but he couldn't be sure. Eyeing the torn-up floor he saw only a pile of muddy soil and nothing more.

    With his fingernails down to the quick, his hands and knees caked with mud and his clothes filthy he felt defeated. What am I going to do now? Crazy ideas raced through his mind. Either one of two things happened. Ali came back and found my credentials, or the wind had blown them somewhere and they would never be found. He had to come up with a plan to get himself back to his old life. But how? Who would believe him and this horrible story? He had no proof. Everybody wanted ID these days.

He had no money. That terrible man, that butcher threatened to find me. Does he know what I look like? All of a sudden Max heard sirens wailing, they seemed to be coming closer. He got up, gathered the few things he had and ran from the area.

Certain that the sirens meant that the cops were coming for him, he ran again. He had to get away, where would he go now? He had no money and no place to go. He had closed all his accounts and put the money where he couldn't touch it and he couldn't get back into his apartment. I did all that because I didn't want to be tempted to go back if I got discouraged, that's a laugh now, that was brilliant, wasn't it?

What am I going to do now? Did Ali see my face well enough to search for me? Max knew he would have a hard time convincing the police to believe who he was with all his identification gone, especially the way he looked with mud all over and his hands bleeding, he looked wild. Could he hide during the day and come out at night until they caught Ali for the murder. Wait a minute, that might never happen. All I have as evidence are the voices in my head. This is all incredible! In the name of God what have I done to myself? How stupid could one be? These circumstances make me a fugitive, a night crawler. How will I survive? I didn't intend for any of this to happen. Now I don't have to pretend that I'm homeless and scared, it's true. I can't go back, at least not now, not until the murder is cleared up. What a cliché! This is like a twist of Fate! What am I going to do now I don't have a backup plan?

Max ran until he collapsed on a park bench, too exhausted to go on. The physical exercise and emotional trauma had consumed all of Max's strength and he fell into a deep stuporous sleep.

[Chapter 3]

After several hours, Max awoke and went to the public restroom in the park and tried to get the mud off his hands and face at least. He was as filthy as a pig that had rolled in mud. Afterward he wandered around aimlessly for the next few days wondering how in the world this happened to him and what was he going to do. He knew he had only himself to blame but he had never dreamed he would be an eyewitness to a murder. I guess my grandfather was right when he would say, "nothing's faster than disaster." Maybe I should try and contact Charlene, Max thought. On second thought that was not a good idea she was so into herself she would be totally repulsed by me now.

Stashing his stuff in a clump of bushes Max hung around the park. He was brooding and beating himself up thinking of questions that could not be answered over and over. Trying to figure out his next moves and find answers to his problems, he wondered how long he could survive living on the street now that all his money was gone, and he was hungry and in bad trouble. He felt that his books had become a success because he had done the research and almost literally crawled into the role of his characters. He had the means to devote all his time to writing because he could support himself without worrying about proceeds from his books. He received a monthly salary from the business run by his father's competent staff and there was money, stocks and partial ownership of the business that made him want for nothing. He was lucky, he had been successful at writing, and he enjoyed that so much. He had it all, but he could not touch any of it now.

Often Max questioned his own determination about why he was so intent on having his writing be genuine and valid. Maybe it was because he had experienced how his father lived such a phony pretentious life pretending, he was happy in his marriages and that he liked the bogus way his family lived. Max had come to realize what a lie all that was and that his father had thrown away so much of his life. He always remembered his very early days when his mother, Jessie, was with them, and she tried so hard to make them a family. His father was an arrogant self-serving SOB that had it made mainly because his own father died, and he had inherited everything.

As he roamed the city looking for a new place to settle down, he knew he could not go back to the area of his cardboard house any longer. He approached several places where homeless people stayed but was shunned by the people there who were suspicious of everybody. Max began sleeping on park benches, but this was a tricky deal because the bench had to be one that was very secluded because if the police found you, they would not only wake you up, if you were drunk, they would haul you to jail, or make you leave that area.

On Max's second night on the same bench, he found some old newspapers and he was planning to cover himself with for warmth. As he opened the paper, he saw the social page headlines. Wealth heiress in a deep depression after lover disappears. Max read the article with interest and immediately knew that had to be Joe. The story said that the man was missing for over a week and that they suspected foul play. They found a unidentified male body in the area of an abandoned warehouse, and they were trying to identify it. The article went on to say that an eyewitness had come forward to say he saw a homeless man running away from the area where the body was found. The body had been beaten and there was no identification or valuables on the victim. The description of the vagrant was inconclusive, but it would have fit Max to a tee. A feeling of fear made Max's belly tighten and he felt anxious, he thought, that Son of a Bitch, that asshole, set all this up and now he wants to pin the murder on me. What the Hell am I going to do now? Why did I ever think I could survive on the street, what a fantasy this was. That night Max was sleeping on a park bench when two teenagers began to harass him. He alarmed them when he sat up and began to act as if he were crazy, He swung his fists at them and screamed, and they got scared and left. Max couldn't get to sleep after that and walked around aimlessly the rest of the night afraid to even sit on another bench.

Drifting around for over a week now Max was just about out of steam. He had lived on half eaten lunches he found in park trash cans, getting a bit here and there and drinking water from the park fountains. He even attempted to get food from dumpsters after other street people had taken what they wanted and now he was hungry, tired, filthy, and discouraged.

In a quandary about what to do. Max pulled up the hood of the jacket and walked down the street with the intention of begging on the corner. It began to snow, and Max found a hoodie someone left on a bench, he added that to what he had on and sucked his head in as deep as he could into the hoodie turtlelike and lowered his head. As he walked, he saw a woman coming toward him in the distance wearing a red coat. Maybe if I ask politely, she will give me some money, he thought.

As the woman approached Max, he held out his hand and as nicely as he could he said, "Can you please give me a handout?" She took her hand out of her pocket and handed him a dollar.

He said thank you so much."

Max stood holding the dollar, something was troubling, it wasn't that she gave him a dollar, it was her voice. It was very familiar. He racked his brain trying to think of where he heard that voice before? Then it hit him like a thunder bolt! That was Ellie. She was the woman he had worked with on his first book, she helped him edit it. That was months ago, I must look like I belong on the street if she didn't recognize me, Max decided. He looked up to see if he could catch up to her, she could probably help him if he could get her to recognize him. He started to chase after her, but it was too late, she was long gone. What in the world was she doing in this part of the city, he wondered.

After three sleepless nights Max was about to collapse. He was so cold he thought he was going to freeze to death. He looked for a place where there were outdoor workers who warmed themselves at intervals. Max found a warehouse that had a heated office. He watched the workers go in and out from time to time to get warm. After they left for the day Max piled up some wooden pallets next to the side of the building that was still warm and fell asleep. The noise of the workers arriving the next morning woke him up and he went back to the park. He sat in a secluded part of the park that had a good view of the benches, and he watched people as they sat and ate lunch to see if they would throw away any food.

As he waited, he dozed on and off and awoke when he smelled the faint odor of bacon. He began to salivate and immediately assumed he was dreaming. He sat up. And saw a man sitting on a rock near him eating a sandwich. The man grinned showing his only three teeth as Max rubbed his eyes in disbelief. The man didn't say much just broke off part of the sandwich with bacon and handed it to Max. Max wolfed down the food quickly and said, "Thank you so much I haven't eaten in a few days."

The man said nothing just nodded and put his hand in his pocket and brought out a scrunched-up pack of peanut butter crackers and handed them to Max. Once again, Max wolfed down the crackers as fast as he could swallow and then sat down next to the man.

"What ya doin out here son," the man said with a twang in his voice. You're lucky the cops didn't see ya or you would be in the hoosegow by now. You can't be sleepin in the park. Especially now cuz the boys in blue have been beatin the bushes for some reason lookin for somethin."

"I did have an encounter with the police earlier last week in another part of the park, but I had nowhere else to go," explained Max, "my old shelter was destroyed by the storm, and I went to a few other places where people were camped out, but they wouldn't let me stay with them."

"No surprise there, you gotta understand the then ways of the street, else you won't survive," the man advised. Unless you're a real badass you gotta be tuned in every second and be hip to everybody you meet. If you ain't a good judge of character, then you ain't gonna make it. Out here you need to figure that everybody you meet is up to no good until they prove themselves otherwise. And worst than that, there is always somebody tryin to save us street people. "Just start prayin," they say, and the Lord will come and fix everything for you and life will be one happy day after another. I tell ya, ya gotta to be with it every minute out here and be ready for anything, mostly be able to run from trouble."

"I think I'm finding that out the hard way," Max replied. How long have you been out here?

"Well let's see now I guess it's been quite a few years now, I used to keep count but then I lost interest," the man said, and chuckled.

"Do you mind if I ask why, you're out here?" questioned Max.

"It's a long story son and I'm pretty sure you need to be thinkin about more impotent things like where you're gonna sleep tonight," he said with a grin. You have a good lookin watch there maybe we could trade," the stranger said winking.

"Trade?"

"Yeah, yeah, trade. You give me the watch and I try and get you in the camp, I can't promise for sure I would have to check it out with the leader first."

"What do you mean the leader?"

"Ya sees it's not a real camp or nuttin like you think of a camp with picnic tables and fire pits an all, it's just a bunch of people with some tents, I don't know about all places but most of the tent cities have someone who is sort of like the grand poobah. The group has rules, they gotta, they don't just let anybody in. Some folks ain't who they pretend to be. They come off like they wanta be your friend and then after they have you sucked in; they rob you blind. To get to a camp you have to say how you would contribute to the group to earn your space there. Or there's other ways, like you could have someone talk up for you, but you can't just barge in."

Really," Max said surprised by the explanation, "I didn't realize there was a hierarchy in such places."

"Son, there is what you call a pecking order everywhere you go, even in Hell. I see I'll have to get you up to speed on what's goin on out here. Ya knows a couple weeks back we had a dude and his chick get in camp. They seemed cool at first and then we noticed that they stirred everybody up."

"What do you mean stir everybody up?" Max asked.

"It means they got all up in their shit and then wanted to fight and act like they was better than all the folk there. Talked trash about what they did before they hit the street and how they made a fortune, all that swill. Come to find out he was a snatch man and stole a few fancy cars and sold them and the woman was supposed to be a dancer, but she was a hoe and robbed the joint she worked at one night after everybody left out."

"What's a snatch man? asked Max.

"That be the dude that snatches your ride when you don't pay the man what's due. He come and haul them wheels away."

"Oh yeah, I get it."

"Lenny kicked them out as fast as they come. Then we had this old lady. Looked like a sweet old gray-haired thing. Pretended her kids did her wrong and kicked her out of her own place. Lenny let her stay. It took about a month before one of her sons showed up. Truth be told, she stole her own son's disability check and all his vittles for some crack, smoked it up and then got arrested and wanted him to bail her out. They put her in a halfway house, she split. She tried to rip off everybody in camp. Went through all their tents and their stuff and took what she wanted. Lenny kicked her out. A real rachet. There are some mean, nasty, common, suckers out here. You gotta remember that."

"Would you be willing to try to get me in, I don't have any place else to go and I don't want to go to jail," Max said as he handed the man his Rolex thinking he had to weigh his words about cops looking for people because they might not be too anxious to take him in at the camp if that were the case.

"Let's do a walk around, see what we can get before we go to the camp, by ought the way they call me Hog, what's your name?"

"I'm Max, it's good to meet you," Max said extending his hand.

When the man shook Max's hand, he was surprised at how strong it was. From that Max suspected that he was not as old as he looked. Hog hoisted his ratty old backpack on his back and Max carried his two plastic shopping bags and off they went. Max pulled his hat down over his face as much as he could as they walked around the city. He found out that Hog knew many people in the city and not all of them were homeless.

They walked quite a distance and were in the more prestigious part of the city when Hog stopped at a street corner and told Max to wait there while he took care of some business. Max waited for 2 hours and was about to give up on Hog thinking he had been dupped and kicking himself for trusting a guy who promptly conned him into giving him the only possession he had left and now he was really hopeless. Max was about to start walking down the street when Hog came around the corner.

"Where you goin?" called Hog.

"Hey, you were gone a long time what were you doing so long?"

"I had a little job to do, and it took a lot longer than I thought," Hog explained, you probably thought I was just gonna rip off your watch and you would never see me again, right?

"Yeah, that thought did cross my mind. You have a job?" Asked a surprised Max.

"It's not a real job, like workin in a store or nothin like that it's more like a favor I do for someone."

"What does that mean?" Max said.

"If you wanna survive out here you gotta learn how to make a little scratch once in a while to get you through. So, I did this favor and got a little something. Let's wander over to the pawn shop and see what we can get for your Rolodex."

"It's a Rolex not a roll-a-dex and, let me ask you one thing, "Why would you do this for me?"

"I know where you're at, I've been there before myself, and someone helped me. I been thinkin we should give as good as we get. Besides you look as if you are about to fall out," Hog said, looking at Max who could hardly stand up straight.

"Yeah, I'm pretty worn out," Max confessed.

They sat on a bench at a bus stop for a rest after walking another far distance. Hog said, "We need to get some grub, what are you up for?"

"You mean I have a choice?" inquired Max.

"Well, sort of there's the Kindly Kitchen that serves box lunches, or the soup kitchen that has one hot meal every day but that's in the evenin."

"Why can't we go to both?" asked Max, "I'm starved."

"They're a good piece apart, I give it a shot one time and tried to go to both but sometimes if you ain't there early, they're out," Hog explained.

"Let's go to the closest one then because I'm running out of steam," Max declared.

"I see you're on your last legs," Hog observed.

They got box lunches and sat in the park near the water fountain.

"Soon the sun will be going down we might have to do a makeshift for the night," Hog suggested, "cuz the camp is far off and it's gettin dark I know you're dog tired. Your ass probably wouldn't make it to camp, we'll do a makeshift."

"That's Ok by me," Max said relieved that rest was near, I'm bushed, "what is a makeshift?"

"I'll show ya," said Hog. He took Max to the junk yard. They entered through a hole in the fence that was concealed by some bushes and found a comfortable old sedan. Hog took the front seat and Max the back, it was still light out, but Hog said that was where they would spend the night. Max was so tired he didn't care; he was asleep as soon as he got horizontal. The next day before dawn Hog woke Max up and told him they had to leave quickly. When Max asked why Hog explained that the people who worked at the junk yard fed the dogs just before daybreak, so while they are eaten we need to leave out. They rest all day and then they are free to roam around the junk yard at night guarding the place."

"Dogs? Are they vicious?

"Ya could say that if one of them gets on ya, you would have a bad day, that's why we had to find a crib early because they let them dogs roam around the junk yard at night and they don't take too kindly to strangers."

Max was surprised and grateful that Hog was helping him. He followed Hog through the city with his hat pulled low over his face. He wondered how soon it would be before the cops found him. Every time they passed a policeman Max's gonads were in his throat. Max was certain that Ali would lie if he was caught and tell the police that Max killed Joe. He knew that Ali would come up with a good alibi for himself and every cop in the city was probably looking for the killer. What will ever become of me? Max didn't even want to think about that.

[Chapter 4]

Max was very grateful that Hog had taken him under his wing and helped him survive, else he would have starved or been thrown in jail. They went and sat on a bench in the park waiting for someone to leave a half-eaten doughnut or bagel and maybe a paper cup with warm coffee left in it. Max pulled his hoodie over his head to hide as much of his face as possible. They watched as people walked through the park heading for the subway station to work. All of them walk fast with a determined look on their faces.

They had no luck finding food that morning. They waited until the pawn shop opened and Hog went in, Max waited outside. Hog took Max's Rolex out of his pocket and asked how much it was worth. The young man behind the counter said he would have to go ask the owner because he was new at the job. The owner came out and looked at the watch then he asked Hog if the watch was hot. Hog told the man that he found the watch and didn't know who it belonged to, so he wanted to pawn it. The man offered twenty dollars, but Hog told him that was not enough. The man pointed to a case that was full of watches and said take it or leave it. Hog took the money. When Hog came out of the pawn shop and told Max he got twenty dollars for the watch and Max was furious.

"That's ridiculous Hog. That watch is worth at least fifteen times as much," Max declared insistently.

"That's what the man said he would give. Do you wanna go back and get the watch back?" Hog said, "That's all he would give me.

"No, no I guess I'm disappointed I thought it would be worth more, I paid a lot for it."

"Things out here ain't like they are in other places Max, if you're gonna survive you need to grab onto that. Let's go get some day-old donuts, then we can go to see if Lenny will give you the ok to stay at the camp. If he's good with it, we will go to the Salvation Army store and buy you a sleeping bag."

Lenny agreed to let Max stay at the camp on a trial basis but warned him that if he got drunk and started a fight, or anybody complained about him, he was out. Max agreed and was thankful. They got an old sleeping bag for a few bucks and Max traded his shopping bags for a backpack and they went back to the camp. Hog said he could put his sleeping bag at his place. Hog's place was not a real tent but a tent like thing that was actually two tarps hung over some poles on a wire strung between them tied together with twists. It wasn't great but would keep the rain from soaking the sleeping bag. Max was still tired from his days of sleeplessness, and he was still cold, so he crawled into the bag and fell asleep almost immediately.

The next few days went by quickly because Max slept most of them away.

On the 4th day Hog told Max it was time he started moving around and told him he had to get his ass up. Hog wanted to show him a few things he should know about in case of an emergency. Max gave no protest knowing all Hog had done for him. They walked to the business area and again Hog told Max he had a small job to do so Max set his backpack down on the grass near the walkway and waited. He had picked up a book someone left in the park and began reading when an uber pulled up and the woman in the same red coat got out and started walking. Max wanted to contact her but didn't want to scare her. He started walking slowly behind her and began whistling, which is what he did a lot in the office.

Finally, Max called out, "It's Max Ellie can you turn around?

Ellie hesitated for a few seconds and then turned around. "Max, Max is that really you? She asked hesitantly.

"Yes, it's me don't be scared I'm not crazy I would like to talk to you and tell you all about why I'm here. Lets' just sit on this bench, and I will tell you

everything," Max pleaded.

Ellie shook her head in agreement. They sat down one on each end of the

bench, Ellie looked as if she had seen a ghost. Max told Ellie the whole story but left out the part about him seeing a murder.

"Ellie, I really need you to help me because I need someone to record all that I've seen and get it down before I forget the details. You were so helpful to me when I wrote my first book, it would be wonderful if you could do the same again. What do you say."

"Max, you must give me a few minutes to compute all this in my brain. It's so

strange and I never in a million years expected to see you again, especially like

this," Ellie expounded.

"I know it's a shock, but you know how I work, and this is something I feel I must do. You are like a godsent to me if you can help because I have no one else to turn to, of course I can't pay you right now but I'm good for it I assure you. I was ready to come back to my old life but then I met this guy and I'm in a better position than I was before I started this."

"Before we go any further there are things you need to know about, and we have to discuss."

"What things?" Max asked curiously.

"You probably don't know this, but the police are looking for you Max, you are considered a fugitive. I thought it was very strange when the newspaper publisher asked me to come to his office because it's been a while since I worked there and when I got there, there were police detectives waiting to question me."

"What did they want?" a worried Max asked.

"They wanted to know if I had seen or talked to you in the last few weeks. They said they were looking for you and that I should tell the truth, or I could be held as an accomplice to murder and go to jail."

"Oh my God, I know you told them the truth because you haven't seen me until today. But murder? How?"

"Don't worry as you said I didn't see you until today, so I didn't lie. Max, they

suspect that you murdered someone! Before I got there your editor told them that you left your office and apartment in a rush and didn't tell anybody where you were going and that made it all sound worst."

"Dear Jesus!! This is awful. What am I going to do. Ellie, you know me I didn't kill anybody," Max begged.

"I don't think you killed anybody Max. But the story is even more serious than just the questioning about that murder. The detective told us that they were following a lead because they discovered that you knew all the victims."

"What do you mean all the victims," he blurted out, "what victims?"

"You don't know about what has been happening do you?"

"No, I haven't been exactly following the newspaper or TV News out here on the street, what did you mean by all of them?"

"A lot has happened since you have been gone Max. You dropped out of sight

about the time the boyfriend of Sadie Jenkins the actress was found murdered and within a week the male friend of the rapper Smokin Hot's was murdered and then Chas Dunkin, the famous designer was in the news several times for beating his partner and was found dead by gunshot. Two weeks later a Wall Street heiress's boyfriend was found dead in an alley. The police are thinking that there is a serial killer who was preying on male figures in celebrities' lives because the killer thinks that they abused them. On the last murder they said, they have an eyewitness report of a homeless man running away from where the body was found in the alley. The witness insisted on having a sketch made of the face of the person he claims he saw. The police think it's you.

Police Wanted Posters of you are plastered all over the subway and on the news, they're everywhere. The people you know from your old watering hole, the Winning Circle bar, were questioned by the police too. They identified you from the police posters. It seems that at least two of the deceased hung out

there too. The police questioned the people considered regulars at the bar, they all wanted to cooperate and told the police that you knew all the victims, but you had not been in for weeks. The cops came back to the office too, they wanted to confirm whether you have been in or not and asked who had worked closely with you. The police detective said they talked to all your close friends and asked if they thought you were capable of murder. All except this one guy named Thomas Kane said yes."

"Jesus! I didn't know any of that. Ellie, you don't think I'm the serial killer. do you?"

"No, of course not it's just that things are tense in the city and with you missing, there are a lot of questions. One or two of the people from the bar told them you got into some heated arguments with some of the victims about human relationships and how people treat each other badly etc.," Ellie explained.

"That part is true, but they were heated discussions not arguments, I'm not a serial killer I only dropped out of sight because I needed to get material for my book.

"Can you help me, Ellie? I'm begging you," Max pleaded.

"I don't know Max all of it scares me," Ellie confessed, what if they think I'm involved in the murders somehow, I don't want to go to jail," Ellie said with a quivering voice.

"Please, please Ellie, I have no one else to turn to and I don't have enough material to come back yet. I'm going to level with you Ellie. I don't want to scare you any more than you already are, but I did see a man get murdered and if I came back now, they might recognize me and think I killed him and maybe those others too."

"Oh my God Max that really happened?"

JESUS God YES! I mean NO I didn't do it, but yes, I saw it and it did happen. I knew this would happen when they found that guy. The killer was so mean. I was in the wrong place at the wrong time Ellie, you know I wouldn't hurt a fly. You must believe me and help me."

"Max, I don't know I don't want to be mixed up in any investigation or I would never work in this town again. Why can't you just come back now and clear your name and then when all this is over, write the book.

"I can't do that yet. They would probably arrest me the minute I came forward." Then you really are living on the street Max?" Ellis asked, "I'm still very astounded by that."

"I don't know how I can come back now I've lost all my IDs and outside of you no one else knows I'm on the street. If I came back now, I would have to implicate you and I know you don't want to be a part of a murder case."

"No, I definitely do not. I have to think this over," Ellie stated, "If I decide to help you, we will have to have certain rules. We would have no personal contact; it would be just you getting the material to me. Besides how would we do this I don't think you can write all this down."

"Maybe I can get a small recorder and get the tapes to you, and you could put those on your personal computer and then when I got back re-work it all."

"I'm scared Max, I never did anything like this before, though your boss offered me my old job back and I could work part time. If I did that, maybe I could find out more. I don't know Max it's all so unbelievable that things like this could happen."

"I know me either. I never stopped to ask you what you are doing in this part of town anyway?"

"I volunteer at the soup kitchen twice a month," Ellie professed.

"I don't want to put any pressure on you so how about this if you decide to help me then I'll go to the soup kitchen the next time you come there, and you can let me know what you decide. No pressure, I don't want you to feel burdened with my problem."

"Ok that's fair, I have to go now. But if I accept and work with you here's the deal, we would never be able to use any public communication devices. We could make the exchange at the soup kitchen. I'm taking a big risk here I don't want to go to jail as an accomplice. Come back in two weeks and meet me at the soup kitchen and I will give you my answer," Ellie promised.

"Ok," Max said, now very distraught that Ellie didn't agree to help him, "keep in mind you are my last and only hope. Thanks for talking to me."

Though Ellie didn't agree with Max's methods, she was intrigued by Max's book idea and really admired that he was so dedicated to telling the real story. She thought about what he asked of her for the next few days. If they could work covertly, then she would do it. They met in two weeks as agreed. Max was very anxious to see if Ellie was going to work with him.

As Max walked back to meet Hog he began to worry. My God if they somehow connect me to Ali's crime, they will think I'm the serial killer. How did this ever happen I went from innocent bystander to serial killer. My Lord, I hate to think of what will take place if they decide to pin those murders on me.

In next two weeks they met at the soup kitchen as planned. Ellie told him she would work with him but that no one else must ever know about it. Max was so happy he swore that he would never tell anyone about what she was doing. He told Ellie he had it all worked out. He would get a small recorder and they would communicate by having Max give Ellie the tapes at the soup kitchen, she would download them and begin the manuscript on her personal computer.

"One thing Max how would I know how to contact you if I need to? Asked Ellie. "I could get you a throw away phone and I would have one to. If anything happened, we could call if we had to. If anybody saw me with it, they wouldn't be suspicious because that's what the people on the street use and it can't be traced. I don't know how often I would be able to contact you, but we would have some identifying words like passwords before talking.

"The final thing Max, is if by some crazy way the authorities found out I am helping you, you will tell them that you threatened me and made me go along with you."

"I agree," Max said immediately.

[Chapter 5]

Max's father Erol was the third generation of a family who grew up during the great depression in Chicago. His grandfather, Eli, earned a lot of money bootlegging whiskey and it kept his family very comfortable during the depression when most people were starving. Bootleggers became rich selling illegal alcohol and Erol's father was one of them. Though the sale of alcohol was banned during the Prohibition period 1920-1933, organized crime, violent criminals, and illegal sources of alcohol ruled the day, crime, and bootlegging was big business. The prohibition laws didn't stop Americans from drinking alcohol although almost a quarter of the population of America was jobless.

It was reasonably easy to make moonshine and almost anything could be distilled, berries, fruit, potatoes, even certain tree bark, so the natural resources were almost always available and cheap. There was a constant demand for alcohol and once you had established customers who knew your alcohol was safe, which meant that nobody got sick from it, and it tasted good you were in business. The only big risk, if you were willing to take it, was the chance of getting caught because making illegal alcohol was considered a federal offense.

There were many loopholes that would allow people to have alcohol. One way was to get a prescription from your family doctor for medicinal whiskey. Some vowed they would use it for relief of aching arthritic joints by rubbing it on their skin. The truth was that almost every family had some form of alcohol in the household for health or religious purposes.

Erol's grandfather prided himself on his homemade batches of whiskey. He often told stories of how when the family first started out making whiskey, they had a hidden still in the garage and had to bury the left-over mash from the distillation process in a nearby field. Erol's father loved telling the story of how one evening when he wanted to go to a baseball game, his father told him he couldn't go until he buried the mash. In a hurry and not wanting to miss the beginning of the game he took it to the farm and fed it to the neighbor's cows. Later that evening, Eli got a visit from the irate farmer who told him that his cows were staggering around the field, and he was afraid that one of them would break a leg. The worst was yet to come, the next day at milking time all the cows gave sour milk. Eli made Erol go over to the farmers place all that week to do choirs for him after he did his own at home to pay him back for the spoiled milk. Martha, Eli's wife told them about the times when they would go on a date and the empty bottles would tinkle against one another and Eli would tell her they were milk bottles because he got up very early in the morning to deliver milk. Eli and Martha had many stories like that, and Max loved to hear them.

When Erol joined the business there was enough profit and money in the business that he could refine the liquor and get a higher price for it. He also talked Eli into expanded the business to include liqueurs or cordials which were favored in the Speakeasies by women. Although technically they were distilled spirits that were sweetened with various flavors, oils, extracts, and herbs. they were the rage. Originally, they were used as remedies for ailments like coughs and sore throats, but the most popular use was fancy cocktails. They were favored by women because they disguised the taste of alcohol but were more expensive than plain, distilled whiskey and appealed to wealthier clients. Erol's father hit the jack pot when they started making them. Ladies no longer had to worry about what they would order because liqueur cocktails tasted good and were very popular.

Speakeasies got their name from an 1889 newspaper article which came out in McKeesport Pennsylvania defining them as, "a saloon that sells liquor without a license. They were called speakeasies because you spoke quietly about such things in public, and definitely did not want to alert your neighbors that you were going there. Some speakeasies had a small window cut into the door and when you knocked, the small door opened you whispered a password. Speakeasies were often disguised as cafes, soda shops and other store fronts, with the real action in the back room. When these places got shut down by the police moonshiners began using basements and attics. These gathering places played an important part in American society because they created changes in society and culture, especially for lower classes and women.

Eli was no fool. He knew one day that alcohol would again become an accepted commodity and become a legitimate business, after the laws were changed. Because of that insight he invested a lot of his money in other things like railroads. His success was not of the magnitude of the Vanderbilts, Harrimans or Hills but less he was successful, and alcohol made him a millionaire, which meant something back then.

The business of social drinking and alcohol skyrocketed under Eli's watch. This family, which would ordinarily not be welcomed into high society, were embraced now because they had wealth and were considered among the privileged. Also, after alcohol was again legal Eli was prepared to do big business with his products. Erol's father had insisted he go to college, so he went. He hated it and it didn't matter he was at the bottom of his graduating class; he got that sheep's skin that said he graduated from college and daddy bought him a brand-new car, he had his own apartment and plenty of money. Daddy was pleased.

Erol was both handsome and rich and he had women coming out his ears. Then as Fate would have it, he met Max's mother, Jessie, at a party one night and fell head over heels in love. Erol's family was not pleased when he brought Jessie home. Although she was beautiful and loved Erol she came from the wrong side of the tracks according to Erol's family. She was not sophisticated enough for their high society status, and they thought she would probably embarrass them. At first none of that bothered Erol and when he came home to tell them Jessie was pregnant, they said, "I told you so."

Erol and Jessie eloped and were happily living in his apartment until the baby came. They had dreamed of buying a house and having enough room for little Max but when they began looking for larger places Erol discovered that his father had cut off his so-called monthly allowance and cut his salary. Erol and Jessie had a hard time scraping by because Erol had no idea how to handle money and spent every penny before it reached the bank. Worse Erol began to drink heavily and often got in fights, sometimes getting arrested. One evening he passed out at the bar and when he awoke, he was in jail. He called Jessie but she had no money to bail him out. Erol had no choice he called his father.

"Dad this is Erol. I'm sorry I have no one else to turn to, I'm in a jam and I need your help."

"What is it son?" asked his father. Erol explained what happened. His father agreed to come and get him out if he left Jessie. Erol became angry and told him he could never do that, and he stayed in jail at first. The next day Jessie came to see Erol, and he told her what happened with his father. She cried and told him she didn't know how she was going to get him out of jail because she spent the last of their money on groceries.

"Erol, you know I love you very much and I would do anything for you, maybe the only way you can get out of here is to take your father up on his offer, Jessie said in the bravest voice as she could muster with tears running down her face. I know you don't want that but it's the only way to get you out of here."

"Jessie we can't do that it would mean that I would not see you and Max and that would kill me. Let me see if there is another way. I love you and Max and don't want to be separated from you," Erol choked out.

Erol contacted all his friends and people he knew from the past that he thought he could count on, but they had been told by Eli not to help Erol. One friend who had known Erol in college told him, "I would love to help you Erol but I'm in business myself now and your father gave me a loan to get started. I'm sure he would not be happy if he knew I helped you and would call in my loan. I just don't have that kind of money now. I'm sorry Erol I can't help you."

After three weeks in jail and seeing no way out, in desperation Erol called his father and asked him once more if he would help him. His father's answer was firm, he said he would only help if Erol did what he asked and leave Jessie. Erol didn't know what to do, Jessie couldn't work and watch the baby and the rent was due soon. Erol had no choice, he told his father he would do what he asked. Erol's father relented and after he was out of jail, he gave him his job back, with the understanding that he would leave Jessie. Erol told his father that he needed a few months to break the news to Jessie and find her a place to live that was close by so he could see Max. His father agreed.

Erol was happy and forgot about what he promised his father. It wasn't very long until Erol fell back into his old routine of spending beyond their means and soon they were in debt again. During those months Erol had taken his family to a few family gatherings and Jessie complained she didn't have the right clothes and his parents made her feel out of place. Erol didn't think that was true and made excuses for his family and their behavior. Then the worst thing happened, Max had a terrible accident, he pulled over a boiling kettle of water that was on their fireplace insert and got burned. He had burns over his legs and abdomen. Erol and Jesse did not have medical insurance and Max needed extensive health care for the burns. Erol's parents helped, and Jessie took care of I Max full time and spent little time with Erol. Soon she and Erol began to fight.

They argued over the least little thing and in his heart Erol blamed Jessie for the accident. His parents had given them money for Max's medical bills and his burns healed and he recovered quickly. Jessie was so happy that she bought a bicycle and had a child carry seat attached and rode Max everywhere. One day Jessie had a very minor accident with the bike. It tipped over and threw Max out of the carrier onto the ground. He was ok except for a few bruises and cuts but when Erol saw the cuts and scrapes, he went crazy. He took Max to his mother and told Jessie he wanted a divorce, told her she was an unfit mother, and she would never see Max again. She tried to explain but Erol would not hear anything she had to say.

Jessie waited a few days and went to her in-law's house and begged to see Max, but they wouldn't let her in. She waited until dark and broke into the back door. She went to the room Max was in and woke him. Her initial intention was to take Max and run, but Max began talking about all the things he had now new toys and even a pony and his grandmother told him they were going to the circus and the movies and Jessie began to feel that Max might be better off without her. Jessie knew she could never give him all the things they could. She tried to explain to Max she would always love him and left quietly the same way she had come in. When Max began talking about Jessie's visit to his father and grandparents and told them that she said she was going away, his father just said, "Good riddance." Jessie had no money for an attorney and was brokenhearted that she was not able to see Max. She fell into a deep depression and left town not telling anyone where she went.

When Max became an adult and saw for himself what kind of guy his father really was. After his grandfather died and the business was willed to him and his father. Max had no interest in the business. Though his father lacked business knowledge that didn't matter, the company flourished due to the dedicated people his grandfather had hired and the fact that most of their customers had been loyal to him and stayed with the company after he died. Max realized he knew more about the business that he learned from his grandfather than his father ever would. Maybe one day he might consider running the company but not now. He wanted to do his own thing and didn't think he would be happy being a businessman or having a fake life. None of that mattered now he had to find a way to make it back to his old life.

[Chapter 6]

Max met Bonnie at the camp one evening when a few people were sitting around outside their tents talking. Bonnie was a slim woman with graying hair pulled back in a ponytail and had a weather-beaten face. To Max she looked about 60 years old from her appearance, but he didn't think she was that old. It was hard to tell how old people on the street really were, because they were exposed to the elements and their skin became weathered. Max didn't dare ask her. It quickly became apparent that Bonnie had been at the camp for some time and most of the group knew her well.

Someone found an almost full bottle of wine and it didn't take much for the group to get high. Bonnie had two or three long pulls from the bottle and then became talkative. Max started asking her questions.

"Bonnie how do you like it here?" Asked Max.

"You're new here aren't you," Bonnie asked, suspiciously.

"Yeah, I'm a friend of Hog's and I'm staying in his tent. He is such a good person to let me crash with him."

"He is one of the few here who has his shit together, people look up to Hog. If he brought you in, he must think you're ok," Bonnie ventured.

"Bonnie," Max questioned, "who brought you in and how long have you been here?"

"I don't rightly remember now who it was, but it's better than my last place because it's not far from the park where there are water fountains and toilets."

"Yeah, that's for sure." Max agreed, "Did you grow up around here?" he asked.

"Oh no I grew up out west, I'm not a city girl," Bonnie said, slurring her speech a bit.

"Do you ever think you'll go back?"

"Back? Back to what? My life there is over, it has been over for a long time, and I have only this crowd here to count on. It was different for me once but all that is gone now."

"Do you have any family?" Max asked.

"Maybe, probably out west somewhere but I'm not sure where, truth is I'm not sure if I want to know where they are," Bonnie blurted out.

The wine bottle came around for the last time and Bonnie took a big slug. Max thought this might be his chance to ask Bonnie more questions, but she got up and went to sit next to Lenny and she was tipsy. Hog came over and sat down.

"I see you're jawing with a few people," Hog told Max, "That's good. That's how to build up their trust."

With that he got up and went to his tent and Max soon followed.

Max was a deep sleeper in the past, but since he had been on the street, he slept with one eye open unless he was utterly exhausted. As he lay in his bag, he thought he heard some noise outside. He got up, put on his jacket, and stepped outside the tent to see what the noise was and saw Bonnie sitting on a log crying. Feeling guilty that his questioning may have precipitated Bonnie's crying Max went over to where she was sitting and asked if he could help.

"No there is no one who can help me now," Bonnie said. Max could tell she was feeling the effects of the alcohol, and she had another bottle with her.

"It's too late," Bonnie let out.

"You shouldn't think like that Max," recommended, "Things may be able to turn around."

"Maybe for others but not for me," Bonnie intoned in a garbled voice, and then blew her nose.

"I'm a good listener if you want to talk." Max offered.

Bonnie sat quietly for a while and then she began talking. "When I was sixteen years old, I was a typical teenager, a cheerleader, and I was a good student. My secret was that I fell in love with a guy named Jeremy on the football team. I was shy and I didn't have much contact with boys or dating and so I kept my love for Jeremy to myself and told no one how I felt. And because Jeremy already had a girlfriend named Dixie and I didn't stand a chance. Dixie was very possessive of their relationship and talked constantly about how much Jeremy loved her. I know she would have just died if she knew that I kept a picture of Jeremy hidden in my notebook, it was from the church group we both belonged to. One day when I was coming back from the library with a stack of books in my hands, I rounded the corner too sharply and Jeremy and I ran smack into one another. My books and notebook and I went sprawling and I began scrambling to collect them. When I got to my notebook my picture of Jeremy had come out and as I went to pick it up Jeremy saw that it was a picture of him. He looked into my eyes and asked why I had his picture. My heart pounded in my ears, and I could hardly speak but I managed to squeak out because I like you and then I fainted. Jeremy was holding me in his arms and shaking me asking if I was ok when Dixie ran over to us. She told Jeremy to immediately put me down and demanded to know what happened and started to pull me up to my feet. Jeremy told her to stop and gently lifted me and stroked my hair. Dixie was furious and stomped around saying I was trying to steal Jeremy away from her and I faked fainting, and I was nothing but trouble. Jeremy told her to be quiet and told her to stop all her drama. She looked as if she had been slapped and turned on her heel and ran off.

The next day Jeremy came to my house to see if I was ok. I told him I was fine, and he should go because Dixie would have a fit if she knew he came to my house. Jeremy told me he broke up with Dixie and asked if we could go to the movies that night. From that night on Jeremy and I were a couple and Dixie hated me with a passion. She did a lot of things to make my life miserable, I never told Jeremy about her mean and hateful pranks, because I could stand that as long as I had Jeremy. Everything was going along fine until graduation day. On that day right on the stage just before he graduated Jeremy proposed to me and I accepted. All the kids cheered and were so excited for me, and Dixie was green with envy. The sad part was that Jeremy was going into the military and we wouldn't be able to get married until he at least completed boot camp. I didn't mind that he had always dreamed of joining the military and I wouldn't stop him from doing that, I had one more year of school and then after I graduated, we would get married.

Dixie made my life even more miserable after Jeremy left. She got me thrown off the cheerleading squad by lying to my homeroom teacher telling her that I cheated by looking at her paper during an exam. She and her friends put sand in my gas tank, so my car died on my way home from work. She threw paint on a poster I was going to present for history class and the list goes on and on. I never mentioned these hateful things to Jeremy, not wanting to upset him.

When Jeremy came home for Christmas, Dixie had her brother who was a friend of Jeremy, had a huge party for him, and she practically threw herself at him. Jeremy would have none of it. He was polite and stayed at the party and held my hand the whole time. Dixie latched on to Jeremy when I went to the bathroom. She pulled him under the mistletoe and put her arms around him and wanted him to kiss her, but he refused and told her that he and I were going to get married as soon as I graduated. Jeremy had a 30-day pass in June, and we had planned a small wedding and then we would leave, and I would go with him to live on the military post. On Thursday night, two days before our wedding Jeremy's old friends from the football team set up a bachelor party in Las Vegas, which was not too far from our town in Spring Valley. They rented rooms and would stay the night and party and be back on

Friday afternoon came and went, and Jeremy did not show up. I tried his cell, but it went straight to voice mail. I called all the guys I knew were there and no one was answering I was beside myself worrying. I paced the floor and waited and finally at 9:00 PM two cars pulled up. Jeremy and his brother, Dixie's brother, and Dixie and they all came into the house. I was shocked to see all of them. I asked what happened and no one answered. Jeremy took my hand and said let's sit down.

We sat on the sofa, and he put his arm around my shoulder and began talking. The guys had set up a room for the party and began to drink heavily. Several hours later Dixie and some of her friends crashed the party and started dancing and drinking. Jeremy said it was all a blur and he could not look at me. They were all drunk and went to a 24-hour wedding chapel as a joke because one of the guys and Dixie's friend decided they wanted to get married and somehow it all got mixed up and Jeremy and Dixie got married too. I couldn't believe my ears! Jeremy and Dixie got married, was this a joke? If it was, it wasn't funny? I could not believe my ears. I tried to pull away from Jeremy.

Jeremy said, "Honey don't be upset it was a total mistake and we can get it annulled fast."

That's when Dixie piped up and said, "I don't think you are right about that Jeremy. You were not in a hurry to get away from me that fast last night. You kept telling me you wanted more of me. So, lover boy that means that our marriage was consummated last night several times she purred and so we need a real divorce not an annulment."

"What are you talking about Dixie?" Screamed Bonnie, "tell her Jeremy, tell her it's not true."

Before Jeremy could answer Dixie pointer at Jeremy and said, "You screwed me before and after we got married so that's pretty good evidence of who he really loves, isn't it? No matter even if he wanted an annulment, I would contest it and we would need a divorce, so it would take about 3 months till a divorce is final," Dixie gleefully said and smiled like a smug Cheshire cat.

"You are a royal bitch Dixie you know Jeremy doesn't love you, he loves me, and you are just doing this to hurt me," I screamed.

"Well, all I can say is that I didn't force Jeremy to have sex with me last night if you know what I mean," Dixie said with a snicker and giggled, and she came over and stroked Jeremy's hair, and said, "isn't that the truth Lover Boy?"

Jeremy pulled away and jumped up and yelled at Dixie, "You little lying shit you know that your brother and the guys set me up and got me so drunk I didn't know what I was doing, and I would have never done anything like that if I were sober. I want an annulment or divorce or whatever is quickest so that Bonnie and I can get married I love her not you, you cheap little fucker."

"You all can do whatever you want but I have a piece of paper and a ring that says I'm married to you Jeremy and if you want to change that you will have to do it the legal way," Dixie declared with confidence.

"You know I'm on leave and have got to go back in a week, you planned it this way, you're a sneaky bitch," Jeremy said vehemently, "And you all," Jeremy said pointing to Dixie's brother. I will never speak to any of you again for doing this to me. You all know it was wrong and still did what Dixie wanted. I will never forget you for this."

Dixie's brother grabbed her by the arm and said, "We're getting out of here you have caused enough trouble."

We tried everything to get that marriage annulled but the court date was set for three months in the future and Jeremy had to go back. We called and wrote but it was not the same. Something was lost between us. Jeremy wanted to set a date to marry right after the divorce, but we didn't know if he could get the time off or if the divorce would come through in time. Three months passed and Jeremy came back to go to court for the divorce. It was to be the next day. We decided to go out to dinner in town. While we were waiting for our check Dixie and her brother showed up and asked to talk with us, they said they had something important to tell us. They followed us to the house and once we were inside and sitting down Dixie stood up and poked out her belly.

"I don't want a divorce I'm pregnant and I don't want my baby born out of wedlock," Dixie triumphantly declared with her hands on her belly and a big grin on her face. What do you say Papa?"

Jeremy hung his head in his hands and cried. I got up and told them both to leave. Jeremy and I cried together for a long time. He held me tight and told me he loved me and was sorry he had been so stupid and made such a drunken mistake. He said he was going back in the morning and would write soon.

Weeks went by and Jeremy kept on writing, and we talked on the phone about everything that he was doing and how my job managing the café was going but never a word about the situation. Then the next day a letter came. I was surprised because we had just talked two days ago, and Jeremy said he was going on an assignment and wasn't sure when he would be back. You always hear about Dear John letters, but I guess this was what you could call a Dear Jane letter. Jeremy wrote and said he had come to a decision that I was the one he would always love but he had an obligation to take care of his child. He and Dixie would be living together when he got out and he wanted to be the one to tell me that. He ended by stating, "I don't know if it's true but Dixie and her brother vow, she is having my baby and I feel I have an obligation to the child and need to try and make sure the baby is raised right."

My tears fell on the letter. There was nothing I could do or say. There was no remedy for it. I lost it all. If Jeremy felt that way, I couldn't stop him. I don't really remember how I got through the next few days. I felt as if my world had stopped turning. Jeremy was no longer mine, I told myself that I had to wrap my brain around what happened and learn to live with it.

I stayed around and watched as Dixie's pregnancy became more and more apparent and then I heard she had a baby boy. Jeremy came home and began living with Dixie and the baby. Every so often Jeremy would send me a note or call me, but I had a hard time talking to him. The last straw was a picture in the hometown newspaper of Jeremy, Dixie, and the baby, with the caption, "A Very Happy Family." The article said the happy couple were thrilled with the arrival of their m new son, that killed me and was about all I could take. I left Spring Valley and went to live with my aunt in a town on the other side of Nevada. It was almost a year before I heard from Jeremy again. He had called a few times, but they were brief and lasted only a few minutes. Just routine stuff, how was I doing? How was my job? etc. This time Jeremy kept the conversation going and ended with a question.

"How about if I come and see you and we have dinner together over the weekend?"

"I was taken aback and didn't know what to say, so I said, "I guess that would be ok."

Jeremy came that Saturday night, and we went out for dinner. We talked about our school days, and it was fun for me because I had not gone out to dinner with anyone in a long time. Of course, I had to maintain control for in my heart of hearts I still loved Jeremy. Some part of me said he had to do what he did, and it was not really his fault. We went back to my apartment, and he kissed me, and I thought I would faint. It was so unexpected I didn't know what to think, but that was the beginning of the real end.

After that Jeremy came around quite steadily for the next few months. One evening after we had sex and were starving, we got up and sat at the kitchen table eating. Jeremy asked me if I would like to do this all the time. I asked him what he meant, and he said, be together you and me. I told him that would not be possible unless he got a divorce from Dixie.

Then he spilled the beans. It seems that Dixie began drinking heavily after he left to go back to the military. She drank so much that her mother had to come and take care of the baby. When Jeremy heard about that he got a hardship discharge from the military and came back home to take care of the situation. He said he tolerated it because of the child and that Dixie constantly told him how she knew he hated her and loved me, and it would never change, because no matter what she would never give him a divorce because I stole you from her and she would see to it that I was punished for it. Jeremy told me that Dixie's mother had been diagnosed with cancer and would not be able to take care of the baby any longer.

Dixie had been in rehab twice because of her drinking problem, and each time she came home she was ok for a few weeks then she fell off the wagon. Jeremy didn't know what he was going to do because now he didn't trust her with the baby. He said no more about it that night.

One evening when we had the perfect meal and saw a movie, I was getting ready for bed and Jeremy asked me to come out to the living room so we could talk. He asked me if I would think about coming back to town and taking care of the baby. I looked at him as if he had gone crazy. Did he realize what he was asking? I asked if that meant he was going to divorce Dixie and take the baby and be with me? He said he couldn't do that right now because Dixie had to have help too. She had drunk so much alcohol that she had liver problems, and they had a lot of financial problems, because of her drinking he had to pay for her rehab because their insurance would not cover it.

"Just think about it Bonnie, we could be together always and be a family like we once planned."

Yeah, with Dixie sleeping between us, I thought but didn't say anything. I was stunned. I couldn't believe my ears. Jeremy didn't say he was planning on divorcing Dixie just that I would be there to take care of Dixie and the baby. He never mentioned marriage. Why would he think I would want a life like that?

How could Jeremy have ever thought I would go along with his plan? The first thing I thought of is that the last few weeks had been nothing but him buttering me up to ask me to do this for him. How could he do this to me? How could he ask this of me? I looked at Jeremy in disbelief. How in the world would he expect me to take care of Dixie and the baby while they were married, and I would live in the same house and be his mistress? My God what kind of fool did he take me for? Did I come off that I was so needy I would do anything to have him. I stood up and told Jeremy to get his things and get out. He told me he loved me and wanted to be with me no matter what. I looked at him and I thought I loved him once, but he was no longer that man. How could he ever think I would go along with putting myself in a situation like that. I would never be able to hold my head up in that town and I would be the laughingstock of everybody who knew me, let alone look at myself in the mirror.

"What about Dixie? What was she going to say and go along with this arrangement?" I screamed, "She hates me you know that."

"She will do anything I tell her to she is out of it on most days if it's not the bottle it's the pills. I can handle her," Jeremy insisted.

"I had enough I yelled, Get out! And take everything you left here with you. I thought you loved and respected me but now I know that your love is not true you love only what's best for you."

Jeremy became livid, "You selfish bitch I thought you loved me, and you would do anything in the world for me but that doesn't seem to be true. You will be an old maid if you don't do this for me."

Without any warning he reached out and slapped me across the face. I was so flabbergasted I began to cry and ran back to the apartment. That slap was not as painful as the tearing apart of my newly repaired heart. I got his backpack and threw it out the door at him and said, "I never want to see you again." I slammed the door and that was it. My heart was broken, and my life of loving Jeremy was over. My soul was empty. I left that night and wandered around. I was a zombie I stayed in a few motels for a few days and then moved on until I ran out of money and ended up on the streets of the city here."

Bonnie stopped talking then her tears turned into sobs. She took a long swallow from the bottle she held tightly in her hand and tears of her past flowed down her cheeks. She stood up and gave a small wave and said, "Good night, Max I have to go," Bonnie choked out and she got up and staggered to her small tent. I tried to think of some way to comfort her but couldn't come up with anything. I was stunned. I tried to find something to write it all down but that was not necessary because I knew I would remember this story as one of the saddest stories I had ever heard. I went back to Hog's tent, and just sat in the dark. Hog asked Max if everything was ok.

"Hog I just heard one of the saddest stories I ever heard in my life."

"I saw you talkin with Bonnie earlier and she is a sad case. One time her ex came looking fir her. I don't know how he found out where she was, but he came askin about her. Lenny heard the commotion when he started calling out Bonnie's name looking for her. He was so drunk he could hardly stand. It's a good thing she and Mary went to the hospital because Ben got in a fight, and they beat him pretty good. They went to bring him back, so Bonnie was not here.

"What happened? What did Lenny do?" asked Max.

He told him that there was nobody here named Bonnie and if he didn't go, he would call the cops. He told him not to come back here again. He never came around again that I know of, and we never told Bonnie that he was here. She would have been all stirred up again by that greedy bastard who wanted her as his slave. Max lay back on his cot and thought how lucky Bonnie was to have someone to protect her.

[Chapter 7]

It was early evening and everybody in the camp was around, Lenny called them all together to tell them that the police had come around earlier that day to ask if strangers had asked to stay in the camp. The police asked if anybody strange came around, we should let them know.

Lenny said, "I told the cops that every person who was in this camp was known to the group and there were no strangers among us. They told me that someone was hiding out pretending to be a homeless person and they suspected he was the serial killer they were looking for."

Max's mind silently went ballistic when he heard what Lenny said, but he cooled his jets when he realized that once more Hog had saved him. Hog interpreted Max's nervousness as being restless. He thought maybe they should find something to do, maybe some work for a couple of days. He talked to Max about it, and Max agreed so they went to the 7-11 and stood on the corner and hung out with about 10 other guys to see if anybody would pick them up for day labor.

In the next hour nearly all the men were picked up by construction companies. Hog and Max didn't want heavy labor jobs, so they decided to wait to see if anyone else came looking for lighter work. A little later a van with a painter's logo pulled up. The man got out and asked if anybody was interested in some light work moving furniture from room to room while they painted. Hog looked at Max and he shook his head giving the ok and they got in the van.

The house was a huge old place, and the owners were remodeling. The job was easy in that they only had to move the furniture from one room to another while the painters finished the room, then move the stuff back again. There was a furniture dolly, so the work was not that strenuous. Hog and Max spent a lot of time just waiting for the painters to finish a room. Later that afternoon when Hog and Max were taking a break, they were sitting on a sofa that was in a corner when a woman came into the room but didn't see them. She was carrying a notebook and opened it and began looking at a color chart and talking to herself. She was a beautiful woman, and she was walking through the rooms making notes. She didn't see Hog and Max because they got up and went out to the garage when she was in another room and when they came back, she was gone. At the end of the day the painter boss asked if they wanted to come back the next day and they agreed. Max and Hog worked with the painters for three more days the next week and Max had seen the same woman twice. Once was from a distance outside and again when she was talking with an older woman about furnishings and curtains or window dressings as the older woman had referred to them. Max heard the older woman call her Deidre. Deidre and the woman were talking quietly when suddenly Deidre said loudly, "Why did you do that Mrs. Gray?"

Mrs. Gray got huffy and responded by saying, "Whatever do you mean by why did I do that? I have creative license here and I have purchase authority. That means that I can and will do whatever I think is needed for this house and I don't have to consult you!" she snapped out.

"Those lamps and sofas you showed me pictures of are ugly and don't go at all with the décor in this room. I'm sure Joseph would positively hate them," Deidre spit out in an angry tone.

"Joseph, you call him Joseph. Why Mr. Collins is a very important member of society in this city, and he would be appalled if he heard you call him Joseph. Only his closest friends call him by that name," Mrs. Gray informed Deidre.

"Really, I don't know what century you're stuck in, but he asked me to call him by his NAME! "Which is Joseph," Deidre screamed sarcastically.

"You can't talk to me like that I'm going to call my office and you will soon be without a job young lady," Mrs. Gray declared.

"Go ahead," Deidre dared, I don't care if you call, but you should be careful because Joseph left me in charge."

Mrs. Gray took her phone out of her purse and called her office. She asked to speak to the manager and then explained the situation. Mrs. Gray was quiet for a few minutes listening and then said, "Well I never," dropped the call and left the room called back over her shoulder saying, "I'm leaving for the day I'm not sure I will be back."

That's all Max heard, and Deidre seemed to carry on with her work. Later that day he ran into Deidre literally as he was moving a tall piece of furniture back in the room and didn't see Deidre until it was too late.

Deidree called out, "Whoa, Whoa!"

Max immediately put down the piece and apologized.

"It's no problem," Deidre said laughing, "It was my fault I was not watching where I was going."

"Are you ok?" Asked Max, "I could have run you over."

"Yes, I'm fine no harm done, have a good day and she was gone.

Max was unnerved but said nothing to Hog about it but now that he had seen her up close and personal, she was beautiful. At the end of the day when Glen, the paint company boss was paying them, he asked, "Would you guys be up for another job tomorrow?"

"I don't know we're being bustin our buns the last couple days," Hog answered, "Moving furniture is hard work."

"Oh no not here and not moving furniture. This is a job over on Green Street. I'm doing it for a friend of mine. I can't even get started because the place is filled with all kinds of junk. It's not heavy furniture but odds and ends the owner collected over the years. If you ask me, I think she was actually a hoarder. If you take the job, you could have anything you find in the house. The guy doesn't want anything from there. I bet you could make a killing at a pawn shop. There's no hurry because I have a few more jobs I must finish up before I can start there."

"Well, let us think on it and maybe," Hog said, "we can help you out."

Glen cut him off. "Let's do this you take a look at what's in the house and if you like what you see you can start on your own. There is a key in the left urn on the porch so you can get in to have a look. If you want to do it leave me a note on the door. You can do this at your own pace."

"Ok Glen we can do that," Hog said looking at Max for confirmation and Max shook his head to say yes.

The next day they went to see the house on Green Street. They opened the door and went inside. The foyer led to a living room and Hog and Max looked around. Hog let out a low whistle and said, "Look at all this stuff, it could bring us some nice scratch and it's easier than moving furniture. We could do this at our own pace and sell it piece by piece and still make some money, plus Glen said we could go all over the house and collect the stuff and then sort it out. What do you think Max?"

"That sounds ok, I guess. I don't know anything about old stuff, so I don't know what we would do with this mess."

"Well, I do, and I know the dude who runs the antique shop, and if nothing else we can get a deal just on the weight alone of some of this junk," Hog nodded, "Are you in?"

"Why not," Max agreed.

So began their treasure hunt.

They started sorting out the trash the next day. Anything that they thought might be worth something was put in a separate pile. Some of the items were in good shape like the old lamps and small appliances that still worked. They took those to the thrift shop. They made a few bucks and the guy in the shop told them to bring in whatever they had, and he would give them a fair price or tell them where else they could take it. Hog and Max were having a good time doin this job. They shared their good fortune and bought food for the camp group twice. Hog was happy because he told Max that some of the people really needed a pick me up because they were feeling low, as the cold weather was coming on.

[Chapter 8]

Max had gone to the Goodwill store and bought a suit coat, shirt, and tie. He wore it to the library because they would not allow any who looked as if they were homeless and only wanted to come in out of the weather. He dressed in the coat and tie and the first thing he did was to introduce himself to the librarian. He told her he was doing research, and she would be seeing him quite often. He said, "I might be asking for some of your expertise with finding records as I know your knowledge of the library is very superior to mine."

The librarian was pleased and flattered, and Max began using the computer there frequently. He had no idea that homelessness in the US is so prevalent. In 2021 in New York City alone there were 122,926 homeless, and 14, 946 were children that slept in shelters. Throughout the US there are about 552,830 people who have nowhere to live. The average life expectancy is 50 years old and about 25% of the people are mentally ill. That number increased when mental hospitals closed, and many patients had no one to take care of them and nowhere to go and began living on the streets. Around 38% have substance abuse problems. Research shows that the primary cause of homelessness, particularly among families, is lack of affordable housing. Surveys of homeless families have identified the following major reasons triggering homelessness: eviction; doubled-up or severely overcrowded housing; domestic violence; job loss; and hazardous housing conditions.

Each night thousands of unsheltered homeless people sleep on city streets, in tents, in the subway system, parks and in other public spaces. There is no accurate measurement of the unsheltered homeless population, and recent surveys significantly underestimate the number of unsheltered homeless. Max felt sad and depressed after looking at the numbers.

Another thing Max researched was the house they were working at on Green Street. While they were working to clean out a closet, they found some old papers and journals that may have been kept by a housekeeper or someone who was responsible for payment of the maids, butlers, and the gardener. It was fascinating stuff reading about the wages and cost of food and seeing the long hours they worked for almost nothing. There were notes about the guests that visited the house. It was always the mayor, or some senator and other important people that were often entertained there. The notes mentioned how many people would be attending the function, the menu and cost of the event. It was a popular place for parties. The papers also described how the house was modeled after a famous house in London called the Green Street House. It was not as large or elaborate as the London house but close in design. When Max and Hog first saw the place, they were impressed with its size. Max had questioned the painters about the house, but they knew nothing about its history. They told him that it was not the house itself that was of interest but the fact that it was on three acres of prime city property and was the only completely intact parcel that had not been cut up to make way for other houses or businesses.

Now Max understood why the house was so valuable. Max googled the Green House in London and according to history the London Green Street house belonged to Anne Boleyn's family. It was thought that at this house Henry VIII courted Anne Boleyn. The story of her fate and how she was beheaded at the King's order is well known. It was uncertain where she was buried but many said that she always talked about how her spirit would always be at Green Street House and to this day she still haunts it. Max enjoyed reading about the house. Its history was fascinating.

The guys who ran the painting company seemed to take a liking to Hog and Max and they kept on asking them to work with them. Hog liked that it was not a full-time job only a few days a week and often not that much because the painters were finishing their other site. And even when they started the paint had to dry before the furniture could be brought back. It was a source of a few bucks for Hog and Max, and they went to the Green Street House when they were not working with the painters at the original site. Today they were all at the Green Street House and they had Hog and Max move all the furniture to one room except for an overstuffed chair. Hog told Max he had to go to see one of the other people he sometimes worked for and that it should only take a few hours and he would be back later that afternoon.

Max continued to sort out the pile of items alone, going through all the small pieces. Concentrating on the chore at hand Max didn't hear the people come in the front door. Once inside it was easy to hear their voices because the house was so empty. Luckily, they were on the other side of the house, and didn't see Max. Max didn't know who they could be but didn't want to explain why he was there either. He assumed it must have been alright for them to be there because they had a key. He listened closely at what they were saying and knew they were about to tour the house and would soon be near where Max was. Wanting to stay hidden he went up the back steps to the upper level as fast and as quietly as he could.

Out of breath and gasping, after running up the steps he leaned against the wall to catch his breath and see if he could still hear the voices. As he leaned on the wall it suddenly gave way and before Max realized what happened he was in a very dark room lying on the floor. He got up as fast as he could and looked around. The room had a musty smell but there was another odor also. It seemed to be a mix of mold and decay. Max was covered with cobwebs and tried to brush the cobwebs from his face and eyelashes. At first, he could see nothing but darkness, as his night vision kicked in aided by a small sliver of light peeking through from the roof, he was able to see. Max looked around at where he was. It looked like a huge bedroom and study combination. There was a bed and dresser on one side of the room and bookshelves and a desk on the other side. This confirms what I read about the elaborate old houses that were built back then. Some of them had secret rooms where they kept their treasures or had clandestine meetings with people they didn't want the rest of the family to know anything about.

    Breathing heavily, Max felt anxious and tiptoed across the room. He saw the outline of a wing backed chair and decided to sit down for a minute. Still not being able to see well he reached back to find the edge of the chair when his hand felt something strange. He explored it a bit and moved his hand over the object and had an idea of what it was, it seemed like a head wrapped in something, but it couldn't be. How would a head get here? Then the realization hit him. A HEAD!! A FUCKING HEAD! He pulled his hand back as quickly as if he were scalded. He turned around and could see it wasn't just a head it was a whole body. He almost shouted, "LET ME OUT OF HERE!" What the Hell was a body doing here. As he turned around and squinted to get a better look, he saw the body was seated in the chair with a coat around it. He wanted to bolt. His mind kept saying Run, Run, Run, Get the Hell out of there. But where could he go and not be seen? He couldn't believe this. He was trapped now what? He tried to calm down, but he was still petrified, stuck in one spot as if his shoes were glued to the floor and he could not move. He closed his eyes and told himself he must have hit his head when he fell and it was all a crazy dream and when he opened his eyes it would all be gone, but that didn't happen.

    It took a while, but Max finally settled down and concentrated on how he was going to get out of there and when he heard voices from downstairs, they brought him back to reality. A new threat crossed his mind what if they were on their way upstairs and knew about the body and were coming to get it? He tried to listen, but the sound was muffled. He moved closer to where the chatter seemed to come from, and it brought him close to the fireplace in the room. Max moved on tender feet to get closer to the hearth and bent down. He guessed that the sound must have been coming up from the fireplace downstairs with the flue acting as an echo chamber. He cocked his head to one side and listened. It was the same two men's voices that entered the house earlier, one seemed to be doing all the talking the other only saying a few words in between.

One male voice said, "I'm trying to get a feel for what you want and how to make the changes, but you need to give me some idea of what Marlene wants."

"Marlene has not settled on a specific theme yet, so I don't know, but I do know that there is not much you can change drastically with the design of this house."

"Maybe you should give me a chance to talk to her then," the man's voice replied tartly.

At first Max didn't know why but the hair on the back of his neck began to stand up and by the time his brain caught up with that, he realized he was once again listening to the sound of Ali's voice! With that realization he collapsed to the floor in a silent thud. How could this be? I must be hearing things! My mind must be playing tricks on me. This is so stupid. It can't be! It had to be a nightmare and he reached down and pinched his arm. No, I'm awake maybe I'm just going looney. No matter I need to get out of here before anything else happens. My God if it is the same man maybe he is going to kill this guy to.

"What to do! What to do! His first thoughts were. Run, run, run, his brain kept saying but there was no place to go, he was trapped. My God, he found me!! Max knew he was dead meat now. He had seen Ali kill Joe. Ali had even followed him for hours and probably would have killed him then if he found him. Max got up from the floor, should he go and confront him? Ali was with someone so surely; he wouldn't harm Max in front of him. This is like DeJa'Vu. Max's heart was pounding out of his chest as he started for the door. Wait! Wait! Wait! His gut said. You can't go down there. They don't know you're here. Just stay put and get your act together and see what happens. It could be a coincidence and Ali has no idea you're here. If he was after you, he wouldn't have brought a witness. Max let out some quick breaths and sat on the floor. Ok I'll ride this out.

As he began to get his wits about him again, he began to wonder, what door was I going to leave through I don't see a door, no matter I'm gonna lay low and listen and when I'm sure they're gone then I'll look for a way out. He sat and listened and rubbed his special coin.

Ali was explaining what Marlene wanted and how she wanted to try and recreate what her father had told her about this place. She was so distraught after he died, and he had been sick for so long. "She couldn't even make the funeral arrangements. I had to do all that for her. Enough let's get this wrapped up and get the Hell out of here."

After what seemed like forever the house was finally quiet and Max heard no more talking and assumed the men left. Now he had to find his way out of this room. He got up and walked as far away from the corpse as possible and made his way to where he thought he had come in but there was no door there. Don't panic you jerk you got in here through a wall and you're not a ghost, so there must be an opening somewhere he chided himself. He carefully moved his hands up and down the walls and after searching for what seemed hours, he found a small latch near the baseboard. He worked trying to get it to move, but it was stuck. After breaking a few fingernails, it finally flicked open, and part of the wall moved just enough for Max to squeeze out. He stood there shaking! Freedom at last. He cautiously went downstairs and sat in a chair and held his head in his hands trying to pull himself together. He leaned back and kept his eyes closed. His head ached and his shirt was drenched with perspiration. The he heard the click of high heels, and a beautiful woman came into the room.

Max crouched down and tried to make himself smaller. That's the woman from the other house he and Hog worked in, he noted. What was she doing here? He watched as she had a palette of colors with her again. She laid them out in the light from the windows. Max thought she must be the interior designer or furniture and color coordinator. She had such a serious look on her face and seemed so intent on the sketches and colors, she'll never even noticed me he hoped as he slowly got up and tried to get away.

Thinking he was almost out of her sight when she suddenly came up behind the chair and said, "Hi there haven't I seen you before? Are you the contractor working on this house?"

Max almost jumped out of his skin but stayed still and turned around.

"No, I just work for the company that is doing the renovations. We are moving the furniture for the painters and cleaning the place out. What are you doing here? I saw you in the other house we were working in," Max said straightening up.

"Oh yeah, I have been asked to come up with some ideas for this house also, for the remodel, so I'm checking it out," Deidre answered. It's sort of a coincidence. I was in the other house and saw you. But no time for talk, I have to go I have an appointment I'm already late for. I just stopped by quickly to pick up my color chart."

"Great to see you again," she called over her shoulder.

Max answered, "I'll see you again sometime."

With a deserved whew!! Max let out his air. He sat back down for a while trying to cool off and pull himself together. Then he left. He was walking fast and heard the siren behind him but kept walking thinking it was not meant for him, would the police stop him for walking too fast. Then the police cruiser pulled up. Max was scared but stood quietly.

The officer motioned him over to the car. He went over to the cruiser and said,

"Yes Sir Officer, you want to talk to me?"

Both officers got out of the car and looked Max over. One asked, "Where are you going in such a hurry?"

"Oh, I just got off work and I was going to meet a friend at the diner a few blocks over and I'm running a little late," Max lied.

"What's your friends name?" asked the policeman.

"Deidre," answered Max, "she's, my girlfriend."

"Where do you work?" asked the second cop.

Max had on one of the painters' hats and motioned to the hat, "You know that big old house on Green Street, well I'm working there with the painting company."

"You sure you didn't break in and steal anything?"

"Oh no Sir," Max said as he dug in his pocket and pulled out the key to the house.

"Here's the key I use to get in, my partner is usually with me, but he had to go out of town for an emergency. The company I work for, it's this company on my hat." The cops looked at the key and said, "how about taking us there."

"Ok," Max agreed, but there's no body there who can vouch for me they are all gone home for the day."

That's ok we'll be the judge of that," the other officer said.

Max got in the car with the cops, and they went back to the house. Max went up to the door and put in the key and they went in.

Max said, "As you can see, we're not ready to paint yet we have to clear away all the junk before we can start."

The First cop looked at the other and said to Max, "Let's see your ID."

Max began to dig in his pockets as if to find his ID, just as he was about to panic the cops radio began squawking. "That's us," The second cop said to his partner, and they started to leave and stopped at the door. One of them turned around and said, "be careful around here there's a serial killer at large and he is targeting mostly men."

"Thanks for the tip," Max responded breathlessly, and they left.

Max collapsed once more in one of the overstuffed chairs with a huff of expelled air. "My God I thought I was a goner I don't know what else can possibly happen today. I'm going back to camp and spend the rest of the night in my bag," Max said to no one. He sat for a few minutes and thought, funny, how a little thing like a painter's hat could save the day.

[Chapter 9]

Hog and Max were walking home after working on Green Street one evening feeling full and content. They had stopped for the blue-plate special at the Silver Diner and were planning their day tomorrow because the paint group wanted to move all the boxes and furniture from the front rooms to the back. Hog was telling Max a story about when he was in the military when they heard noise that sounded like moaning from a wounded animal. Max hesitated to see what it was for fear it could be a rabid animal or some kind of problem they wouldn't know how to deal with. Hog wanted to plunge in and took a few steps toward the sound. Max took Hog by the arm when he started to go into the bushes, "Hold on man we don't know what's going on in there, it could be dangerous. We should go and flag down the cops an let them handle it."

"Max, I'm not digging it, I can't shuck on down the road when I hear somethin that sounds so pitiful as if it's in a lot of pain and turn my back on it. I gotta see what's going on," Hog answered.

He shrugged off Max's hand and when over to the bushes and parted them. It was dark and he could see a human figure but couldn't tell if it was a man or a woman. Hog bent over to get a closer look at the person, then he let out with, "Oh my Lord!"

Hog knew who it was, he stood up and called Max.

"Max get your ass over here it's Angie and we need to give her a hand and get her home."

Max walked over to the bushes and saw Hog kneeling down next to a woman and talking to her softly, "Angie come on baby we going to get you up and take you home," Hog said in a small, kind, coaxing voice.

A surprised Max asked, "Hog, you know this person?"

"Yeah, I know her, I seen her like this before," Hog answered in a woeful way.

Angie continued to sob and moan and lay still on the ground holding her hands over her face, she reeked of alcohol.

"Come on now, Angie girl. This is my friend Max. We are going to get you to your crib, and you'll be alright," Hog crooned, "Max come mere, step on the other side of Angie and we'll lift her up."

Max did what Hog told him and between the two men they got Angie and sat her up in the grass. Hog found her other shoe and put it on her foot. They steadied her so she wouldn't fall backwards and after a little while got Angie to her feet and began walking or more realistically dragging her between the two of them, one on each side of her, then Angie passed out. They put her down gently on the grass and rested a while.

"Angie's place is a few blocks from here I think we can get her there if we keep her upright, she might be able to get her ass moving," Hog said hopefully. They shook her awake and got her up again and started off. It took a long time because they had to stop several times to rest and once to let Angie vomit, but they made it to her basement apartment. Max held Angie up while Hog got the key which was hidden in a container with an artificial plant and opened the door. The efficiency apartment was as neat as a pin. They sat Angie in a chair while they pulled out the bed and then took her over to it and sat her on the side. She held her head in her hands and her hair cascaded down from her braid as she rocked back and forth, whimpering and crying, calling out the name Cassie several times. Each time she said that name a new stream of tears would come down her sad and foreloin face. Hog had his arm around her shoulders and stroked her hair with his other hand and had tears running down his face too, he kept telling her it was ok.

Angie stopped rocking and said in a slow whimpering tone her voice cracking at times between moans, "Hog, the pain, the pain is so heavy it penetrates every pore in my body. Sometimes I'm able to push it down, far down to a place deep and keep it away from my heart where it's tolerable for a time, but it never goes away. It's always there just below the surface, like a perpetual, ceaseless, unrelenting beast waiting to spring forward like a hungry tiger, ripping at my heart and trying to devour it yet again. That's when I can't control it anymore," Angie choked out, "and it bites, gnaws, and claws at my heart until I can't stand no more the pain makes me weak, then I'm helpless and I would do anything to get rid of this devil that chases me and won't let me forget."

"Oh! Lordy Angie. You'll be alright Angie girl, everything will be ok, Cassie is in heaven where she should be, and you can't fret about that anymore. Come now my sweet girl let's get you to lay back and get some sleep, I feel your pain I know your heart is broken," Hog said keeping up a gentle rhetoric and helping Angie down on the bed and said as he brushed her hair back from her eyes with tears continuing down his face, "you gotta rest now." Hog went on lamenting, and comforting, "tomorrow will be better now don't you cry no more now, and he kept talking to her in a soothing and gentle voice till she drifted off to sleep. When he was sure she fell asleep he said, "Ok she done drifted off to sleep and we need to get some vittles for Lucy the dog and then let them be."

Max was so taken back by the display of emotion and empathy Hog emitted. He could not remember when he had seen such a sincere act of comfort and caring, probably never. Hog covered Angie with a blanket and found the dog food and fed and watered the dog. He let the dog out. When the dog came back from outside, she hopped up on the bed, got close to Angie and curled up beside her. Hog checked Angie's breathing once more and when he saw she was in a deep sleep, he turned to her side. We locked the door and placed the key where it was before. We both stayed quiet the whole way back to camp, Max thought he saw Hog wipe his eyes a few times. Max said nothing, he was so blown away by this experience. Of course, he wanted to know the whole story about Angie but felt this was not the time to ask Hog about it. He knew when the time was right Hog would fill him in, it was just all so pathetic to hear Angie in such pain, it made him sad just to think about her and remembering her mournful sounds, she sounded like a wretched animal in distress. Whatever happened in her life that was so egregious stayed with her and she carried it with her in her heart always.

Several weeks went by and one evening when Max got back to the tent, he saw a tin of cookies sitting on Hog's cot. Max smiled to himself glad that someone other than himself recognized Hog's good nature. Max sat on his cot trying to write some notes he would pass on to Ellie and was on his third try attempting to describe the scene when they found Angie, but he couldn't get it quite right. Each time he tried to describe Angie's pain he got lost in his thoughts of her suffering and he could hear her heart-breaking wailing and tears welled up in his eyes.

Hog came in and saw the cookie tin and smiled. He picked it up and opened it and found a small note on top, "I'm coping once again thanks to you Hog, many thanks. The cookies were still warm, and Hog gobbled one down in two bites and offered one to Max. Hog took out the bottle of bourbon they found at the Green Street house, and it was hard to say how long they sat there eating cookies and drinking bourbon.

After a few drinks of the liquor Hog began talking and said, "I know you have been wanting to know Angie's story, I preciate that you waited instead of askin cuz it is a sad one and I feel for her. Not many know much bout her but one day when she was not nearly as drunk as when we found her, she told me about her life and the devils that chased her. She lives by herself and wants to keep it that way. She told me once she was not fit for prime time. I wasn't sure if I dug that, but I know what she meant.

Angie was a very happily married woman, and her life was sweet. She was married to a man who was well off and though she didn't have to work, she was a substitute teacher and she loved kids. Her husband wanted a family very much also and they were trying, but after 5 years it seemed as if it was not going to happen. She told me once that she felt bad about not getting pregnant, but her husband was the one she worried about. He had that natural thing like an instinct, that some people have with kids, and for whatever reason they liked him very much. They would go to the park and sit on a blanket and soon there were about 5 or 6 kids around us, and Jake would be telling them jokes or a story and they were mesmerized. The kids in our neighborhood would come to our door and ask if Jake could come play with them. I was not jealous, but I worried about Jake because I know he longed for a child of his own.

There was a local Boys and Girls club, and Jake and I would chaperone some events. He would buy them treats or birthday presents and make me say the things were from me afraid parents might get the wrong impression if they were from him. We talked about adoption, but I was against it and would not consent. Then one day wonder of wonders I got pregnant. My God you would have thought the sun shined only on me. Jake practically carried me around. Our little girl was so sweet and perfect it was a fairytale come true. We named her Cassie. One day when Cassie was 3 years old, we decided to have a fourth of July barbeque. We had a bunch of friends over and we decorated with small flags and tiki lamps around the patio and had a lot of fun.

The next day I was in the yard cleaning up and Cassie was on the patio playing with her toys. I worked physically hard that day and slipped on a muddy patch in the yard and I hurt my back. It would be sore the next day, but it was not serious. Jake was out of town on business, so Cassie and

I had a light dinner and I put Cassie to bed. She seemed unusually tired. The next morning, the fall had made my back stiff and achy. I didn't hear Cassie crying so I took my time getting dressed. When I went to wake up Cassie she was not moving, I shook her and still nothing then I saw she was not breathing, and I began CPR, but she did not respond. She turned blue and was still not breathing. I called 911 and we rushed her to the hospital, but she never woke up. I was hysterical and paced around the small exam cubicle holding her little body in my arms. The nurse came in and tried to calm me down and asked me to sit down. That's when I saw the blood running down my legs. I was bleeding heavily and knew that was not good. I was pregnant, it was a surprise to me and now I was bleeding probably from the fall I took yesterday, and the stress. I hemorrhaged so badly they told me they had to take me to the operating room, or I would bleed to death. I was rushed to the operating room. They got in touch with Jake, and he finally arrived just as they were bringing me out of surgery. Jake was overwhelmed with all that happened and was in shock. We could hardly believe it when the doctor who had done the operation on me came in to say he had no choice but to perform a hysterectomy and I could never have and more children.

We were both hardly able to cope. It took months to recover, I sometimes questioned if Jake ever got over all that happened, we were both depressed. He was by my side every minute while I recovered. I physically recovered although my mind was a wreck. Jake did everything he could to help me get back to normal and then he began talking about adopting a child. We never disgusted what happened to Cassie. They found a container of the tiki torch oil and it looked like apple juice. Cassie must have found the bottle and drank a lot of it which poisoned her. When I found out I blamed myself for not keeping a better eye on her. Jake did not blame me outwardly but there was something different with our relationship from then on. I was not sure I could trust myself with a child again, any child. In my heart I knew that I would not be able to accept an adopted child when I felt that in the eyes of everyone who heard about what happened to Cassie thought I was a neglectful mother.

When I was strong enough, I told Jake I had to be by myself for a while and got my own apartment. We were still friends, but I knew I must end our marriage, poor Jake would never find happiness with me without children, and I couldn't bring myself to consent to adaptation. Because of that I divorced him and considered myself a negligent mother, I hated myself.

After two years Jake found a girlfriend. She was very different than me, she had bright blonde hair and wore a lot of make-up and dressed in a sexy way. Who was I to pass judgement? If she made Jake happy then that was ok with me. They seemed happy and got married. In the following year they had a beautiful blond little girl, called Mary Jane and they seemed like the perfect little family. I felt comforted that Jake was so content, and I told him I wished them well. The child loved Jake very much and they were almost inseparable. I don't know how it happened, but Jake and his wife Carol began drifting apart. She said she and her friends thought his behavior with the child was abnormal, that fathers didn't spend so much time with their kids. Carol started seeing a psychiatrist then she decided to divorce Jake and told her lawyers that Jake was a pervert, and she didn't want him near their 2-year-old daughter anymore. After Jake left the child became very distraught at not seeing her father, she cried all the time. As so many divorcees do, Carol was unreasonable and couldn't prove the nasty things she said about Jake and after a long period of back and forth he said she said with lawyers, the judge decided Jake should be allowed to see the child.

Carol and I had become friends, I know that sounds odd, but in the beginning, I thought we both wanted the same thing for Jake. After the divorce proceedings Carol began to change, she was so angry all the time now, and livid that the judge was going to permit Jake to see Mary Jane. The first time Jake was to see Mary Jane, Carol asked me to come over and be there when Jake came to pick up the child because she didn't want to see him.

When Jake came to pick up the child for his first visit. I did what Carol asked and took the child outside and I was holding her standing in the yard. I saw Jake begin walking across the street. Suddenly Carol came running out of the house with a butcher's knife and grabbed the child out of my arms and laid her in the grass and began stabbing her. I was shocked. I rushed over and tried to pull her off the baby and she stabbed me to. Jake jumped on her and tried to pull her away from the baby, but she was wild, she had so much strength. She started stabbing at Jake to, but he never flinched and was finally able to subdue her by punching her so hard she passed out. Jake picked up the baby, and began CPR, but it was too late, Carol had cut her throat and blood poured out. I called 911. By the time they got there the baby was dead. Jake's face was covered with blood because he had been trying to do month to mouth breathing on the baby. They took all of us to the hospital except Carol, they took her away in a police car.

Jake held the baby in his arms and wouldn't let go of her little body. Then as if something snapped inside of him, he looked as if he were in a trance. The nurse came and took the baby. Jake would not talk he walked like a zombie, even after many months of drugs and therapy, Jake did not respond from his deep mental depression. After about 6 months he refused to eat. He pulled out the IV and feeding tubes each time they inserted them. He grew weaker and weaker and was near death. I came to see him.

Hs physical appearance was completely changed. He was so thin and wasted looking and looked like an old man. I wasn't sure if he would recognize me as he had not even acknowledged me the last few times I was there.

Jake looked at me and I took his hand. He said, "There in the sky I see Cassie and Mary Jane and I'm going to them." He closed his eyes and drifted off to sleep. That night he died in his sleep. "You see it's all my fault if I had not poisoned Cassie and lost my other baby and consented to adoption, would have had kids around it would have been ok, but I killed them all, all the people I loved with my pigheaded ideas about adoption.

"That's what happened to her heart," Hog said, "it was shattered into pieces." He took a huge swallow of liquor, "and it never healed, she has never forgiven herself."

"Oh Hog, they always say that truth is stranger than fiction and I wasn't sure I believed that until now. Nobody could hold up to the kind of pain that Angie feels."

"And there ain't no one who can take it away either," Hog intoned sadly.

[Chapter 10]

Deidre Ramsey had big hopes and dreams and the idea of becoming a clothing designer since she was a child. Her talents were drawing, designing, sewing, and sketching. She won contest after contest first in her local town, then county wide then statewide. Her college degree in art and design had been a great experience because she loved every minute of it, and she had a 4.0 average. Her first job wasn't really a job at all, it was a non-paying internship in a design firm. She worked in the evening as a waitress to pay the rent and could eat one meal at the restaurant which saved her butt.

The firm had many rich and influential clients and her boss depended on her and the staff to please them, to make sure they came back for more. Deidre's main job was to take sketches from one department to others for input from each department head on what fabrics to use and then to the head designer for final approval. That might sound boring, to most people, but it was not as bad as one would suspect because Deidre met rich and famous people from all areas of life and learned a lot about making selecting designs. With her beautiful long, brunette main curling down her back, her green eyes flashing and her sweet disposition most of the clients found her pleasing some even asked for her each time they came in. Deidre spent time with them no matter if their appointments ran over, she stayed and talked with them. At the end of the workday after making many trips all over the building, until all the people working on the design signed off, Deidre was tired. She left for her other job each night physically tired, but it didn't stop her from dreaming.

Deidre enjoyed rubbing shoulders with the rich and famous when they came in for fittings or looking for outfits for a special event, it was exciting to see how the clothes looked on them. She didn't get introduced to the clients formally but was present when the designers brought out the sketches or when they were there for a fitting, she assisted some as they tried on clothing. They often brought the entire collection and talked about whoever they were dating at the time and gossiped about the rich and famous people they knew. That was the exciting part of her job. In her heart she knew that one day she would connect with one of these people who had big bucks and they would give her a start and use her designs. Then the design house and especially her boss would understand and know how talented she was and that she could bring so much to the fashion industry.

After a few years of playing errand boy and delivering sketches and dreaming of her future plans she was getting a little discouraged. She talked to Chas Dunkin, her boss, about the possibility of getting a paying job with the company and the boss gave her encouragement. Deidre often discussed her ideas with him, and he often asked her opinion on some of the sketches he was working on. On one particularly difficult day when Deidre was erroneously blamed for upsetting a client who didn't like the dress that was designed for her, she didn't throw her boss under the bus when they balled her out instead of him.

After that challenge blew over Deidre asked her boss what her future with the firm was because she said she didn't know how much longer she could stay there and work without being paid. He told her that he thought there was a job opening becoming available soon and that she was the most experienced person they had for it. Deidre was very excited. Her boss intimated that they were looking for someone from the inside and she had a good chance of getting the job. It was not designing but nonetheless a step up from what she was doing and a much-needed-paying job. Deidre had applied for the job and waited weeks for the team to make up their minds. The job was to be awarded on a Friday afternoon.

That morning Deidre asked her boss if she was even in the running, he told Deidre that the design group was secretly meeting at noon. He said this with a smile and a wink, so Deidre was thrilled thinking she had the job. She continued with her work that morning when one of the other staff members rushed by her and knocked the design boards out of her hands. As she picked them up Deidre began looking at each one closely. She noticed that one of the sketches had some women's trousers which were very much like the ones she had been working on in her sketch book she kept in her cubicle. Another one had a dress that had almost exactly the same design as one she had done weeks ago for a friend. Never mind she thought soon I'll be able to get my ideas across to the team and they will see my talent when I get the new job. After lunch around 2 o'clock she couldn't stand it anymore, so she went to her boss's office, knocked and he called, "come in."

Seeing it was her, "He said, 'I'm busy now Deidre what do you want?"

"Chas, I wanted to know if you heard who they gave the job to? Asked Deidre, point blank.

"Oh, they decided that they should select someone from the outside rather than anyone here because they needed some fresh ideas," he said in an off the cuff way.

Deidre was shocked. That answer plucked Deidre's last nerve and she said, "New ideas, new ideas, I have been trying to get someone to see my NEW IDEAS and no one wanted any part of even looking at them. But what I did see today are some of my ideas on your sketch board. Can you tell me why they looked so much like my designs?"

"Are you accusing me of stealing your work? He asked. "Because if you are I will see to it that you never get a job designing anything, anywhere, ever."

"What a bunch a conceited pricks you all are, you think you are so high and mighty. You know the truth of You, Chas knows the truth of what you have taken from me, and I will make you pay for that, I'm out of here.

She ran back to her cubicle, packed up her desk and left. She went to her apartment and cried for two days then she knew she had to do something else to make a living, so she began looking for a new job. What now! Certainly, I have to make a living, and although her waitress job kept her rent paid that was about all it could do; in fact, it was a blessing that she was able to eat one meal a day there. It was at this time Deidre's boyfriend asked her to marry him. In her desperate situation, feeling she was going to starve and never find a job, she agreed. They were married at the courthouse the next day and for the next 6 months they were happy newlyweds. Then Deidre realized that the man she married had no ambition of finding a better job and living in a small one-bedroom crummy apartment was ok with him. She began to dream about her career again and started looking for a job in design. The couple soon grew apart and got divorced mutually.

Deidre thought about what else she could do and came up with the idea of becoming a personal service assistant. After all, hadn't she babysat important clients and kept them occupied and happy doing the dance of the dumb dumbs while the designers put their final touches on their new ensembles. If she stayed close to that kind of people, she might get a break and that was what she thought would be in a way staying close to rich clients.

Deidre found a job as a personal assistant a far cry from designing but exposure to clients who had money, so it was ok. Money often meant they were well dressed and could spend money on good clothing. Maybe she could see her way to doing something with this job. Thinking back to her first personal service client Shane Blake was a downer. Wanting to make a good impression she began to do too much for the man. He came to rely on her for everything and Deidre hated that. She had been at the job about 2 months when he first began asking her to help him in the bathroom. She would set the water temperature and lay out his shaving kit, toothpaste, and clean clothes. When he demanded that she begin washing him that's when she had enough. She told him she was leaving, and he said if she didn't have sex with him, he would tell the agency that she stole money from him and she would never work in the industry again. After working extra hard to avoid getting close to him, she decided to take a chance and quit anyway, explaining to her boss what happened. It seemed her boss was surprised that she stayed as long as she did with him because he was notorious for demanding sex from everyone who had taken care of him. Deidre felt so good that she had not given in to him.

Her new job was no easy task. Though it was nothing like the role of Andy the character portraited as Meryl Streep's junior personal assistant in the movie, "The Devil Wears Prada", but it was a very demanding job. Assignments came and went and after about a year and a half she finally got lucky and was hired by Joseph Worthington Collins, heir to the prestigious line of clothing his family owned. She stayed with Joseph until he recuperated from his surgery, luckily for her that had lasted much longer than expected. It worked out so well she left the agency and began working directly for Joseph.

The job did not turn out as she expected but she was becoming familiar with his line of clothing. Joseph was an older man and decided he was tired of traveling the world. He wanted to come home to the family mansion. The problem was that no one had lived in the huge house for the last 50 years and its maintenance and upkeep had been neglected, so he set about restoring it to its former elegance before moving in.

His plan was to oversee the restoration and he needed an assistant to do the leg work. Deidre had been working for Joseph for only 3 months when he was called to Paris where most of his clothing line was made, to make some corporate decisions. He left and told Deidre that she was in charge of the restorations while he was gone and that since she was familiar with color, art and design, he would trust her judgement on the remodeling of the old place until he got back. Besides, the major repairs and changes had already been made. Deirdre was so grateful to Joseph he was such a good and kind man he had turned her life around and given her a chance and she would always remember that.

Deidre was happy and scared at the same time. Although she loved design she had never dabbled in any home or furniture designs. With the thought of working with Joseph on the remodel, she had taken a crash course in the home design basics. Joseph had tried to hire an interior decorator before he left but did not have time to select one. Deidre would continue the search. She had been in on a few interviews Joseph had with a few interior designers, but he did not like any of them. The basic repairs continued, and Deidre spent a lot of time at the house itself trying to get a feel for what was needed.

Max and Hog were working on Green Street one day when the front doorbell rang and it was Mrs. Gray standing there carrying a small brief case immaculately dressed in business attire who introduced herself as Mrs. Charlotte Gray of the New York Firm Goldman, Gamp, Gamp, & Stein, Chief Interior Designer. Max invited her in.

Deidre came and said hello to Mrs. Gray. They met briefly before but it was not a good encounter. "I see you are still here," Mrs. Gray said, "May I to speak to the person in charge." Deidre told Mrs. Gray that Joseph left her in charge and the woman seemed to look down at her as if she didn't believe her ears.

"Oh, I see Mrs. Gray," Said. "Will he be back soon?"

"I'm not sure his business is keeping him quite busy in Paris and we communicate only through email and the phone," replied Deidre.

"I see when I was here before I didn't think Joseph left you in charge. Have you had any experience with Interior design," Mrs. Gray inquired, staring at Deidre.

"I majored in design and art in college," Deidre told her, "But mostly in clothing design not in interior design."

"Well then, I expect you will be wanting me to make all the decisions and that is just fine with me. I have redesigned many homes like this in the past, that's why Mr. Collins hired our firm.

"Mrs. Gray before we go any further, I was under the impression that Mr. Collins didn't hire anyone."

"I believe his nephew attended to the details of hiring our firm and of course they understood he would want the very best person for the job," Mrs. Gray intoned in a haughty voice.

Deidre thought a minute and decided she would investigate that later. "So, "she said, "could you give me some examples of your work?"

"Examples of my work?" questioned Mrs. Gray.

"I mean are there some homes here in the city I could visit to see your work?" Deidre amended.

"Well, I sent my credentials to Mr. Collins, and I thought that was sufficient."

"As you see Mr. Collins is not here at the moment so if I could, I would like to see some of your work in person," insisted Deidre.

"Very well I will send you the addresses of some of the homes I have redesigned, and I will call and set up appointments for you to go and see them without disturbing them. I will leave you my card and get back to you. Good day Miss., ah I …I don't remember your name. I'm not sure we can work together but for Joseph's sake we should try."

"Deidre," Deidre said, "Deidre Davis and don't worry I won't go unannounced and will not upset or bother your clients in any way."

To say the least Deidre was annoyed by the pretentious Mrs. Gray who had looked down her nose at her. I wonder why Joseph hired this wretched woman and never told me about it thought Deidre. I guess I should not be so judgmental and give the great Mrs. Gray a chance to show me what she has in mind for the old place. With that thought Deidre fired off an email to Joseph and asked if he had really hired Mrs. Gray. She hoped it would be a logical explanation. Joseph emailed back to say he wasn't aware that Mrs. Gray was hired and that it must have been a misunderstanding. He suggested that if Mrs. Gray had come from one of the firms, he said he thought she must be experienced. He suggested that Deidre have her come and give some suggestions as a consultant. If they are good and we like them, we can use them or see if we want to find someone else. Deidre thought that was fair and that she would go to see the woman's work and then decide. Deidre wondered if the other people who were on the job had heard the exchange between, she and Mrs. Gray, if they did, they might complain to Joseph. The next time I see Mrs. Gray I will apologize to her and hope she will not hold any grudges against me, after all she was trying to protect Joseph.

[Chapter 11]

Max came out of the tent and looked haggard. He sat down on a bench and held his head. Soon he saw a woman come out of her shelter and light a cigarette and walk slowly over to where Max sat.

"Hey, how are ya doing you look upset?" Candy in her deep sexy voice.

"Oh, I just can't sleep because of the noise and I'm trying to shake it off," Max confessed.

"What noise I didn't hear anything," Candy replied.

"I know it sounds silly but it's that stupid, wad of paper stuck to that pole right there above our tent and when the wind blows it flaps and kept me awake," Max explained, then he paused and looked at Candy and said, "that certainly makes me look like a prima donna doesn't it," and he choked out and laughed.

"It sounds like the princess and the pea story," Candy said with a grin, and they both began to laugh uproariously.

After they recovered from the enjoyment of pure delicious laughter Candy took Max's hand and pulled him to his feet. "Come Momma can fix this for you."

They walked over to the tent and Candy who was about 8-9 inches taller than Max reached up on her tip toes and pulled down the offensive flapping papers.

"Oh my God!" Max exclaimed, "You are my hero." Come on let's go over to the diner and I'll buy you a coffee and a donut for saving my life," Max invited, and they continued to laugh and talk as they walked.

Max and Candy were friends after that. Candy didn't leave the camp much. Sometimes she would get dressed up and be gone for a few hours and when she come back, she would stay in her shelter most of the day. Candy and Max talked a lot, and she would wave to them as Max and Hog went off for the day. Candy and Max and Hog sometimes ate together when the group had a common meal.

For the next few weeks Max and Hog didn't find any jobs so they just wandered all over the city to see if they could find some good "stuff" that was free. They found a beat-up bicycle that was left abandoned under the bridge and Max told Hog he thought he could fix it up, so one of the things they were looking for were old bike parts to restore the bike. They walked almost to the end of the city limits but had no luck finding anything useful. By the time they walked back to camp they were tired. They ate the food they brought back and had some wine and went to sleep. Max and Hog slept late that morning and would have slept longer except for the noise outside in the camp. They got up and went out to see what was going on. Hog and Max walked over to where Lenny was standing and Hog asked, "What's happening man?"

Lenny said to Hog, "I was bout to rouse you because the cops will be here soon, and I know you don't want them to see you."

"What happened." asked Hog, did someone get caught stealing or something?"

"It ain't that, it's worse, it's Candy, Mary found her this morning she finally did it, she cut out. Mary went to check on her because she hurtin bad last night."

"You mean Candy is dead asked Max?" stunned.

"Yeah, she gave up the ghost," Lenny answered.

"What do you mean?' Max blurred out.

"She couldn't stand the pain no more. She said that when it got to where the narcs didn't fix it, she would take care of it her damn self," Lenny said.

"Candy did just like she had a mind to," declared Hog.

"Yeah, she had been saying that her good days were not coming like they was a couple of months ago. She had been saying this for months now and everybody thought it would pass. Then she fell out a couple of times and she couldn't take it anymore." Lenny agreed.

"Oh God! Why? Why would she do a thing like that?" Max said very emotionally.

"Son she was in misery and taken more and more medicine. Then it stopped working and the pain got worse, and it got to her." Lenny said, "she could stand but so much, you know Max if it you can't cure it you have to bear it."

Max had tears in his eyes and told Hog he was going to the tent to sit for a minute and walked off. Hog followed Max and sat down on his cot and said to Max.

"Don't fuss too much Candy suffered a long time and here lately she had been livin on weed and crack," Hog said.

"Hog what was she suffering from," asked Max.

"She had HIV," Hog said.

"HIV? HIV? They do a lot with HIV these days why didn't she get treated?"

"Yeah well, she got treated but she didn't get in the know until it was too late. She got the heave ho from her job. She used to work at the drag show place and made good money but spent it all on clothes and make-up for the show. She didn't have no education. Her family was all out in California, and she hadn't seen or heard from them in years. Candy was desperate and started selling her body. When her partner heard about that, he went off. He busted her up pretty good. Somebody called the cops, and they took her to the hospital. That's when she found out she had HIV. When she was released, she got in the dude's face about it, and he threw her out. She waited a long time before she came around to what her diagnosis was because she couldn't believe it at first," Hog explained.

Max knew from a few articles he had written that the final stage of HIV infection is AIDS, which occurs when the immune system is severely damaged. People with AIDS lose weight rapidly and have recurring fevers and liver problems and many physical symptoms.

Hog said, "When Candy started having big time pain, she also had serious liver disease. She had no crib. She was hanging in the park or in old cars. Lenny was in the park one day and saw two teenage punks trying to rip her off and he scared them away. He brought her here and she has been here ever since. Candy was a looker before she got sick, I seen pictures of her when she was in good health. "Hog sighed and gave a moan. "Shit happens to a lot of folks on the street. When you feel so hopeless that you got nowhere to turn that's when you sell your soul to the devil and sell your body to get money to buy drugs to get you through."

Max was floored, there was another surprise he would have never dreamed of. Candy seemed like an ordinary person, she was not bitter and never mean and never let on she was so seriously ill.

[Chapter 12]

Max contacted Ellie and asked her if it would be ok if they met outside her apartment. This was breaking the rules they set up in the beginning about not having any contact, but the soup kitchen was closing for renovations, and they had not found another site to startup. There was a small, wooded area near Ellie's apartment that no one ever went to. Max wanted to give her an outline he had worked on so that she could start putting the information he sent her into some kind of order. Max was building his literary straw man so that he could follow it and make the book writing easier when he was ready. Ellie agreed and they got together that evening.

Ellie met Max just after the sun went down. He brought two 5-gallon buckets to sit on and an old blanket. She brought a carry out box with two huge sandwiches and a salad. She had a bottle of wine and glasses in another bag. They sat and ate, and it was the first time in a very long period Max had some of his favorite food and good wine. He drank most of it and became very talkative. He began telling Ellie about how much he wished that his life was different when he was growing up. "For the first part of my life Max began, I had a real family, my mother tried to keep us together, we were all happy and loved each other. Then things changed. It just seemed that every time she planned a dinner for us to have as a family group my father didn't make it and me and my mom were left on our own. When he was home, he constantly complained and criticized my mother, for her lack of sophistication and accused her of spoiling me by loving me so much, is there such a thing? I don't want to bore you with my story Ellie, so I'll just shut up."

"No Max I would love to hear about your life I know so little about you though we worked together for so long,"

"Mom went away when my father first took me to live with his parents. She returned because she missed me so much, but he wouldn't let her see me very often. The last thing that my father did that my mom couldn't tolerate was deciding that I would go to boarding school. They argued about that for weeks. The day before I was to leave for school, mom and I biked to the beach and spent the whole day together. She tried to explain to me that she had to leave because my father made her life miserable but that she would always love me. The next day she was gone. When I told my father that she was gone he said, "Good riddance."

I ran away from the boarding school several times, so my father decided that he would keep me at home with a tutor. It wasn't long after that, that Erol got married to CJ. She seemed ok and was nice to me, but she wanted no part of being a stepparent. Erol and CJ had an "open marriage," which of course did not include kids or family.

A typical week for me now was something like scheduled chaos and confusion. When Erol or CJ were having an extra marital affair, they didn't come home for 3- 4 evenings a week or sometimes the weekend. They had no close friends or for that matter didn't even know their neighbors except to wave when they passed them in the car. Erol thought it sure beat the way he grew up in a small town where everybody knew everybody else's business.

Erol and CJ would ask each other mundane questions and pretend they both had very busy schedules and it seemed to work out for them somehow. Erol liked the idea that he could come and go as he pleased with no explanation. One time when Erol was hot and heavy with the new receptionist, "Miss I answer phones well and give a good roll in the sack, but that's all I can do," he didn't even remember her full name, but they were having a ball sneaking around at the office thinking no one knew about them. Meeting in closets for a quick feel, that was fun for a while until someone spotted them and asked him about the cute little receptionist.

"Hey Erol, I saw you with the new receptionist downstairs. Her name is Sherry, isn't it? and she has a body to die for," Erol's account manager asked.

"I sort of met her yesterday, and she is great eye candy," Erol said with a sinister grin.

Erol just smiled to himself and thought about the firmness of her butt. At the same time, since someone from the office saw Erol with Sherry together, she had to be history. He mentally admitted he was sorry he had to do that to her but now she would have to go. No room for rumors to start and then corporate would be all over him for breaking yet another rule. This too would pass and someone else will come along they always did. Tonight, he would buy CJ some flowers and call and tell her he was taking us out for dinner so she wouldn't have to microwave dinner or get carry out and she would be none the wiser. In Erol's mind, he would forgive himself. The receptionist would be upset with him for a few days, he would stay away from her, or maybe she would quit, if not he would have her fired and then it would all be ok.

We ate out often and most of the time it would go like this my father would think that the hostess at the restaurant looked at him with hungry eyes and he could had sworn that she would have given anything to jump his bones, but he martyred himself and shrugged it off. CJ would chat on about how she found the perfect dress for the party they were invited to, and she was going to have some shoes dyed to match the dress. The rest of the conversation went like this.

"How was your day dear?" CJ asked Erol just as the appetizer was being served.

"It was a little busy today," Erol answered, Anthony the assistant executive officer was in a car accident and got banged up a bit and needed surgery. The gossip is that he had too much to drink and hit another car."

"Oh, that's too bad," CJ responded. Thinking to herself that Anthony did drink like a fish and sometimes when they were together, he couldn't get it up. "Are they going to send flowers from the office?"

"Oh sure, Sarah my secretary will take care of all that. How about you what did you do?"

"I went to a charity luncheon and then shopping," answered CJ.

"That's lovely dear," Erol said, trying to conceal the fact he was bored to death.

I mostly kept my mouth shut. I was busy texting my fellow game players with my new iPhone under the tablecloth, so no one really saw me. No one really cared anyway, especially my parents. I hoped my stepmother wouldn't notice the $1252.00 dollars I had racked up on buying game time online that month. It didn't matter when she noticed, I would just tell her how sorry I was, and she would forget she told me not to use her card. A sniffle here and there wouldn't hurt, and I would tell her how nice she looked and soon I would be back in her good graces. She probably wouldn't even mention it to my father. I really thought that a little larceny might get her at least angry with me, but she was in a hurry getting ready to go out with her friends and she really didn't say much. Maybe it would hit her later if dad questioned her about the bill.

As a young guy, I didn't really understand all that stupid fake, rhetoric they were spewing as long as I could continue to play games on my phone and keep buying new ones, I was happy. I wanted my own credit card, and I was pretty sure my father was going to give me one for my birthday, but for now I had my stepmother's card which I managed to get access to, so it was working ok. I didn't have any friends except those friends I played games with online. As far schoolwork I had a tutor, Ronny who did my homework, and had been doing that for a while now. Once I stopped turning in my homework and thought that getting failing grades would get my parents attention. I had tried several other things that didn't work. They did notice the failing grades after a call from my teacher. They responded by firing Ronny and getting me another tutor who was a real geek and was almost at my house full time because I had great computer equipment and updates of every electronic gadget you could think of and Lenny the tutor loved them all.

When school was out, I would go to camp in the Hampton's for 8 weeks and then to Hawaii for the rest of the summer. I would see my parents off and on when they came to their house in Maui, mostly separately. It didn't matter if I was getting a good education my father would get me a place in college because the business donated a lot of money to the university and the university would have to accept me there. For right now I had to play his game for the next few years because soon I would be driving, and I wanted a car. Not just any car, but a BMW convertible I had already picked out. It was just a question of dropping the hint to my stepmother and she would tell my father and next thing you know; it would be there in the garage with a big red bow on it waiting for me to be surprised.

Essentially, I spent my early years going back and forth from home school with tutors to vacations in the Hawaiian house where I saw my parents for a few weeks and then go back to college. On several occasions after I got my car, and I got in trouble my father gave me a lecture and that was it.

Then my father had a stroke and a strange thing happened, it changed him completely. It was like a life awakening. He had to work hard at physical therapy to get his strength back and when he was fully recovered his persona and views on life changed. Now he not only insisted that I go to college, but I do well. He wanted to know what courses I was taking etc. And he started to care about work. He and CJ divorced, and he became a workaholic, so, I tried to do my best in college."

"What about college? Asked Ellie, "Didn't you meet any one you wanted to be with?"

"No not really, I dated a lot of the girls but none every really made me think of marriage. Besides I don't have much respect for marriage, it seemed like a waste for my father."

My father and I spent many hours discussing why I took English and Literature courses and wanted to become a writer and not go into the family business. He threatened that if I didn't graduate from college, and at least go to work for the business for a year he would cut off my inheritance. I knew my father was serious about this, so I took a few business courses and graduated from college.

"Wow that was a mouthful," said Ellie," I'm sorry you didn't have an ideal life growing up but not many people do. It was a lot easier than growing up under the same non-caring parental attitude with money."

"I'm sorry," Max said, "I was just feeling sorry for myself because I'm feeling badly about something that happened."

"Do you want to share that?" asked Ellie. And Max told her about Candy. Ellie was very empathic and said she was sorry.

"I have the story on tape so you will hear the details anyway. I have been accepted by the homeless camp group and I don't want to blow that cover. I know that what I'm doing, writing about them, is a breach of the group's trust and if they knew I would be kicked out of the camp. I'm hoping as I get the stories and the book together and give the people who told them to me fictious names they will agree to let me use the material. I'm trying to help them. I want to do something good for them and I hope they will forgive me when they find out about the book," Max said hopefully. "I think I bored you enough already."

"You didn't bore me Max, but I have to go. I hate to end our session like this but there was another police questioning session and this time your old girlfriend Charmayne was there. She told them that you are unstable always wanting to do wacky stuff and that you sometimes thought people were being mean and not treating others well. They ate that up and wrote it all down. I tried to explain your motives, but they were eager to hear the nasty stuff Charmayne said and not what I had to say, Ellie reluctantly told Max.

"Thanks Ellie, I appreciate that you believe me, even though no one else does, my relationship with Charmayne was over before it started because she was not the kind of woman I want to marry. I'm sorry to say I kept her around because she was good at parties and entertaining, outside of that she has no depth."

[Chapter 13]

Max continued to be disturbed by Candy's death and moped around for days. Hog asked him if he was ok. He had been sitting on his cot most of the day and Hog saw that he had a coin he would bring out of his pocket and look at.

"What you got there Max is that a lucky coin?"

"Yeah, it helps me de-stress when I'm upset. It's a coin my grandfather gave me when I was a boy. He carried it with him when he was in the military during the war, and he swore that it saved him several times. A few days before he passed away, he gave it to me and made me promise to keep it with me all the time. I have kept it in my pocket since then. He believed that it would save my life one day.

"Them old folks have visions before they pass so I would latch on it," Hog said sincerely.

"I think I'm suffering from cabin fever Hog and missing Candy. She was so kind to me and such a gentle person when you got to know her."

"Let's beat feet and go to the diner for a while," Hog suggested.

At the diner they had coffee and sandwiches. Hog did most of the talking.

"Yup, you're right. This was a bummed-out week and I miss her too. What do you say we go down to the 7-11 tomorrow and maybe pick up a hustle for a couple of days. Workin may take our minds off Candy for a while." Hog proposed. Maybe the painter will come by and need something."

The next day they went to see if they could find something to do. Sure enough, their timing was just right, and the same painting company people came by and when the foreman saw Hog and Max, he signaled them over and asked them if they would like to work with them again. They readily agreed. The next day was Saturday, and the painters didn't work on weekends. Hog and Max hung around the camp most of the morning and did nothing.

It was early afternoon when David Strong came up to Hog and communicated to him that he wanted to go fishing. He didn't talk but Hog had done this with David before and now he had his beat-up fishing pole in his hand and kept gesturing that they go.

Hog turned to Max and said, "Wanta go fishing with David here, he looks like he needs it."

"Hog I would go but I don't have a fishing pole and I haven't done a lot of fishing in my life," Max confessed, "I really don't know a lot about it."

"Hell, no need to worry about that," Hog said, "We'll just find a stick, or a branch and I got some fishing line and you'll be ready to roll."

Off they went to fish off the old dock and see what they could catch. Max was doubtful they would catch anything, since he had nothing else to do, he went along with them. They were there for about an hour before David thought he had a bite. Hog encouraged him and he tugged and pulled at the fishing pole and soon brought up a pile of plastic, the kind that a six pack comes in with other debris hanging on to it. When David saw what he caught he was visibly upset. He grunted and groaned and threw his fishing pole on the ground. He stomped his feet and picked up the pole and walked away.

Max didn't know what to think.

"What just happened Hog?" Max asked, taken by surprise at David's outburst.

"Well don't be to be worried about David he has a hard time accepting things, this water is so polluted I doubt there is a fish within miles of here," Hog replied, besides this happens every time we come here."

"Why do you keep coming here then?" Max inquired.

"Ya got me, it's because David likes to come here, I guess. It might could be that he remembers going fishing with his father when he was a boy. At least that's what the psych guy told us once when he came to see what happened to David when he didn't show up for his appointment at the Free Clinic. Some of those clinic folks are mighty good to people and they came looking for David. One day they found him sittin in the basement of the clinic building and he wouldn't talk to anybody. They didn't know what to do so they took him back to the shelter. After a few days the shelter called the clinic and asked for help because now David not only wouldn't talk but he wouldn't eat and refused to come out of the dorm. They took him to the hospital, and he escaped from there. One day Lenny was walking close to the bridge tunnel and heard a dog barking. He saw David and the dog, and they were both shivering with cold. He brought them back to camp and they been here since. David and the dog were buddy, buddy."

"Wow," Max said, "That a great humanitarian story."

"I don't know nuttin about that but it's what happened," Hog declared.

"So, what happened after that?" asked Max, intrigued by yet another story about one of the people in camp.

"Well one day the dog got sick and couldn't walk, and David nearly lost it. Lenny carried David and the dog to town to the animal shelter and begged someone to look at the dog. They called James who was a veterinarian and volunteered at the shelter. James took care of the dogs in Iraq and stepped on a mine. It blew off his legs and part of his face. He was with it, but he was in a wheelchair and had a hard time because of his messed-up face, it was pretty hard to look at him. He came to the animal shelter to take care of the dogs. The dog was very sick, and James ended up bringing David and the dog to his house so he could treat the dog every day. David stayed there until the dog got better.

James didn't have much family and never married so when his parents died, he just stayed at the house. His parents had taken out a reverse mortgage on their house to take care of James when he first came back. He needed a lot of medical care, and the VA was slow to get him help. When his parents both passed away James's monthly pay wasn't enough to pay the tax man, they took the house. He stayed with his sister and her husband but one day he overheard them arguing about the fact that they were planning to get a divorce but with him there they put a lid on that.

One day both his sister and brother-in-law let out of the house and never came back. His sister left him a note and told him she had lost her job and she had to go away to work. James was left alone in the house for days with no food, he couldn't get around well and wasn't capable of taking the medicine he needed. Some neighbors found him out in the driveway half naked covered with crap and looking half starved. They called the police, and they took him to the hospital and kept him. Weeks later when his sister came back to see him, she didn't know what happened and asked the neighbors where James was, and they told her. She went to the hospital and apologized to James saying she thought that her husband was coming back and would take care of James. If that was the real scoop or not James didn't care. His sister told him that they were going to sell the house so in a few months he would have to find another place to live.

James went to a men's shelter but there was nobody there to help him. He met up with David again when David brought the dog to the clinic again and asked for James and they told him what happened, and that James didn't come there anymore. David went to see James and wanted to help him, but the shelter wouldn't let the dog stay.

They didn't know where they would go but they wanted to stay together. David brought James and the dog to camp. Lenny didn't have the heart to say no, he feels for military people, besides they could take care of themselves cuz James had a pension from the army, not much but he could get his medicine and other things he needed.

Where is James now," asked Max, "I haven't met anybody named James, where did he go?"

James died a few months ago, right before I met you, it seems he got a real bad infection after he had another surgery at the hospital, and they couldn't cure it." "Holy cow what a story," Max mumbled.

"Lenny doesn't have the heart to send David away so we all just sort of keep an eye on him, he really is harmless, it would be a shame to have him go someplace where someone might take unfair advantage of him because he can't take care of himself his head is screwed up," Hog spewed out. "Best he stays here cuz after the dog died is when David stopped talking. He has not said a word since."

"Hog honestly before I met you and came to this place, I thought most of the homeless were druggies or alcoholics I never heard any of these other things," Max uttered quietly.

"Yeah, there is a lot, a whole lot of that too, people see the drifters and the ones who don't want to work. The ones who are alcoholics, who walk around the streets high or drunk and some who are just plain lazy and will steal whatever they can to get by. They don't care about other people who don't want the public eye on them. They have dropped out of society and their will to be what others call normal. They want to spend their last little bit of life with what they have left. Especially the ex-military people," said Hog. For most folk here, not counting the free loaders, it is sorta a place where empty souls live."

[Chapter 14]

One evening just past 10 PM when the weather was getting nice Max and Hog were sitting on an old wooden bench just a short distance from camp. They had split a pizza and six pack and were on their last cans of the six pack, when three motorcycles rolled up making a lot of noise. Max immediately got his shackles up, but Hog just sat still like nothing happened. The three men stopped the bikes and got off and walked toward Max and Hog.

"Hey guys," the huge man called to them, "Can you all give us a clue where we can find a place to get some grub and some beer. We took a wrong turn and got off the beaten trail if you know what I mean."

Hog gave a little chuckle and said, "I can help get you turned around cuz there ain't nothin to eat here and definitely no beer, we just guzzled the last that we had."

"How about if you hop on the back of our bikes and show us where to go?"

Hog looked at Max and said, "Come on Max let show these fellas where they can get some chow and something to wash it down with." With that Hog got up and hopped on the back of the leader's bike and Max got on another, and off they went.

They drove to the "Open 24 Hours," diner and sat in a large booth. Duke made the introductions of his traveling companions, Spike and Ziggy. They ordered burgers and beer and ate as if they had not had any food for days. Duke told Hog and Max that they were on their way out west to attend a motorcycle rally and planned to make stops in different states to pick up other riders. He had been in touch with some bike clubs, and they were all headed to the same rally.

"We're gonna hang out here for a few days, get the road dust off our hides, get our bikes tuned up and then get back on the road. Where's a good place to spend a few nights that's clean and cheap?" asked Duke, and get our bikes tuned up?"

"There's Motel 6 a few miles on the other side of town," Hog suggested. We could show you where it is then you can bring us back."

"Where is your hovel?" asked Duke.

"We stay at a small camp close to where you first saw us, Hog revealed but there ain't no room there."

"I'm not messen with you," Duke confirmed, "I was just curious."

"No harm, no foul," Max said, "We just have a small group that sticks together."

"I get it," Duke acknowledged, "We have some places like that back home, I didn't mean to question I was just wonderin."

Duke and the other riders took Max and Hog back to the spot where they found them. Hog explained they wouldn't take them into camp because the noise of their bikes would wake some people up.

The next day Duke left his bike with the others outside of camp and walked into the camp area. Before he could get far Lenny stopped Duke and asked him what he wanted. Duke told him he was with Hog and Max last night and he wanted to talk to them again.

"Hang loose," Lenny demanded, "While I go see if they feel like singin."

Lenny went to their tent and called out to them. Hog answered and asked, What's goin on?

"There's a biker guy in the front of the camp asking to talk to you guys do you want to see him?"

"Is he a tall guy with long hair and a biker's jacket?" asked Hog.

"Yeah, that's him," Lenny said.

"Ok, we'll be right there."

They walked out and Hog called out "Mornin Duke how's it going?"

"We're chuggin along," Duke said, "but again I need a little help."

"What's up?" Hog said.

"My bike has been making a funny noise when I cranked it up this mornin and I need someone who knows about bikes to listen to it cuz I don't want to get stranded in the middle of our trip, do you know anybody around here that could help me with that?" Duke inquired.

"There is a guy who has a garage over in the next town that I know of, but I don't know if he's open. Let's go down the road a piece and I'll see if I can hear it. I used to know a little something about bikes, but it has been a while," Hog let out.

"Sounds like a plan," Duke said with a smile.

"You go on for your ride," Max told Hog, "I'm going back and have some breakfast. If you need me, I'll be here."

Duke and Hog came back in a few hours and told Max that Duke needed a part for his bike that was not available in the shop close by, so the mechanic got on the computer to see where one could be located.

"The guy found one several towns over and they were going to ride over there to get it, Hog said, "I come back to tell you that the weather doesn't look so good and if'n a heavy downpour starts we might have to stay and find a crib there. Spike and Ziggy are stayin at Motel 6 they must be out riding cuz we can't seem to get them. If they come looking for us tell them what's happening ok?"

"Yeah sure, You guys be careful on that bike, I heard they are not good in the rain," Max replied.

"We got it covered," Duke assured Max, and they rode off.

Hog and Duke stayed in the town where the part was located and the next day when they got back Hog came to the tent and grabbed his backpack and began going through it.

Max woke up and saw Hog and greeted him, "Hey! Hi Hog, how did the repairs on the bike go? Did you find the part you needed to get it back in shape?"

"Oh, Hiya Max, Yeah, we got the part, but it took the better part of the night to get it in right, it was in a tight spot. Hog sounded so excited, "Max I'm cutting out with these boys to go to the motorcycle rally they have been talking about. It's something I've always been wantin to do all my life and never got the chance. We will be goin in a few days and I should be gone for a couple of weeks. I might even get a chance to ride a bike or two, outside of Duke's and the other guys I mean. I'm stayin at Motel 6 with them to get all the bikes tuned up. I can't wait to see all of the hogs at the rally, some will be super modified with everything you can think of on them, some are pullin small trailers. I'm sure there will be some classics too, folks like to show off their bikes."

"That sounds like a lot of fun Hog, you sound excited to go, it's a good thing to look forward to, I hope you have a great time. I'm going to the house on Green Street today and poke around. If I find anything I will get our antique guy to look it over, but I won't sell anything without you. Hog one thing I want to ask, do you need any money? I would be happy to give you what I have for the trip I mean." Max said seriously.

"That's might fine of you Max, but I'm cool. These guys asked me to go to help service their bikes. That will get me enough bucks to get by. If you need some scratch, you go ahead and sell whatever you need to," Hog advised.

"When will you be leaving?" quarried Max.

"Oh, in the next day or two, I'm hangin with them till we get Duke's bike running without any problems. I'm stoked about this Max it's one of my life's dreams." I think it's great Hog and I know you'll have a wonderful time," Max said grinning.

[Chapter 15]

Jessie couldn't wait. She was out to have some fun. She was 17 years old and had never been to a concert before and loved the rock groups that were playing. Her best friend Kendra was able to get her father's van and all six of them were going to stay and sleep in the van overnight if traffic was bad or they couldn't find a place to crash.

At the festival the wine was flowing, and hookahs and joints were everywhere. The outdoor arena was packed, and Jessie and the crew brought blankets and sat along the perimeter listening and taking in the sights. Clouds of smoke drifted over to where they were sitting but none of the girls had smoked dope or even knew what hookahs were. Jessie had never seen anything like it, she was mesmerized. There were a bunch of guys several blankets over and they had beer and were very loud. Jessie had to go to the bathroom and got up and headed for the nearby woods. When she got back, she saw three boys sitting on the edge of their blanket and her friends were laughing and talking with them. The boys ran out of beer and the others with them went to get more supplies. Jessie joined the group and soon she was part of the mix. When the other boys got back with more beer, they offered the girls some. Jessie looked at her friends and they giggled and then Jessie said, "Oh, what the Hell." And they were off to the races. Soon the girls and the guys were drunk, and the boys began lighting up joints and offer drags to the girls.

It didn't take long for the laughing to start and now they all were ravenously hungry. Not having much money, the girls had packed a cooler with sandwiches and snacks and now they brought all the food out and devoured it like a dog eats a fly. It got dark, and a lot of the crowd started small fires and people brought their guitars or other instruments and began to play and sing. It was such a good time Jessie hardly noticed that Earl was making moves on her. But soon they were in the tall grass making out.

The girls had planned on staying in the van anyway, so they didn't have far to go. They said goodbye to the guys and settled down for the night when someone noticed Jessie was not with them. They looked out the windows and saw Jessie and Earl holding hands and kissing as they walked toward the van.

The next day they woke up and were not feeling so great. They gathered up their things and were getting ready to leave when Earl and some other guys drove up in a beautiful convertible.

Earl honked the horn until Jessie came out of the van and they all sat around talking. Soon they came up with a plan to go to the local diner. Earl took Jessie's hand and insisted they sit together away from the others. Earl had been shot by Cupid's arrow and had stars in his eyes. They talked and Earl asked if he could drive Jessie home. She refused knowing that her parents would be very upset if she was not with the girls but alone with some strange guy. That was ok with Erol, he told her he understood, and he would come to her house and date her the way her parents would approve of.

All the attention and dating were exciting and new to Jessie. She had always been a quiet bookworm happy to get good grades and please her parents. Erol wanted to see her every day, but Jessie held him off. She suspected he came from money because he always had plenty to spend and of course his flashy convertible. He brought her flowers and jewelry and several times he took her shopping, but she had to be careful because her parents did not approve of all the things Erol did.

Tragedy struck one day and when Jessie came home from school her mother and father sat her down in the kitchen. Jessie knew it was going to be bad news because her mother was crying. her parents told her they were going back to Italy because her father's brother and his wife were killed in a terrible train accident. That left no one to take care of their children, bring in the crops and run their farm.

"Jessie," her mother said, "I'm sorry but we must go and help there is no one else to help their children and keep the farm going. We will all live together as a family should, my parents are too old to do this on their own."

"No mom no I can't leave I have to finish high school and I don't want to leave all my friends and Erol is here. I only have a few months before I graduate then I can come to join you," Jessie begged.

Jessie begged and cried, and her parents tried to explain but Jessie was not listening. She didn't want to leave. She ran next door to her best friend's Nancy's house and cried for hours. Jessie stayed there for 2 days and would not talk to her parents. On the third day Nancy's parents came to talk with Jessie's parents. We know this is a difficult time for you, but we think we have a solution. Let Jessie stay here with us until she graduates. We will send her to you and by that time, you will know if you have to stay over there or can come back," they offered.

Uncertain what they would find when they went back, it seemed like a great solution to a weighty problem, and they reluctantly agreed.

That was the beginning of a new life for Jessie. Nancy's parents were a throwback from the old hippie era. They were as liberal as Jessie's parents were strict and often went away and stayed for weeks. Jessie and Erol and Nancy and her boyfriend partied and smoked and stayed out and did literally did whatever they wanted. Erol and Jessie began to have sex every minute they could, they even did it on the kitchen table which blew Jessie's mind.

Nancy's parent philosophy was, "you only live once." If it was late when the group got back from their night out or they were drunk, they slept at Nancy's. If they wanted to have a party Nancy's parents would go out or sometimes join in, Jessie thought they were so cool. Erol and Nancy's boyfriend practically live there. Money was no problem, Erol always had a tank full of gas and a pocket full of cash and off they would go.

Time moved on and it was a good thing that Jessie's past grades were good enough to carry her through the final months because she just about had enough to graduate. Earl had asked her to marry him, and she had been to meet his parents and attended a few social gatherings at their home, which Erol did not encourage because he thought they were boring. Jessie got the distinct feeling that Erol's parents did not approve of her, but she went along when Erol asked her to come with him. One night when they all had a lot to drink and stayed at Nancy's house Jessie and Earl had sex all night. "It was great," Jessie told Nancy the next morning and when Nancy cautioned Jessie about getting pregnant it was like a light went off in Jessie's brain. She had never given any thought that could happen, but next time she told herself they would be more careful, no need to worry now. After that Earl used condoms but they were in lust and sometimes they forgot to use protection.

Jessie's parents were insisting she come to live with them after she graduated but Jessie was having too much fun and didn't want to leave Erol. Erol had asked Jessie to marry him on several occasions, but Jessie blew him off, not thinking he was serious. After several serious phone calls with her parents who were insisting, she came to live with them Jessie said yes when Erol asked her to marry him again. Earl was thrilled and he and Jessie went to tell his parents.

Erol's parents were very upset when they told them they wanted to get married, but even though they were disappointed in Erol's choice they gave Jessie and Erol their blessing. Jessie's parents were not happy with the news. They always thought Jessie would go on to college and have a career since she loved art and dancing so much. Jessie's mom had married young, and she always wished she could have gone on to college but that didn't happen for her. After some disagreement about having a big wedding Jessie and Erol decided to elope. They left and Nancy and her boyfriend went with them, and they had a great time.

After they got back and told Erol's parents his father came to see them. He asked Erol where he was going to work and Erol said he hadn't decided yet since he didn't find anything he loved to do. Erol's father told him that since he was now a married man his monthly allowance would stop, he could work at the brewery, but he would have to start at the bottom and work his way up. Erol said he had no problem with that he was certain he could master the jobs quickly and be ready to be on the family board of directors in no time. Jessie's parents didn't say much but were relieved that Jessie was married and not just running wild. They told Jessie she should stay where she was and make a good home for, her and Erol.

The newlywed couple were thrilled that Jessie didn't have to go with her parents they would be happy just being together. They lived in Erol's apartment and had sex every spare minute they had. Jessie worked in a music and bookstore and a few weeks later Jessie found out she was pregnant. Erol was thrilled at first and then as time passed and Jessie didn't feel like partying and going out, he was disappointed. When the baby came their life changed. Erol felt Jessie paid more attention to the baby than to him and she spent a lot of money on things the baby needed. Erol's parents remained distant and cold and had only seen the baby once.

Erol's job at the brewery was dull and boring and once the other employees found out he was the boss's son they stayed far away from him. Erol was treated differently by the supervisor and the other employees resented it. Erol was habitually late and took longer than everybody else for lunch and often left before the shift was over. He got into the habit of stopping at the local tavern with his friends before going home and often arrived home drunk. They say there are two types of drunks, those that get happy and want to sing and dance and tell jokes and those that want to fight or fuck and can't do either. Erol was not interested in singing or dancing.

Jessie tried to have dinner ready when Erol got home from work, but most of the time Erol didn't come home at the time she expected him and when he came home much later, Jessie asked for an explanation. Erol would get angry, and they would fight. Jessie tried to talk to Erol, but he did not see that he was doing anything wrong, "I just have a few drinks with the boys, and we discuss work Problems, that was Erol's excuse. Some of these nights when Erol had too much to drink he would call his father and complain about Jessie not treating him well and told him that she was not a good wife or mother. His father believed him and felt sorry for him.

One evening Erol came home with a beautiful brand-new set of golf clubs. He was so proud of the deal he struck buying the clubs.

"Erol," Jessie said in an angry voice, why did you buy a new set of golf clubs when you have a perfectly good set that you used only twice. You know we don't have that kind of money to spend, besides Max needs a new crib he has outgrown the small cradle."

"Jessie all you ever do is tell me about what Max needs, and what I shouldn't do. I work hard and I should be able to buy whatever I want. You buy all kinds of useless stuff for the baby so why shouldn't I have what I want?"

"The baby needs things; he's growing and needs new clothes. I go to sales and thrift stores not to the country club to but expensive golf clubs."

"Jessie you're not the same girl who loved to party, when I married you, you have changed. What happened?"

"Erol, we have a baby, and we need a bigger apartment, and we should be watching every penny, we spend so that we can give the baby what he needs but you don't seem to care about all that."

"That's all you ever think of is the baby, I'm going out where I can be me," Erol said, stomping out he went back to the bar.

This went on for several months and then Jessie and Erol stopped talking to each other except for minor things and their relationship began to dwindle.

Erol's father came to the brewery section where Erol worked one day and asked to see him. The supervisor made an excuse and said Erol went home early because he was not feeling good. A few days later Erol's father came to Erol's work area again, this time at the start of the shift and asked for Erol. As usual Erol did not come to work on time and again the supervisor covered for him saying he sent him on an errand. Now Erol's father was suspicious but decided he would try again. At the end of the day, he came back again and was told that Erol left early. Now he was pissed. The next morning, he again came to the work area and waited until Erol showed up and was 45 minutes late.

Erol's father was super pissed. He called the supervisor and Erol out in front of the entire crew and asked what the working hours were for that section. The supervisor told him and then he asked Erol why he was not at work at those times. Erol stammered and shuddered making up lame excuses and was visibly shaken. Erol's Father told him that not showing up for work on time or leaving early was just as good as stealing money from the company.

In a loud voice, Erol's father screamed, "Your fired Erol and you Mr. Lying Supervisor are fired too.

Erol was bummed. He went to his usual watering hole and began to drink. He was angry and got into a fight and was arrested and ended up in jail. Erol called Jessie and told her he needed her to come and bail him out. She went to see him and reminded him that they did not have enough money in their account to bail him out. Erol knew that was true but expected Jessie to somehow get the money. He told her to go to his parents to get the money.

"Go to your parents to get the money," Jessie questioned. "Are you crazy, they hate me they wouldn't give me anything."

"Well lie and tell them that it's for the baby but get me out of here."

Jessie tried but when they questioned Jessie about why she needed the money she broke down and cried.

Erol's father came to see him in jail. He told Erol what a cheat and a liar Jessie was and that she tried to get money from them. He asked Erol why she didn't come and get him out of jail. Erol told him she refused to bail him out and had squandered all their money.

"Erol I will come and get you only if you do what I tell you."

"What is that dad," asked Erol.

"You will leave Jessie and bring the boy to us to raise. From what you have been telling me she has ruined your life and made it miserable. If you won't do that you can stay in jail and rot."

Erol was dismayed at what his father said, knew the only reason Jessie went to them was because he insisted, but he was not going to tell his parents that. Erol also knew that most of the problems between he and Jessie were his fault, most of all he didn't want to stay in jail, so he called his father back and agreed to the deal.

[Chapter 16]

Hog and Duke came back in the early evening with Spike and Ziggy. Hog walked into their tent and asked Max if he wanted to chow down with them. Max was happy about the invitation because he had not eaten all day.

This time they went to a small Mexican restaurant called Juan's Surprise. They had quite a few rounds of Mexican beer and tequila and were feeling no pain. Duke began bragging about Hog and how he knew exactly what was wrong with his bike just by listening to it.

"You should have seen it Max, the Hog had to put the bee on the mechanic and had to show him how to install the part because it had to be placed perfectly. I want you all to know my hat is off to Hog, I was impressed, and the mechanic offered Hog a job right then and there at his shop," Duke said.

Duke sang Hog's praises all night long. They ended up closing the place and tried singing on the way back to camp. They dropped Max and Hog off and both men helped each other stagger to the tent. Each laid on their cots and were soon out like lights.

Max was taken aback at Hog. He was of course surprised that Hog knew so much about bikes but the fact that he divulged something about himself, that part really blew Max's mind. He sat on his cot thinking and his mind began to wonder and think about what happened this morning between Hog and Duke. Then feeling like Gomer Pyle, he said out loud, Shazam and Golly e e e! How could I have not thought of this sooner. Hog, that's slang for a motorcycle. Duke, Ziggy, and Spike have been throwing the name hog around all night. I'm surprised that Hog didn't tell me about his mechanical skills. The reason his name is Hog is because he had or knew about bikes or both. How could I have missed that giant clue? I would love to know his story, but I would never risk his friendship by prying into his past. His past is something he might want to forget. Wow what a revelation, Hog! Who knew?

About 3 AM Max got up and went out to go to the bathroom and when he got back, he saw Hog sitting on the side of his cot.

"Hey Hog, are you ok? I know we both had a lot to drink, and I have a headache I know you probably do too, right?"

"Yeah, yeah I got a headache and a heartache too and I'm still drunk," Hog vented with a long sigh.

"I reckon that hanging with Duke and the boys and working on his hog brought back a lot of old memories, not all of them good. Ya sees some of them are ones I thought I had pushed away so far; I would never think about them again. Riding a bike and workin on one is just what I used to do. I don't want to think about all that at all. You held up all this while from asking me about my past just as I have for you. Sometimes it's better that way, just to take a person at what their face value and not care about what was in their past or where they came from. But then somethin happened to trigger my mind and all those sad, miserable memories come flooding back like a huge black cloud and washed over me and made me remember those horrible days. Those desperate days when I had no control over what was happening, but I was in the center of it."

"You know Hog I don't care if you tell me about your past or not. I know you for who you are now, and I like that man." Max hesitantly said, "I'm right here though if you feel you want to talk."

"You maybe never noticed when I put my rags on, I ain't got any short-sleeved shirts or if I do I put my jacket on. That's because my arms and hands are ugly with scars. That's why I had to give directions on how to install the part on Duke's bike and couldn't do it myself. I've had so many operations on my hands, but they're still ain't right and probably never will be. I never dreamed of taking the mechanic's offer to work in his shop, although I would love to do that," Hog said in a melancholy way, I could never handle that."

"Sorry Hog I never thought about that, go on."

"Thanks Max I think it's time I spilled, and I know you have my back.

Anyway, here goes, "I had a bike most of my life. When I was coming up my father bought me a beat-up old Harley he got from the junk yard for my 14 th birthday and I began working on that thing for the next several years. The parts that I needed to restore it were very high priced, so the going was slow because I didn't have much money and had to save up for each part. All the parts had to be re-chromed, painted or powder coated along with the fenders and tanks. Of course, it needed re-wiring and complete overhaul of the engine and transmission. I worked at a mechanics shop after school to get the money to do all that and the guy who owned the shop was good to me and let me use his tools and I studied all the manuals and watched the other mechanics to learn what to do. I just about had it all restored, and somebody stole it from my yard. They found it in the next town wrecked and out of fuel and it looked as if someone just took it for a joy ride and crashed it. I was broken up about it. But I got it towed back and started work on it again. It took me until I graduated from high school to get it all done. I finally took it to my first rally. A lot of people looked at my bike and admired it and one bunch of guys who were in a club asked me to join. I was thrilled. Do we have any liquor here?" Hog asked.

Max got up and found a half full bottle and asked, "Do you really want more liquor Hog?"

"I gotta stay drunk to tell you this story or else I won't be able to do it and I want to," and he took a swallow of the whiskey.

"Ok," Max uttered.

"One night I got all liquored up and had an accident with my bike and totaled it. I didn't have the money to repair it and didn't have a job, so I joined the military. They saw that I was good with engines and put me in the motor pool. I was happy with that and saved every penny I got and did some work on the side for the officers' cars and bikes. When I got out, I had saved enough to buy another bike. After that I just went to biker's bars and rode my bike. I joined a bike club and had a part-time job fixin hogs."

Hog stopped for another swallow. Hog began again, "I ran with that club for a couple of years and then joined another one and was away from home most of the time. It was a wild way of life till I met Janey. From then on, she took first place in my heart. She was my life, my heart, and my soul, I tell you she took the place of my bike in my heart, that should say it all. Once we got together, I ditched the club, and we did everything together, just the two of us. She rode with me on the back of my bike.

We got married a year later and tramped around doing odd jobs to survive and rode anywhere we wanted. Then Janey got pregnant and wanted to settle down for the baby. I agreed it would not be a good life for a kid, so we went back to my hometown and found a small place and I got a job, and we started our new life. A few months into the pregnancy, Janey seemed unusually tired, the doctor said that it was normal for pregnant women to be tired and that it would pass as the baby grew, but it didn't. I came home from work one day and found Janey was still in bed, and I freaked and insisted she go to the doctor. The doctor discovered that Janey was going to have twins. We were happy and sad at the same time. It would cost a lot to have two kids at the same time, so I got another job and now with two jobs I was never home. Janey was upset but we needed the money, so I kept on working. After the twins were born everything seemed fine. Then the baby doctor discovered that one of the boys had lung problems. The medicines he needed cost a lot, and he needed them every day.

I had been working two jobs now with no days off and I was tired, but it was worth it to me that my family got everything they needed. Janey couldn't work and take care of the babies, so it was up to me. Then one night after my second shift a few of the guys from my old club rode up to where I worked, and we began talking about old times. They wanted to have a drink with me, and we met at the local bar. I tried calling Janey but there was no answer. After we had a few rounds of booze, I told them I had to go. They began to talk about some fast money, and I was suddenly very interested. They had a plan to rob the bank in the next town and they needed another man they could trust. They planned on getting away on fast off-road bikes where the cops couldn't follow, and they needed someone who was an ace biker. I told them I would have to think about it and went home. At home Janey was up with my son who was having trouble breathing. We took him to the hospital, and they helped him, but the doctor had bad news. He said that the boy needed a lung transplant, or he would not have long to live. We were broken up about that. After a week we brought him home and I started thinking about the money it would take to get care of my son. That night at work my buddies came looking for me again. I decided to do the job with them.

We pulled the job, and everything went off without a hitch. My son had the operation, and it made him better and he was home and feelin good. A few weeks later my friends contacted me and said they were up for another job. This time it was the bank in our town, and I was scared to do it. They said it would be the last one cuz they were all moving to the west coast after it was done. So, I agreed. We did the job at dawn on Sunday and afterward went to a cabin they had in the area

We got to drinking and it got late, and I had to go home. I tried calling Janey to say I was on my way but there was no cell service. I wasn't used to drinking and I was tipsy. On my way home a car came speeding toward me and I recognized it as Janey's mother's car, so I turned around and followed, trying to catch up with it. Now Janey's mother was a sickly lady, why she was driving was a worry to me. As I got closer, I saw the car weaving badly and suddenly I saw it go off the road down an embankment. I drove my bike down the embankment, but it was so steep I spun out of control. I flew off the bike just before it hit the car, and both burst into flames.

It was very dark in the tent and Max could hear the change in Hog's voice as he described the scene and became moved telling the story. Max knew that Hog began to cry. Max didn't know if he should tell Hog to stop or maybe he had a need to tell his story to get it out, so he sat still and said nothing. After a short pause Hog took a drink out of the bottle and began talking again.

Max said gently, "Are you ok Hog?"

Hog replied, "I'll never be ok." He paused for a few more minutes and then went on. "I tried my best, my very best Max, with everything in me but I failed, and I couldn't fix it," Hog said between sobs. No matter what I did it was not good enough." Then silence except for great gasps of breath between cries and moans.

Max was paralyzed not knowing what to do.

Hog began again. "I could hardly see in the car because of the smoke and the flames but somehow, I managed to pull them all out of the car and someone driving by must have seen the flames and called the police. My mother-in-law was unconscious but seemed to be breathing. Janey had a terrible gash across her head where she must have gone through the windshield, but she was moaning, and her leg looked as if it was broken. One of the boys was crying so I knew he was breathing ok. The worst one of all was my other son who was not moving. When I picked him up, I saw he was not breathing."

"Oh my God," uttered Max astonished at Hog's story and so engrossed in the story he was re-living it with Hog and began to weep himself.

"I heard sirens as I laid him on the ground and started to breathe into my son's mouth trying to make him take in some air. I kept it up until the paramedics arrived and pulled him away from me and began CPR. But they couldn't do any better. Janey was unconscious, the other baby I could at least hear was still crying. When they got us to the emergency room, they told me that my mother-in-law and one son were dead, and Janey was on a respirator fighting for her life. I had burns all over but especially on my hands and arms and they were severely burned, and I was in shock. The cops did a blood alcohol on me and thought I was the one who caused the crash, so they arrested me, but I was in too bad a shape for them to take me to jail."

Hog stopped and took another taste and began crying again. "When Janey's father came, he said he wasn't home so his wife went with Janey when she called to ask for help, and they called me from the car and said the boys had a high fever and one of them was having a seizure."

I was in a fog because they gave me drugs for the pain I had. Then came the surgeries. Janey was unconscious most of the time during the accident, so she was not able to tell the police that I didn't cause the accident and they had no clue I did the robbery, so they investigated the accident but found only skid marks from the car, but Janey blamed me for not being home to help with the boys. Somehow, I don't know if the cops told her, but she knew I have been drinking and she blamed me for her mother and my son's deaths. The surgeries were grueling and the cost high. I was at the mercy of the state for medical care. Janey didn't come to see me at all and when I was ready to go home, I had no place to go because Janey told me she didn't want me there and she wouldn't let me see my son. I took some odd jobs and hung around that town hoping Janey would change her mind. I stayed with my father and mother for a while, but they were struggling to keep themselves fed, so I called Janey one last time and begged her to let me see her and my son and she said no so I left."

Hog paused and took another mouthful then he said in a very soft woeful voice I lost my wife, my son, my bike, and my livelihood all in one big swoop. When I was a little boy my mother made me go with her to listen to a preacher talk. I remember one thing he said. He told the people there to remember one thing, it was a quote from somebody named Immanuel Kant or Kent, he said to be happy you don't need a lot of money, or a big house. To have a happy life you just need three things, something to do, someone to love and something to hope for. Now for me there was none of those things left, I now had nothin, every piece of me, all of me, every hope and dream were gone, I had no one to love so I left and wandered around until Lenny found me just like I found you."

Hog was quiet again. Max asked him if he needed anything, and he heard the now familiar laments and wails and sat waiting for Hog to calm down. Hog tried to talk again, but the words came out in jerks and sputters. Max went over to Hog's cot and put his arm around his shoulder.

"It's like I can see the whole accident right now every detail as clear as if it were happening right now and I can't do nothin to change it," Hog said softly. Whispering to Max as if to tell him a secret, "There's more, several years back one of the guys I did the robbery with found me and told me that somehow the cops found one of the other guys and he spelled his guts and told them who all of us were, so I' a fugitive from the law. But the most awful part Max is that I called Janey a few years ago. My son answered the phone, I told him who I was and told him I loved him and asked if I could come and see him.

He said, "you are the monster that killed my twin brother and my grandmother, and I hate you and never want to see you again. You don't deserve to be alive. I wish you were dead, dead, dead," and hung up the phone.

"That's what he said Max and he's right I couldn't save them and don't deserve to be alive myself."

"No, no, no," Max voiced with emotion, "you are a good person with a big heart who would help anybody you could, they are wrong about you Hog."

Hog seemed to slump over so Max laid him down on the cot. And sat near him on the edge of the makeshift bed and listened to his sobs and felt his body wracked with pain. Max just patted him on the back until Hog finally fell asleep.

Max knew now why Hog understood Angie's pain so well and had been so good at comforting her. Max was in tears himself not knowing what he could do to help Hog knowing his life was a living Hell each day he remembered what happened and how his wife not only blamed him but taught his son to hate him too. Truly, she will be sorry for that one day, Max felt sure of it. Although it made a lot of things seem clearer Max knew why Hog didn't want any part of the police. It was possible he could still be charged with the robberies and go to jail. Max's second thought was that he had been so anxious to hear Hog's story and now he wished he hadn't heard any part of it. He wondered how a human, Hog or anyone could sustain such pain on a daily basis. The next day Duke and the boys came for Hog, and he gathered up his few belongings and put them in his backpack and they were on their way.

[Chapter 17]

Deidre Miller felt good about her work on the old house so far, she had little input from Marlene who was going to live there except that Marlene had definite likes and dislikes. They communicated via faxes and texts and email about changes to the house. Although some of the furniture and colors were not what Deidre would have chosen that's what Marlene wanted, so she went with that. The Green Street house project was something Joseph asked Deidre to look at to see if she could work with Marlene. Joseph told Deidre that he had been a friend of her father and she had taken his death so badly she needed a project to get her mind grounded again.

 Deidre always felt she had to be challenged to do a good job. She had never met Marlene in person, but it seemed she took Deidre's ideas and made only a few changes. Deidre had to go and walk around the house again before she went any further so she went to peruse the house. After walking around and making copious notes she came upon two men who were sorting through all the items in the living room. She was curious about the two men that they had hired to get rid of the garbage that was left there. She thought the one guy looked familiar. For the mean time she was going to work hard to please Joseph and he might give her a nice bonus for taking this job. Now that she had put Mrs. Gray on notice that she, Deidre, was in charge and not Mrs. Gray. She did not want to get her completely out of the picture because the old lady had good ideas and might help her with the Green Street house. She would ask her questions without being specific and think it was for Joseph's house. Deidre needed ideas because of her lack of experience. I will listen to her ideas because she does have design knowledge and then transform them into what I think is the best and no one will be the wiser.

Deidre had felt so alone and abandoned in the last few years after she quit the design house and went from one unsatisfying personal service client to the next. It drove her into a short marriage. Theye were happy for about 7 seconds and then other women began to look good to him. It was a good thing she had another source of income that she didn't have to pay taxes on. Being an escort for wealthy gentlemen was not really her dream job but it paid very well, and she got a few very nice, expensive baubles for her work from a few of the men. The part Deidre hated was the servicing of the old boys who just couldn't do it anymore but wanted to still be considered masculine and sexy. She had to be careful the old guys could easily get attached quickly and then it was a real problem getting rid of them. But I have to face it they have the money and the power to give me the tools I need to become a famous designer, if the money was right, I would consider it. At a party one evening when she was escorting someone there was a police raid all the women at the party were escorts and taken to the station house for questioning and probably would be arrested. Deidre was questioned by an officer and unlike the others he seemed very understanding. He explained that since she did not have a previous record and if she gave him some information she might just be questioned and released. Deidre sang like a bird, and she went home that night. Two nights after that the police officer came to her apartment asking more questions. They had a few drinks and nature took its course. They started a romantic relationship and it seemed to flourish.

Joseph, her new boss, was Deidre's newest personal service client and was different than the others. The circumstances were much more businesslike. He did not want daily living to help, he really wanted help with business chores. Joseph was not at all like her father, which was a good thing because he was a pain in the ass most of her life as she was growing up. Her mother was a quiet lady, who believed that the husband was always right. It always seemed that whatever her brothers did was, oh he made a mistake, or he didn't mean it but when Deidre did something that was out of line it was World War 3 no matter how small the mistake was. Deidre couldn't wait to get out of that house and go to college but even then, it was constant knit picking about her grades, her class standing, her friends etc. Things didn't really change. They were just further away and not daily. Every time she came home from college, her father reminded her of all the money he was spending on her education and how they all sacrificed so much to send her to a good school. How would she be able to repay them when she was done with school. Deidre grew sick of hearing how terrible she was and reminded her father that her brother had taken 6 years to finish law school and three times to pass the bar. He didn't want to hear that. When she complained about him to her mother, she would just say how Deidre must respect her father because he worked so hard and did so much for them.

    When Deidre quit her job at the Design Company her father was the first to say I told you that taking those fluff courses in college the painting and design were worthless now what will you do because I don't plan on keeping you for the rest of your life. That was part of why Deidre would never tell her family what her extra- curricular job was, she knew her father would put her further down on the food chain than where she already was. Deidre was glad to tell her father she didn't need him to pay her rent anymore and she was making a good living, she lied and said she found a new job with another design company. It almost seemed her father was disappointed to hear that, surely, she was going to fail and make all his predictions about her failing come true.

    Thinking back to her first personal service client, Shane was a downer. Wanting to make a good impression she began to do too much for the man.

He came to rely on her for everything and Deidre hated that. It wasn't long before he first began asking her to help him in the bathroom. She would set the water temperature and lay out his shaving kit, toothpaste, and clean clothes. When he demanded that she begin washing him that's when she had enough. She told him she was leaving, and he said if she didn't have sex with him, he would tell the agency that she stole money from him and she would never work in the industry again. After working extra hard to avoid getting close to him, she decided to take a chance and quit anyway, explaining to her boss what happened. Surprisingly her boss knew the man did this before and that Deidre stayed as long as she did with him because he was notorious for demanding sex from everyone who had taken care of him. Deidre felt so good that she had not given in to him. She stayed and then was assigned to Joseph, until he recuperated from his surgery, luckily that had lasted much longer than expected. She left the agency and began working directly for Joseph.

Deidre's job with Joseph was her fifth personal service job. Two of the others had been with people who were recuperating from medical conditions and although they did not need medical attention, they needed help with being driven to the office or help dressing for an event or shopping and other chores of living. After they regained their strength, they no longer needed her. It was interesting to see people from their personal side, especially rich clients that could afford her services. Some were celebrities or dating famous people. Most of them were so self-centered that they acted one way at work and another totally different way at home. What an eye opener it was to hear her clients talk about the other people at work or that they associated with in a despicable way. They were either too fat, didn't know how to dress or wore too much make-up. Surprisingly even the men talked about other men and how they had body odor or wore cheap suits, were out of shape or had bad breath.

Joseph was out of town for 2 months, but they talked on the phone daily and she would give him the progress of the house renovation and send him pictures and he seemed quite pleased with her work. He would never know what an opportunity he had given her and now she could say that she rehabbed houses and put that on her business cards.

Preparing to go to work the next day Deidre made a mental note to get to know the two guys who were working with the painters because they were the sort of referrals people often looked for. She would give them some of her new cards which said she had experience in home restoration and historical preservation. It didn't hurt to fudge a little and what the Hell titles and credentials meant different things to people so she would go to the library and read about restoration and besides when it came to structural things her brother's bestie was an architect so she could always ask him for advice. At any rate she would try and do her best to break into this business after she got established, maybe then she could once again think of being a clothing designer. Maybe she would get lucky and instead of being a clothing designer she could be an interior decorator.

[Chapter 18]

Marlene was what you would call a poor little rich girl. She was lucky enough to be born into a very rich and prestigious family and was the darling of her parents' eyes. Part of that may be due to the fact that her mother had had three miscarriages before Marlene was born. In order for her to carry this pregnancy she had to stay in bed and keep her feet elevated for months before the birth. Of course, Marlene always had the best of everything and loved every minute of being the center of attention. She commanded so much attention in fact that she and her mother didn't get along well because after Marlene grew up, they began vying for the position of queen of the castle. As Marlene's mother began to get older her father seemed to turn his attention to Marlene more and more so much so that her mother and father argued frequently, and most of the time it was about Marlene. Her mother wanted her to establish herself in a career and eventually get married, but Marlene didn't want to settle down. She was too busy partying and going to the country club and playing tennis.

When Marlene was 21 her father had a heart attack. Although he recovered and the doctors told him he was doing well he became what they termed a cardiac cripple. He became over cautious, would only eat a special low fat, low cholesterol diet and exercised far more than was recommended.

He got at least 8 -10 hours of sleep each night and would seek medical attention with the least little sign of a problem. He also insisted that Marlene take a serious interest in his business. Marlene wanted to please her father, so she began working with him closely. She actually surprised herself and began to enjoy and understand the business process so much more than she realized she would and often joined her father at board meetings. This new partnership she enjoyed with her father left her mother to fend for herself. They often found her mother extremely inebriated and asleep on the sofa when they came home from the office. Of course, this was an additional turn-off for Marlene's father, and they eventually divorced.

In a few short years, Marlene's mother was found dead lying in a pool of vomit on the kitchen floor of her apartment. The realization and guilt that she had driven her mother away became a reality to Marlene and she grieved for a long time, needing care from mental health people.

Although Marlene became very knowledgeable about business, she was still a complete airhead when it came to the facts of living and the difference between real friends and gold diggers. After her father's death she had come to rely on Ali his business manager heavily. Ali always seemed to be there when she needed him and didn't mind being her escort when she didn't have a date and needed to go to a business dinner. He helped her make decisions when she was so down and out after her father died and understood her need to rest.

Once Marlene was feeling better, she still wanted Ali to be her back-up when she made corporate decisions. She would run the deal by him and seek his advice on almost everything that happened at the company. When she began dating again, he would act like a doting father and wanted to know all the details of what they did and where they went. When she asked him once why he felt he had to act like that he told her that he promised her father he would watch over her for him.

For a while it was great having someone always watch your back but after a time Marlene became annoyed that she no longer had a life of her own because Ali wanted to know every move she made. She told him how she felt, and he agreed that he would back off but never really did and always just stayed in the background. On several occasions Ali had introduced several of his friends to her to be her escort but now she wanted to choose who she would see for herself. There was one evening when she was out with a man who drank too much, and they were in an auto accident. He hit several parked cars and then passed out. Marlene was scared but within minutes there was Ali pulling her out of the car and driving them away from the scene of the wreck. Marlene was grateful but when she asked Ali if he was following her, he said he was just by chance in the neighborhood.

From then on Marlene didn't tell Ali anything about who she was going out with or where they were going. Then one night she brought her date home. He was a nice guy she had seen several times and she really liked him. She was planning to have sex with him that night, but it seemed he drank a lot and fell asleep on her sofa while she was changing her clothes and getting into something more comfortable. Not knowing what to do she went to bed and left only a dim night light on. She awoke to see this man going through her jewelry box and was petrified. She waited until he left the room and called Ali. He came just in time as the man was about to leave with a bag full of all of Marlene's valuables. In order to avoid a scandal, he called a private detective friend, and they handled the matter. Marlene was hysterical and again Ali saved the day. Marlene never asked how Ali and his friend took care of the problem, but she was now back to square one with Ali doubly cautious about who she was dating. He made her give him the name of the person and had his friend look at their background etc. How frustrating that was in that he always knew where she was once again. Except this time, she was torn between being safe and having Ali direct her life. She had again lost her confidence in herself.

Marlene decided that she was not cut out to be married or have a family. Instead, she would become a spinster and just have a good time having parties with groups and enjoy entertaining. Her apartment would not be large enough for what she had in mind, so she decided to buy a larger house and move in. The business had foreclosed on a property downtown that was very interesting. It caught Marlene's eye because it was known to be the largest property with untouched acreage. That she thought would make for an interesting estate where she could entertain in several venues, especially on the grounds. The house had to be restored and the grounds brought back to their old glory, but she had plenty of money and it would be fun to have a place everybody admired. She told Ali about her plans for the house and property on Green Street and he would handle everything. She would only have the final say on furniture and colors. Besides, her new friend seemed to have a lot of party experience and he thought it was a grand idea also. Ali was not so enthusiastic and felt Marlene would be spending a lot of money just to restore the place. Ali introduced Marlene to Sam Neal Olson Oscar Kaiser a friend from college. They were never besties but had worked some deals together. Marlene took to him at once and began calling him Snooky privately to match his initials. They went everywhere together and saw each other every day. Ali soon became annoyed that Sam and Marlene had become so close.

Marlene lavished presents and money on him as if it were going out of style and between the two of them succeeded in avoiding Ali or telling him about their plans. This was a giant piss off to Ali and he had confronted Sam on several occasions about it. Sam always blew him off saying that it was all Marlene's fault because she wanted to be free. When Ali had introduced Marlene to his old friend, he thought that would keep her occupied, but he would still have control of her every move. Now she wanted Snooky, and a new house and Ali was furious, I guess I'll have to show Snooky, what a ridiculous name, who is really the boss around here.

[Chapter 19]

With Hog away Max had become friends with several of the other men at the camp. Sometimes he would ask one of them to come with him to the Green Street house and help him load up stuff or make a run to the junk yard. The painters had let Max use their van to haul away things.

George had come to work with Max at the house and they had become friends. He was quiet and never talked much and as usual Max was dying to know why he was at the camp. They had gone out for a few beers after work several times but had headed back to camp before dark. George was uncomfortable about being out after the sun went down.

On Friday night Lenny gathered everybody together and told them they would have a party because he had made friends with a guy who worked in a food warehouse. They were going to throw away some cases of food that was about to expire. Ordinarily they would have taken it to a shelter, but Lenny had talked his friend into bringing two cases to the camp. Tony was going to have someone he knew who worked at a restaurant cook it for them and they would have a feast. It had to be very late in the evening because the guy had to cook the food after the restaurant closed. Nobody seemed to mind that, and Max told Lenny he would bring a few bottles of wine because the painters had paid him that day. The whole camp was in a good mood and ate the food and drank the wine as if it were a real party. It was the first time Max had heard George say more than a few words. He guessed that the food and wine had loosened his tongue and he felt comfortable enough to talk. He stayed and talked to Max far into the night and then he got quiet.

"What's the matter George you got awful quiet?" Although Max meant that he stopped talking for that evening George looked at him and said, "There are certain things that trigger bad thoughts in my brain and wine is one of them. It makes me think of my old days at school. Funny it's not beer or even liquor but wine. Maybe it's because I used to drink it with my sister. It's not a pretty story Max and maybe you might not want to hear it."

"No George I'm ok with it I think that sometimes telling someone about things that happened to you can be cathartic and good for the soul. So, if you want to, I'm happy to listen."

"I guess it's ok if you promise you will not think any less of me after you hear it." "I try and not judge people by what happened in the past I see them in the now," Max confessed.

"If you're sure because it ruined my family and my life." George confided.

Max was surprised and said, "I'm a good listener George, that is if you want to talk," Max declared.

Ignoring Max as if he were not there and without stopping as if he was in a trance George began talking.

"When I was 15 years old, we moved to a new town. I was a skinny kid, and it was a new school, and I was shy. My sister had to practically drag me off the school bus each morning because I was not a good student and didn't like school. A cute girl befriended my sister, and I had a crush on her. She would sit with us on the bus each day and I would be in heaven when she talked to me. I had no idea that her boyfriend, Boomer, was the school's football star player. She rode the bus because he practiced every day after school. One day it rained, and he came on the bus with us and when we sat in our usual seats, he sat in the next one because there was no room. When the bus began to move, he told me to move because he wanted to sit next to Adele, my sister's friend. I started to get up and Adele put her hand on my arm, she told him, "Why should he move he sits there every day like we all do. Just because you don't have practice today doesn't mean we all have to change our seats."

Boomer looked at her but didn't say anything. As we rode along Adele began talking and as usual included me in the conversation asking me my opinion of the subject they were talking about. I could see that Boomer was getting angry and kept my answers short and tried to ignore Adele's questions. When we got off the bus, I heard Boomer say under his breath, "I'll see you next time."

I was worried for a few days but then nothing happened, so I forgot about it. One day my mother wanted me to stop at the post office to get her some stamps after school, so I rode my bike to school that day. The seasons began to change, and the days were getting shorter, and it was getting dark earlier. There was a long line at the post office so by the time I got the stamps it was getting dark. I wasn't worried, I had a light on my bike so I could see how to get home. I started out and just as I got to the edge of the wooded area my bike tire went flat. I got off the bike and pushed it to the side and saw that the tire was split wide open so I would have to walk it home. As I started back down the road Boomer and some of his friends came out of the trees. They surrounded me and they had Kojo, with them. Kojo was a vicious dog that belonged to old man Sparks, and he kept him tied up and, in a pen, because he was unpredictable and had bitten several people.

"Hi there Georgie boy how you doing? How come you're not riding the bus with my girlfriend today?" Boomer asked.

"Boomer listen, I just ride because I'm with my sister. I don't know Adele at all, and I didn't know she was your girlfriend. I hardly talk to her."

"It didn't seem that way to me, that day I rode with you. It made me feel bad, and I don't like to feel bad. For making me feel bad you're going to pay, and we'll see how talkative you really are.

They tied me to a tree and spilled bacon grease on the crotch of my jeans, then they let the dog go. He came charging and began to lick my pants at first then he began biting and tearing and I was screaming and crying and was in so much pain. They saw that it was going too far when the dog began to bite my arms and chest and neck, but they couldn't make him stop. It was a nightmare and just before I passed out, I heard a bang and thought they had shot me. They later told me that Mr. Sparks had fired a tranquilizer at the dog to make him stop. I was in the hospital for weeks and had to have many surgeries. I also had a temporary ileostomy because the dog had torn my bladder. Finally, I was released from the hospital and was able to go back to school.

Nothing had really happened to Boomer and his buddies because they were high school football stars and without them the team would lose. The football coach came to my father and begged him not to press charges that the families would pay all my medical bills if he would just leave it alone. My father agreed. The night after the big championship football game, which of course they won, there was a big party for the whole school. I didn't go to the party, but I went to school later to pick up my sister. Two of Boomers friends saw me and started heckling me. I tried to ignore them and walked up the school steps. They came behind me and pushed me into the party. Most everybody there was drunk or high and at Boomer's request they made a big circle around me and as his friends held me Boomer pulled my pants down saying, "Let's see what damage Kojo did to your little dick." Just then the catheter that was attached to the urine bag came apart and poured urine out all over me and the floor. Everybody was grossed out and ran away. Boomer didn't know what to do. He just stood there dumbfounded. I gathered up the bag and catheter and ran out of there crying with humiliation. I went to the Emergency room, and they put the catheter back in and I begged my parents to let me stay home. I waited until I was well enough to have the catheter removed, and then one night I packed my stuff and took all the money I could find in the house and left. I haven't been back since."

"George I'm so sorry all that happened to you don't you think you will ever see your family again?"

"NO! Why should I? My father sold me down the river for a few bucks and a high school football championship. None of those guys were ever put in jail or had any charges brought on them."

"What about your mother or your sister?"

"Yeah well, my sister told me she was ashamed to go to school because I embarrassed her so much. My mother gladly took the money and used it for herself. Do you think that means that they cared about me or my feelings or how humiliated I was? No, I had to survive as best I could with everybody snickering behind my back. Some really sweet people wouldn't you say. "Hey, can I watch you pee. But what's the sense of talking nothing is gonna make it better or change it."

George got up and went to his tent. The next morning, he was gone. I felt terrible that I had encouraged him to talk and tell his story, but I felt he wanted to tell it to someone. I don't know if it helped to tell me what he did, but I hope it did. I wonder where he will end up or if he will ever go back to his family, I doubt it.

[Chapter 20]

With all the material he had collected it was time for Max to contact Ellie and see if she could meet him. He left her a note in her mailbox and asked if they could meet next Friday in their secluded spot near her apartment. He would go there and wait to see if she showed up.

Friday after dark Ellie put on her warm coat and headed for the woods. Max was already there and happy to see her. They exchanged greetings and then Max asked if anything had changed with the police since they talked last.

Ellie told him that the police had been by twice more, especially one detective who was the lead in the case. "The way he talked," Ellie described, "He is sure you are the serial killer. Thank God there have not been anymore killings."

"Why do you think he is so set on my being guilty?" Max questioned.

"I'm not sure," Ellie said, "I just think he wants to put a notch in his belt and maybe get promoted. He hates anyone who has money and made some snide remarks that you were a rich guy with big bucks, that could keep you in hiding, but he intends to find you no matter what. Max if I'm not being too pushy outside of your wanting to be accurate and honest in your writing what compelled you to focus on homeless people?"

"I have always had an interest in who these people are. One day the woman who did my taxes came to my apartment and she seemed a bit off, she told me she had a headache. I gave her some Tylenol and told her to sit in my easy chair and rest for a while and see if she felt better. She did and I kept on writing at my desk. After about an hour she came to my office, and we talked a little. She asked me how I found the things I wanted to write about. I told her that I like to listen to people's stories and if I find them interesting and think other people might be to, I write about them."

"Oh, then I have a story to tell you.

"Great I would love to hear it," Max said enthusiastically.

"When I first came here, I knew nothing about living in a big city or about what parts of the city were considered dangerous. I found an apartment close to where I was working and moved in. It was convenient and close to the subway, so I was pleased with it. As I got to know the city better, I saw how many homeless people were around, I felt so bad for them. I asked some of my co-workers about the homeless and they had many opinions about them. One told me that people on the street were all crazy, one said they were all drug addicts, and another said there were some people who just could not afford to pay rent. That the money they made was not enough to feed the family and pay rent. It made me wonder every time I saw one of these people on the street."

"Yeah, we sure have a lot of homeless people around," Max commented.

"I became accustomed to taking the subway home and because I never discussed the area where I lived, I didn't realize it was not the safest place to live. Anyway, every night I would see this same man sitting near the subway. He didn't seem to be like the other people I saw. He was clean shaven, and it seemed as if he took care of himself. When I saw him, he would make a small nod as if to say hello, but he never approached me. He had his hat on the ground but did not ask for money.

I overheard two people talking on the subway one day about how some of the homeless stay around the subway stations thinking maybe someone needed help carrying something and they could pick up a few bucks. Every other Fridays when I got paid, I would give him a five-dollar bill by throwing it in his hat that was at his side. I did this for months. I don't know why but he just seemed to be different than the others. It was just a gut feeling."

"I understand about gut feelings, and I always try to go with them," Max interjected.

"This one evening my boss asked me to work late and I agreed. I concentrated on my work and didn't realize that I was the only one left in the office and it was dark outside. I was a bit hesitant about walking to the subway but didn't want to spend the money on an uber. I began walking to the subway which was a few blocks away and kept looking around because I was a little scared. I saw a man walking behind me, but I kept on going. When I came to the next block, I crossed the street and kept looking back and sure enough the man crossed the street also. My nerves got the best of me, and I began to run, and the man began running after me. Now I was really scared and didn't know how much faster I could run or where to go to get help. When suddenly I heard this voice say, "STOP! Leave her alone she is good." Then from all kinds of places street people popped up and they were all telling the man to stop. I was so astounded. When I looked back again, I saw the man I had given the money to, and he waved me on. I couldn't believe how lucky I was. After that I didn't see the man for several weeks and one day as I was walking toward the subway he stepped out from behind a tree and said, "Thank you I work now." I have not seen that man since but what happened stuck with me and after that I always looked at the street people with new eyes."

"Wow, that's some story," Ellie expounded. I see why that inspired you to write about the homeless. I will have to think about that the next time I see someone like that."

"I got that feeling too," Max agreed, and after I finished my other book, I looked down at the park and decided to know more about these people."

"I was able to get all the information you gave me on my computer, and I have to say as I was entering the details I wanted to know more about each person. I feel as if I have come to know them and my heart aches for all their woes."

"I'm sure you will be very interested in this new stuff I have brought. My greatest worry is that I have this feeling I am somehow betraying these people all of whom have been so nice to me. I hope I can make it up to them somehow and it goes without saying that I would never use their real identities.

"Max, you need to start to plan on how you are going to come back to your old life. It's not going to be easy with the cops watching and waiting for you to make a move. For sure your old office and apartment will be off limits. You could stay with me" ....

Max cut her off, "no way would I ever put you in harm's way. You are doing enough for me right now and you are taking a chance at that."

"What are you going to do?"

"I don't know at this point. I might have to create a new identity until they find the real killer or killers, but my hands are tied with me being on the street now."

"You know you just said it, you need a new identity I bet we can come up with a new person you could become. One that is not around all the time because he travels extensively but enough to do some research and maybe help solve these crimes."

"How about this keep your eyes open to see if an apartment in your complex becomes available, I need a place I'm familiar with. I have a stash of cash hidden in my old apartment, but I can't get to it."

"They probably found it because they tossed your apartment, and it was a total mess it took a week to put it back together," Ellie told him.

"That's good in a way because they won't have to go search there again. The only problem is that I will have to physically go there and get the money myself because it's in a safe place that's hard to get to."

"Let's think about this and I can meet you next week and we can come up with a solid plan. In the meantime, I will check to see if anyone in this building is moving out," Ellie suggested.

"Ok great. Thanks for everything Ellie I like your idea, just know that if you change your mind and don't want any part of this I will understand," Max reminded her. See if you can get more intel on any progress the police have made on finding the killer. I suspect that if they already think they know who the killer is they have not done much more to look for someone else."

[Chapter 21]

Max knew that if he was going to clear his name, he had to come up with some hard evidence and he probably needed to start by getting the money he stashed in his apartment so he could get people to do the leg work for him, Lord knows I can't be seen by anyone, thought Max.

Max decided he could gain entrance into his old apartment by disguising himself as a plumber and get in without anyone knowing. That way he could get away with taking tools in with him and not create any suspicion. Finding a plumber would not be a problem, there were plumbers working on the old house right now. Max was already friendly with all the trade people who worked on the house. Max told the plumber that he was going to fix a leak in his girlfriend's apartment and asked to borrow his truck and some tools. The plumber chuckled and said if you need me, you know where I am.

Max dressed in overalls and had a gray wig and an old baseball hat and looked the part. He had never met the building manager in person so there was no risk of being recognized by him. Max carried the plumber's toolbox with him and knocked at the building manager's door and asked if he could get into apartment two. He spoke to the manager and said his company received a call from apartment one that they smelled gas.

Max knew to say that because the woman that lived in apartment one was an older lady that did not speak English very well. Her daughter did all her communicating.

"It's probably a miscommunication," the building manager told Max, "Mrs. Costello calls her daughter at the drop of a hat and then the message gets all mixed up. Come on I'll let you in and you can check the place out, the guy who lives there travels a lot and is hardly ever there anyway."

As soon as they got into the apartment Max headed for the kitchen and began looking at the gas stove. The manager asked if it was going to take long because he had someone else coming to do some repairs in an apartment in the next building. Max told him he didn't know but he could just lock the door when he left if he didn't find anything.

"I can't do that," the building manager said. I'll just sit here in the living room on my phone so let me know if you find something."

Max got right to it and began to remove the top of the stove. Before Max left the apartment knowing that he would be gone a long time he had the gas company turn the gas off before he left. He had placed the money under the metal plate that held the burners and since the pilot light was not on, there was no chance of the money getting burned. He took the bundles of bills and put them in the bottom of the toolbox quickly and began putting the stove back together, then called the building manager to come in.

"How's it going? Did you find anything wrong?

"No not anything unusual the pilot light blew out so maybe a small amount of gas did leak out and that's what apartment One may have smelled," Max lied, I'm done here if you want to lock it up again, I'll be on my way."

"That sounds great now I can go next door and get the tile guy going."

"Thanks, have a good day," Max called as he walked back to the truck.

Back in the truck Max gave a silent prayer that everything worked out well and he was able to get the cash, but I wish I had some time to look around the apartment and maybe pick up a few things. It's probably better that I didn't. Max hurried back to the old house and took the money out of the toolbox and placed it in a sturdy paper bag, and then put everything back the way it was in the toolbox and thanked the plumber for the use of the truck. Now he had to get some money to Ellie and find a way to contact someone who could find out exactly what kind of evidence the police gathered from the crime scenes of the murders and find out why what evidence they had on him.

Max racked his brain trying to think of who he could hire at first, but then he thought that over and tried to put himself in place of the detectives. He asked himself why would he hire someone if he was not guilty? That's what everybody would think. Ellie couldn't do it because if they traced her to hiring a private detective it would look as if she was working with Max. Then it hit him, Thomas Kane. Thomas and Max had become friends when he was writing his first book and needed some information on some city officials. Thomas was a reporter and although they often disagreed on things, they always understood the others point of view. Thomas as well as Max knew that the city politicians were as evil as sin so he agreed to help Max only if he would never reveal his source and Max agreed.

Max would call him on his burner phone tomorrow and see if Thomas was willing to help. If not, he would have to take a chance on picking a private eye by the dart board theory, that is just look at the names of a bunch of PI names and pick one. The next day when he called Thomas he was at work and couldn't talk freely. He was completely taken off guard to hear Max's voice but was receptive. He told Max to call back later that evening and they could talk. That evening Max called Thomas again and told him he was not in town but on the run and asked if Thomas would help him.

Thomas said, "Max I know we never saw eye to eye on a lot of things, but I don't think you killed anyone, did you?"

"No, I have never killed anyone, and I'm being framed by that police detective who wants to pin the murders on me and get promoted."

"Let me think this over and see how I can help you. I'm not on the police beat at the paper anymore so it might be tough to get anything. Call me back in a day or two and I will let you know if I can help."

"Thanks, Thomas, for even considering this. I'll get back to you soon," and Max hung up.

Max was worried. If Thomas decided not to help him, he didn't know what he would do. He went to the library to try to do some research on murder cases and what was used as evidence. Surprisingly, on some of the cases there was little evidence except for the testimony of the police and other people who knew the victims and it was all that was used as evidence. If it got the sympathy of the jury the person was convicted.

After 5 days Max was in a tizzy and prayed that Thomas would help him. He couldn't stand waiting, so he called Thomas again.

"Hey it's Max. How's it goin?"

"You are one lucky so and so," Thomas said.

"What do you mean?"

"Yesterday morning the editor came to me to ask me to write about the people who were victims of the serial killer. He said the police wanted to get people stirred up about the killings because they are having such a hard time finding the serial killer. He wants me on the story day and night to get the facts and then he would put the story on the front page. He wants me to get inside stories on the victims, you know sob stories that would paint the killer as the worse guy in the whole world. I told him the only way I would do it is if I had the full cooperation of the police and access to everything they had as evidence. I wouldn't print that, but I would need it to start a trail to see if I could get someone to give me something on the victims. They agreed so I will be getting a peek at the whole package soon and then we can go from there. I'm not sure if the cops remember they talked to me at the bar about you or not. If they ask, I will acknowledge but I won't volunteer. Then we'll go from there. We'll talk every other evening at 7:00. I'll get a burner and give you the number and you can call me on that so that I won't have a record of incoming called on either of my phones."

"I can't thank you enough," Max said with a whew, after holding his breath.

Don't go getting crazy just yet, I have no idea what I will find out or if they will be as forthcoming as they say they will. You know how it is they promise you everything and then in reality you don't get much."

"Yeah, I get it," Max said but you are my last hope so I will be praying that you get all you need, or should I say all that I need."

[Chapter 22]

After Max graduated from college, he talked his father into letting him take the summer off to go on a cultural tour in Europe. Max and two of his college friends began in England and spent weeks doing the usual London, Paris, Prague tour and every night they ended up getting drunk with locals in a small pub or in a rural bar off the beaten path. After a few months Max's friends got tired of roaming around and they wanted to go back to America to get started on their futures. Max told them he was not ready to return to America because he had an ulterior motive. Since Max's father had refused to talk about Jessie to tell him anything about her, Max had done the DNA thing, and it came back saying that part of his family may have been from the Mediterranean area. He knew his mother's maiden name was Ricci because he found her birth certificate in some old papers in his father's study and now, he knew the names of her parents. Max had heard his father say once that Jessie was a hardheaded Sicilian. With all that in mind Max went to Italy,

After finding a small apartment Max began to search for his mother's family, but after a few weeks he ran out of money. He called and begged his father to send him money and let him extend his trip for another month. Erol agreed but was not too happy with Max roaming around Europe for all this time. He agreed because it gave Erol some more time to decide exactly what he was going to have Max do when he got back and where he would fit him in, in the family business. He was actually worried that Max would not be able to settle down and would squander all the money the family left him. Max at this point was not aware that when he turned 25, he would inherit a fortune.

Max continued to look for his mother's family. His plan was to go to them to see if they knew where his mother was and if she was ok. Thinking they might not be open to his questioning he went to see them and told them he was looking for Jessie for business reasons. They were suspicious but Jessie's father was a smart businessman and suspected who Max was. They invited Max to come in and join them for dinner and during the course of the conversation Max blurted out that he was Jessie's son. To his great surprise the family told him they knew and embraced Max because he looked so much like some of their family. They began telling him all about Jessie when she was a little girl. They encouraged him to stay and get to know them and Max was thrilled.

He did not dare tell his father that he found his mother's family. Max had been searching for his mother online for some time and basically knew when he came to Europe that he would search for his mother's extended family. Jessie's family was not rich but had a great old villa that had been in the family for generations. They had vineyards where they grew grapes for the local winery and had a small olive grove. Max's uncle took to him right away and told him he looked exactly like his own son who had been killed two years ago. Max knew he had to stay when they told him that his mother was coming for a visit in two weeks.

Max was very nervous about meeting his mother. Would she want to see him? Would she be angry if he was there with her parents? Did she ever think of him? Were some of the questions that went through Max's mind.

The day finally came when Max met his mother, he could not believe his eyes. She is friggen beautiful Max thought to himself, why would my father not want her? She was not painted-up the way CJ was but had a warm and natural beauty. She wore very little make-up, only mascara and her hair were a rich warm, brown and she had big brown eyes. Max was blown away. Jessie was so happy and surprised she was not expecting to see Max in her childhood home. The two talked for hours each day. Telling each other all about how much they missed being in each other's lives. Jessie told Max that she lived with friends for a while and then lived in her car for several months after she left. She got a job in an art gallery cleaning and learned how to restore old paintings. The man who had taught her this craft was now her husband, and they had a small business restoring antique paintings and artwork in New York then moved to Italy.

Max told Jessie that his father told him that Jessie was mentally unstable, and she was uneducated and taking care of Max had been too much for her, so she ran away and never came back. Jessie did not say much about the lies Erol told about her, she just said that sounds a lot like Erol's fantasy world.

Max told her he was going to go back and at his father's insistence he would work in the brewing business. Jessie made no comment about that. Jessie told Max she had followed his life as best she could by reading about the family in the newspaper and that she had attended his graduation from college but from a distance. Over the next few weeks mother and son became re-acquainted and became friends.

Max was very happy with his new relationship with his mother. From then on, they kept in touch. Max had picked up two letters from the pile of mail at his apartment and left the rest not wanting to create suspicion, the letters were both from his mother. Although they did text and sometimes call, she liked to write. Max would read the letters and give her some idea why she had not heard from him for so long. He didn't want her to worry.

Max read the letters and the last one said that she might be visiting in the next few months and was hoping they could get together and spend some time together. Although I would love to do that, thought Max,

I was hoping that if my situation here was not resolved I could go to Italy and stay there with my grandparents. I must write back and give her some excuse for not being here when she visits. Yet another reason is that I must get all this squared away and get on with my life.

[Chapter 23]

Several weeks had passed and one day when Max was at the Green Street house the postman knocked on the door. He had a postcard addressed to Max and asked if he knew who that was.

"Yeah, that's me," Max said.

"Are you going to be staying at this address asked the mailman because I have not delivered any mail here in years. I have seen the trucks here and saw people going in and out, so I thought it was being renovated."

"Yeah, that's right and someone will be here for a while we are doing some work to restore the house so the address will be good in the future," Max told him. It's a good thing I didn't use my real last name just in case anyone was watching he thought. The postcard was from Hog and said they were in Texas, and he was having a ball. He had ridden several hogs and been able to keep afloat by servicing bikes and helping with repairs. He signed it simply, miss ya.

That evening he called Thomas and asked if he had found out anything.

"Well so far there have been 4 murders. Three of them were shot and one was stabbed. It looks as if the murderer subdues the victim in some way and then shoots them multiple times. There were essentially no witnesses except for the man they found in the alley that was stabbed. Someone reported seeing a homeless man running away from the scene. That was the one you saw, and the witness said he was close enough to him to have them make a sketch of you and that's why they were looking for you," Thomas explained.

"I know that part, what about the other victims."

"Same MO all shot, one was drugged then shot, one maybe hit on the head first and the other tied up and there is still a missing person they haven't found. It's a male and he has been missing several months and they have no clues about him, but I think they are going to try and add him to the list of victims killed by the serial killer. So far, no evidence that the victims knew each other or had any commonality with anything, except surprisingly the bar where we used to hang out or at least visited occasionally, but they are still looking into that.

You were right about one thing, the detective, his name is Finley, is hot to trot to get this case solved. Apparently, he has been on the force for some time and is looking to get promoted. He's looking for someone to take the fall for these murders even if the same person did not commit all of them. I hate to say this but it's not looking good for you Max mainly because you ran away.

"I didn't run away because I saw the murder or because I killed someone I went to live on the street because I'm writing a book about homeless people and need to see and hear the stories for myself so the book can tell a story and it will be the truth. You know how I work," Max intoned.

"Sure, I do but the timing is very bad, and it looks as if you ran. It might be that you have to prove you were on the street for that purpose, but I swear I don't know how. No one wants to believe anything about street people who live in that way, or what they say, and people are fearful and suspicious of them."

"I know what you are saying is correct but I'm not sure I could even get any of them to do this for me. Not that they would not do it but because

I would have to betray a lot of people I have come to know and respect some of them and they trust me. They are on the street because they don't want to be in the life they knew before and don't want to be found by anybody. Most of them are here because their lives were ruined in some way by others and if they had to come forward for me it would ruin whatever peace they have now and could make them relive the bad stuff again. There are plenty of messed up people out here, drug addicts, alcoholics, and some people that are plain hateful, they are not the ones I'm trying to protect. I couldn't ask the ones I know who have helped me just because they were good people. If I asked, they would probably come forward and do this to help me, but I can't ask them to do that, I just can't."

"Let's see how the case is going, maybe some evidence will surface, or someone will come up with some clues or some solid evidence and it will change the picture. If not, you may never be able to come back as yourself again, you will need a completely new identity. We're not there yet so don't lose faith. Something will turn up. See ya, keep in touch."

Max was feeling quite low the next day but decided he would go to the house and putter around. All the furniture that was to be salvaged and reupholstered was placed in the room away from the main living area. There were still closets to be cleaned out and a lot of stuff upstairs, but Max was hoping not to do that until Hog came back to help.

Max worked by himself that day, and Deidre came to the house at noon and told him that Marlene was going to come to the house later this afternoon to see if she approved her sketches and color schemes. She commented that Max looked down in the dumps and asked if she could do anything to cheer him up. He smiled and nodded no.

Marlene arrived at 2:00 and had several people with her. Max didn't want to have any part of that crowd so he stuck to the back area of the house hoping that they wouldn't want to see any part of the kitchen or the chef's pantry.

He could hear the chatter of Deidre's excited voice selling her ideas to Marlene. Max caught a peek of Marlene as she entered the front door, and she was quite beautiful. She was well dressed in a classy suit and heels. As he packed up old cookbooks and ledgers in the kitchen, he heard the group coming down the back steps and ran out onto the back porch and listened. The next voice he heard was a dreaded familiar one. It was Ali again. Dear Lord, he must be a friend of Marlene's or connected to her in business somehow. His heart pounded and his mouth got dry. Just as quickly as they arrived, they left the kitchen area for another room. Max was glad of that. The group didn't stay much longer after that and soon Deidre was back in the house after seeing them off. She told Max how much Marlene liked her designs and paint selection and wanted only two changes.

"That was quite an entourage that she had with her, who were all those people?" asked Max.

"Well let's see there was her architect, the construction manager, her business manager, and her personal assistant. You know," Deidre said in a stage whisper in a gossipy way, she, I mean Marlene has had some trouble in the past. She had a nervous breakdown after her father died and then went into a depression when a close companion was murdered."

"Murdered?" questioned Max.

"Oh yeah, murdered as in stabbed to death. It was in all the papers he was found in an alley stabbed to death by a crazy homeless man."

"Is that right," Max said looking surprised. He hoped the panic in his voice did not come through.

"She is much better now, and this is the project that will pull her completely out of her depression for good. I just know it. Then I will get a lot of referrals and be on my way," Deidre said with a happy lilt to her voice.

"That's great for you Deidre I have to go now see you soon." And with that Max turned and walked back to camp.

Max felt better after the walk back to camp but the fact that he had heard the voice of Ali twice now made him jumpy. He was either her business manager or personal assistant. Max went for the business manager role. That would mean he knew everything about her financial status. What if he knew Max was the man he chased and he was just toying with him"? Talking to Thomas had not been encouraging either and now all of it was just churning in his head making him crazy.

[Chapter 24]

Lenny was putting together a group thing for the camp to get people together for the holidays. Max asked him if there was anything he wanted him to do, now that he had some money that he was making from working at the Green Street house. He had as promised to put aside half of what he got from the items he took to the antique dealer and the thrift story for Hog and there would be more to come after some of it got sold. There was not really anything Max needed to buy as his needs at the camp were minimal and the living was so simple.

Max got a list of stuff from Lenny, and he went to the supermarket. Almost all the food would be pre-cooked as they had no access to any kitchen facilities, and it was all in bulk so people could help themselves. He got some wine and beer and since there was a freezer at the old house that they had started up he would bring some ice. The bakery always had day old muffins and a pie or cake, and he would get those too.

Lenny was surprised when he brought all the things to Lenny's tent each day, adding to the party supplies. He asked Max where he got all of it.

"This stuff is not only from me it's from Hog to," Max also declared, "after all we have been really lucky in finding some jobs and able to get a little money."

"That's mighty fine of you Max," Lenny said, "I'm glad Hog brought you in and you have made a good way with us."

Max was feeling so guilty that he had been forced to tell so many lies and make these people think he was something he was not. He would try and find a way to make it up to them somehow. After all, wasn't he here because he wanted to know the truth and here he was lying through his teeth.

The day of the little party seemed to be going well and all the people in camp were enjoying the food and wine. Lenny had silenced the crowd for a few minutes to say a few words about Candy and Jimmy. The people had in turn stepped forward and said a few things they remembered about them, and it was a sad moment. As the wine and beer got to working the party livened up and people began telling stories and there was laughter. Just as they were about to bring out the pies, they saw flashing lights and heard sirens. Soon two police cruisers with their sirens blasting came up the dirt road toward the camp as far as they could drive. Lenny and the others had made no effort to clear more of the road which worked best for them. It assured people coming to the camp had to walk a fairly long distance because it turned into a wooded path, and it gave the people in camp a warning that someone was coming up the road toward the camp.

Soon after the noise about 6 police officers got out of the cars and came walking into the camp. Max was shocked and didn't know what to do. He tried to hide behind the piled-up boxes of trash so he could see and hear all that was going on. He was sure they had to be there to arrest him and put him in jail. He wondered if he should step up and just say, "I'm here take me in and leave these folks alone." His gut told him to wait and see how this was going to play out, but if they began getting nasty and mean then Max might have to come clean. Lenny stepped forward and asked the cops what they wanted.

"We are looking for a felon who has been avoiding the law and we have an outstanding warrant for his arrest. We have been to two other tent cities in the area, but he was not there. We want to talk to all the men that you have here and see if any of them fit the description we have. Here is the warrant we have if you're not too drunk to read it."

"I'm not drunk, and these others here are not either. We are just having a small Holiday party and not botherin nobody," Lenny answered in a gruff voice. I guess you all think that everybody here is an alcoholic, druggie, or plain loser but you're wrong, and none of this food or drink is stolen either."

"Ok, ok, enough crap. Line the men up and have them come over here to the light one by one and then we will see what we came to see."

As the men lined up Max fell in line behind David and saw that he was so scared he was trembling. Max put his hand on David's shoulder and told him everything would be ok. One police officer heard Max talking to David and came over to them in the line.

"What's wrong with him," he said looking at David and shining his light in David's face and David began crying. "Is he an addict that needs a fix or what? Speak up there guy," the cop said and poked him with his nightstick.

Max stepped in front of David and responded, "He's not an addict at all, he can't answer because he can't talk, he has had a bad loss, and he is afraid of the cops. Can't you see he is terrified of all this?"

"Yeah, yeah what's his name?"

"It's David, David Johnson."

"Does he have any ID and what's your name," asked the cop.

"Most of us don't have IDs they were either lost or stolen. He lives here with the group; my name is Max Chambers."

The Sargent came over to the cop, David, and Max, and asked what was happening. The cop said he was questioning Max and David. The Sargent looked David and Max up and down and then said to the cop let's finish up here and get going."

After every male in the camp was questioned the Sargent said, "if for some reason you are hiding this man we are looking for, you will all be in trouble, so if anybody knows anything they should say so now."

Lenny said," What is the name of the man you are looking for and what's the charge?"

"His name is James Clinton Thompson, and he is wanted for vehicular homicide, child abuse and robbery."

"There ain't nobody like that here," Lenny said.

The cops left and the camp settled down. The party was over, and Max helped Lenny clean up. Max was glad there was something for him to do because hands were shaking so much, he felt as if he were going to explode. There were a few bottles of wine that were half full and later they all sat on the bench and drank the rest.

Robert who had helped with the cleanup said to Lenny I guess I will be leaving in the morning, "Lenny. I think they are getting close to finding me."

"What do you mean," Max asked, "finding you?"

"The truth is I was a teacher and a student counselor two states over and got fired. My wife threw me out and drained our bank accounts. My 13-year-old daughter began running with the wrong crowd. I told my wife, and she had a talk with her, but she didn't stop it only got worse. One Friday she didn't come home from school and stayed out all night. The next morning, I got dressed and went looking for her. I went to her best friend's house and demanded to know if she was there and found out she nor the friend were there. They were supposed to stay with another friend. This was a girl I had forbidden her to see so I went to that house next and knocked and when no one answered I broke in the door. They were all there asleep on the floor naked boys and girls, empty bottles, the stench of pot, garbage everywhere and places where someone had vomited it was a total disaster. I found my daughter and slapped her awake along with a bunch of others and took her home. I explained to my wife where she was and what I saw. My daughter began crying and became hysterical saying how I had embarrassed her by slapping her she felt I physically abused her, and she was humiliated. My wife just held her and cuddled her.

The next two days were agony. I made her stay in her room and told her she was grounded for a month, and she was not going to the Spring Prom. My wife went up to her room and they cried together. My wife decided that I was being too harsh and that she was going to let her go back to dating and to the dance. I tried to explain how wrong that was but when my daughter came to the dinner table that evening, she was all smiles and when my wife left to go to the bathroom she said, "you see you can't make me do anything I will just cry, and mom will give me my way."

For several months I just lived with it trying to make my wife see how she was being manipulated but she wouldn't give in. The following week my daughter came home with a tattoo on the side of her cheek, and I had a fit. This time my wife hit the roof also. I sent her to her room until my wife and I could discuss what we should do about this. We sat and talked about what we would do when suddenly my daughter came downstairs, and declared she was going out. I told her she was not going anywhere. She laughed in my face and started for the door. I grabbed her by the arm, and she struggled. Then she stopped and said, "I'll fix you." She made a lunge for her phone which was on the kitchen table because we took it from her, she missed and hit her nose on the table, and it began to bleed. She grabbed the phone and called 911 and when the police came, she said that I had physically abused her. Pinched her arms and punched her in the nose. The police arrested me and put me in jail.

My wife bailed me out and on Monday I went to school as usual. I was called into the superintendent's office and told I was suspended and there would be a hearing, but I was probably going to be fired. To make a long story short my wife and daughter testified against me, and I was in jail for 6 months and got out on probation. I was lucky in prison they only beat me up three times. Most pedophiles get beaten weekly. When I came out, I had no job, my wife packed up my clothes and put the suitcases on the porch and told me to leave. She threw 50 bucks at me and told me to go. I wandered around until Mike and I got to know each other, and he brought me here. If the cops are coming around it won't be long till they come for me. I saw my picture in the post office last week as a known pedophile so I can only guess my daughter told more lies about me and now I'm a fugitive. I will go farther south and maybe they won't find me.

There was silence from both Lenny and Max. What could you say to a story like that? To break the ice Max said, "Well at least they didn't find the person they were looking for here and maybe they won't harass us anymore. You could stay because they probably won't be back now that they satisfied themselves for now," Max suggested.

"No, I couldn't do that because I would be worried that they will be coming back and if they found me then they would harass the whole camp."

"Yeah, that was a lucky break all around," Lenny said.

Max looked at Lenny and asked, "What do you mean? All around."

"It's a good thing James Clinton Hamilton wasn't here," Lenny let out with a puff of relief.

"Who is James Clinton Hamilton anyway Lenny do you know him?"

"Lenny looked at Max with surprise and said, "You mean you don't you know Max? That's Hog's given name."

Max's mouth hung open, but he didn't say a word.

[Chapter 25]

The bike rally was ending. There was only one more week left before it would wrap up and everybody would leave for home. Hog, Duke, and Ziggy had been having a great time showing off Duke's bike and partying with the others. Spike left a few weeks back and went home to see his mother who was very sick. Everything seemed fine until a new bunch of bikers got caught ripping off a liquor store and got busted. They not only stole booze, but they had a stash of cocaine and heroin when the police found them. That was the beginning of the end for the rest of the bikers. After that the cops were present at every event every day watching all of them and ready to pounce at any wrong move. That made Hog very nervous and put a damper on the fun everybody was having.

They were riding back to the motel when they got pulled over by the highway patrol. They asked for Duke's and Hog's IDs. The officer took them back to the police cruiser and then can back. He didn't say anything but told them not to drive so fast. Before they left Duke asked the officer why he pulled them over.

"I got a call from one of the policemen at the rally and he said that a fugitive they were looking for who was wanted a few years back was there. Someone who used to ride with him thought he saw him at the event tonight. You two don't fit the description so your free to go."

Duke and Hog got on the bike and rode away. The next morning Hog told Duke he wanted to go back to his old camp. Duke told him that he had enough to because with the police watching their every move it was hard to relax. Hog told Duke he could take the bus back to the camp, but Duke wouldn't let him do that.

"Hell, Hog we would be within a few miles of your place when we hit the highway it ain't no trouble to drop you off. Ziggy and I were already making plans to go to the rally next year with you and maybe Spike will be going too. My bike can't be, without you now you take such good care of it. Why you could have had any number of jobs with any of the biker clubs," Duke told Hog.

"Yeah, I get that, but I want to go back. It may sound goofy, but I miss my old life, Hog divulged. "Ridin hogs might have been ok at one time in my life but not now."

Hog was extra quiet on the ride back he pondered if he should say something to Duke and Ziggy that the police were probably looking for him. He had recognized the man who told the police that a fugitive was at the rally, was a cousin of Janey's. He must have believed Janey when she said the accident was Hog's fault and he wanted to see him pay for it. It took 3 days for them to reach the camp area and they planned to have some chow and stay one night in the motel and hit the road early. Hog suggested they go see if Max was able to join them, Hog knew he would love to hear their stories about the rally and all that happened.

They rode up the road as far as they could, and Hog got off the bike and walked to the camp. It was early evening and Max was sitting on the old bench writing something. He got up when he saw Hog coming and ran to meet him.

"Hog man it's so good to see you, I missed you and everybody in the camp did too."

"Hi ya Max you look good how you been?"

"Ok same old thing still working at the Green Street house. Wait till you see it now it's really coming along," Max said happily.

Hog put down his pack and said, "Duke and Ziggy are waiting by the road you want to go get some grub?"

"That's sounds great I can't wait to hear your tales. Where's Spike?"

"He left early to go see his sick mom and didn't come back. Let's go to the Chinese buffet place I have had my fill of Mexican food for a while."

The group ate and talked and laughed and had a great time telling their stories until the manager can over to their table and told them they had been there 3 hours, and they needed the table. That brought laughs all around and they left chuckling at the broken English of the manager saying three hour you be here three hours no more eat."

Duke and Ziggy dropped Hog and Max off at camp and as they walked into camp several of the people greeted Hog and welcomed him home. Lenny popped out of his tent to greet Hog and gave him a bear hug.

Back in their tent they made small talk for a short time and then Max felt he should tell Hog about what happened when he was gone, and the police were looking for him. Hog was very unhappy to hear that and told Max he wasn't sure that it was still safe for him to stay there.

"I'm uptight about what you told me. Not afraid for me but if the police think that it's possible that a felon settled in camp, they will start comin down hard the people here and that's the last thing I want." Hog declared. "It could be others here may be wanted on charges somewhere and if the police start to nose around it could pluck some people's last nerve".

"What would you do asked Max? I mean where would you go?"

"In a case like this there is one thing to do and that is to take a hot ass to a cool country. Duke has been asking me to come back with him to where he has his crib. He's thinking of opening a small bike shop and wants me to work with him. That's the best offer I got in a long time. I think I could lay low and go underground for a while, if you know what I mean. I'm gonna level with Duke first though to see if he still wants to take a chance on me. Tomorrow first thing I'm gonna chew it over with Duke and see what happens. If he digs it, then I'm history."

"Oh, Hog I know how you feel. I know everybody says that, but I really mean it I would miss you a lot, but I understand that you need to protect yourself."

"Max hang with me in the morning and if Duke is willing to take me on, I'll ask you to clue Lenny in on me splitting and tell you what he should say to the others. If not, I be back in the tent with you."

"Ok man I can do that." Max agreed.

The next morning, they went to see Duke and Ziggy. Hog told them the whole story. Duke was surprised at first but told Hog he didn't care about the past and after knowing Hog and seeing how he understood bikes and people he knew what kind of man he was.

"You helped out a lot of people with their bike problems and never took a penny from them Hog, so let's let it lay and go on down the road."

Hog took Max aside for a few minutes and told him what he wanted him to say to Lenny. They dropped Max off back at camp. Hog got off Duke's bike and hugged Max. He didn't have to say much more, he got back on Duke's bike and Max had tears in his eyes as he waved them off.

[Chapter 26]

Thomas had been working long days and was trying his best to get the rest of the police files because as usual though they promised the editor they would be forthcoming with everything they had, Thomas knew they were sandbagging and had not come clean. When Thomas asked Detective John Finley where the rest of the evidence was, he told him that the evidence was highly confidential and that only very few people were privy to see all they had.

Thomas didn't believe the detective, he thought that they were protecting a person who was very high up in the city or a political person. Without all the evidence Thomas didn't have much to go on. Frustrated he went back to the bar where they used to hang out to see if the people the police questioned were still going there. He hoped it would be easy because he was considered to be one of the insiders and they would pay no attention to him. Thomas hoped they would talk freely in his presence. He would go there a few evenings and see what would happen.

Thomas went to the bar, and it was like old home week, they were glad to see him and wanted to catch him up on what was happening. After telling him about Max and the gruesome murders they told him that the detective had asked them all to be there that night. Thomas's ears perked up when he heard that. He pretended he got a phone call and stepped away. Instead of going back to sit at the bar he moved away and sat at a small table off to the side with his back to the bar, but still within earshot.

About 30 minutes later the Detective John Finley arrived and gathered the witnesses to him. He began telling them how important this case was and that if he didn't catch this killer, it would be very bad for the city and for them.

"If we don't nail this guy none of you will feel safe walking down the street wondering if this guy will be looking for revenge because you had the courage to come forward. He will probably think that you ratted on him, and he will want someone to pay for that," the detective emphasized.

The two men and woman looked at each other and asked why he would say that. The Detective told them that they had taken the suspect into custody and were questioning him.

"It's too bad my boss, is under a lot of pressure to find this killer, in his desperation to solve this case he went ahead and questioned this suspect this afternoon and told him about getting information from all of you at this bar. Now the fugitive is well aware of who you all are, and he verbalized that he would make anyone who told lies about him pay." That's why I asked you all to meet me here tonight."

"What does that mean exactly," asked one man.

"You know the city couldn't give you 24/7 protection so you would be on your own to watch out for yourselves when you moved about the city and maybe even your own homes."

"We didn't say that he committed the crime we just said that he argued with people about different topics, how would he know what we said or who we are anyway?"

"He's pretty smart and started asking how we got the information we have and once my partner mentioned this bar, he put two and two together, "the detective explained.

"What should we do?"

"I think you need to tell us everything you know about this man and hope that is enough for us to put him in the right spot at the right time. It is circumstantial evidence except for the one eye witness it would be powerful evidence against him if you could pinpoint his whereabouts during the storm. I tell you that Max Stein needs to be put away for murder."

The group began talking among themselves and told the detective that he was there the night of the murder of the man they found in the alley but left at 7 and then returned at 10:30.

"I remember," said the woman, "because it was storming, and I never stay here that long but the weather was so bad I didn't want to leave. We had dinner here and waited for the storm to die down."

"Wait a minute." One of the men said we had another terrible storm two weeks before and Max was there that night. I don't think he was there the following week when we had the second storm, in fact, I don't remember seeing him all that week. Time seems to run together it's hard to remember when you go to a place frequently."

"Well, I do," said the woman indignantly, "and if that means that I get police protection then that's what should happen."

The man protested that she was not correct in what she remembered but the defective picked up on it fast.

"Will you be willing to come to the station tomorrow and give a formal statement swearing to that?"

"Yes, I want to see this guy behind bars I don't want to be afraid to walk the streets or be in my house, I live alone you know," the lady volunteered.

The detective took the woman aside for a few minutes to tell her where to go the next day and then thanked all of them and left. The group talked among themselves for a few minutes and began to squabble, some being critical that the woman was so certain when the rest were not. Then one by one they left. Thomas couldn't believe his ears. Detective Finley had lied deliberately to get one of them to give a statement. He must want that promotion badly thought Thomas to get a witness to lie and put it in writing when they didn't really remember the truth. Thomas slipped out of the side entrance with no one seeing him and went home and began to try and put the pieces of the crimes together. He realized that he needed more information from Max. Max had told him about seeing the man murdered but not the details. Maybe he knew more than he thought but just didn't remember the details because he was so freaked out. He would contact Max tomorrow. Thomas listened attentively as Max told him the whole story about the night, he saw the murder. Thomas asked him about the exact date of the murder and Max told him. "The woman at the bar told the detective it was two weeks later then what you told me," Thomas declared with triumph. "I'm not a detective or a lawyer but I would definitely say that it was a premeditated murder. The guy came prepared to murder, he had the stun gun and the knife."

They talked a bit more and Thomas told Max to call him later in the week. The story gave Thomas some ideas and now he had some facts he could run down and had some investigating to do. Thomas didn't want to tell Max about the detective lying and about the woman giving the sworn statement because he didn't want to discourage Max. He had been very emotional when he related the details of witnessing the murder to him, and Thomas didn't want to worry him further. As Thomas began writing the story for the paper it did not make any sense. It seemed as if the police were basing all their evidence on circumstantial stuff which was not the usual procedure especially for serial murderers and they were being led in a totally different direction by Detective Finley, no matter what his reasons were. Then there was the matter of the witness that gave the sworn statement that Thomas knew was a lie. This is a mess. I know that Max didn't do the murder of the man in the alley but there were other bodies so someone who is going around killing people needs to be found and soon and the cops are not looking for the real killer. If they find Max, they will pin all this shit on him.

[Chapter 27]

Max really missed Hog these days as he continued working at the Green Street house. He was also worried about his relationship with Deidre. They had lunch together almost every time that she came to the house and thank God that it was not every day. She told him that Joseph was back in town for a short time, it had complicated her life, but she did not go into detail.

Max's latest huge worry was that the painting crew was about to move upstairs and paint all those rooms and he wondered if they would find out about the secret room. He knew that he needed to go up there and see if the room was still in the same shape, it was when he first saw it, meaning that the body was still there in the chair. It would be Hell to pay for everyone when they found the body. He would play dumb and never acknowledge he knew anything about it but realistically he knew he would be questioned by the cops again because he was at the house working for so long. They would add the body to the list of serial kills and then when they found out his real identity and think he killed that person to. Max still did not have any ID and the time the police followed him to the house he was lucky very, very lucky. Maybe I should ask Lenny about getting an ID, he might know where I should go to get one.

After all the lights in the tents went off that evening Max approached Lenny and asked his advice about where to get an ID. At first Lenny looked at him questioningly and asked what happened to his ID. Max explained about his cardboard house and the giant storm. Lenny stroked his chin and said, "let me think on it a while."

The next day as Max was returning from the Green Street house, he could hear shouting and cursing coming from the camp. As he got closer Lenny and some of the other men surrounded one of the tents where a couple had been staying and they were wondering if they should intervene or not. Max asked Lenny what happened.

Lenny said that he was going to the tent to tell them they had to leave the camp when suddenly he heard screaming coming from there. When he tried to get into the tent Larry Joe opened the flap and showed him he had a gun and told him to stay away. Lenny asked what was going on and Larry Joe told him that he had to make Kitten pay.

"Why what did she do?" asked Lenny.

"She's been carousing with those hopheads for crack and when they give it to her, she couldn't pay so they beat the shit out of her. But now she gotta pay cuz she lied to me and smoked all the crack by herself. Now I put my mark on her so they will all know who she belongs to. It's there on her face for all to see and I gave a little demonstration of what I would do next time on her chest."

"Larry Joe, you know you're as high as a kite and when you sober up you will be sorry you hurt her. Let us come in and see if we can help her and if she needs a doctor and you can sleep it off," Lenny begged.

"I don't know," Larry Joe called out, I'm gonna think on it," and closed the tent flap.

The banter went back and forth for a while and many of the people in the camp gathered around. Finally, one of the men said, "I'm gonna go to the back of the tent and see if I can see what's goin on and if I can jump

Larry Joe and bring out Kitten. We don't need no body dying here or the cops comin around again."

In the next 10 minutes it was over, the man had Larry Joe on the ground and Lenny and a few men went in the tent. Kitten was on the cot holding what was left of her breast. It had been almost cut off and was bleeding a lot. She had a lot of blood on her face too because Larry Joe had carved his initials in her forehead.

What we gonna do now asked Lenny to no one in particular as a small crowd had gathered. Mary stepped forward and said, "I can help Kitten to wrap the wound and get on some clothes on. Then we can help Kitten get to the street and get somebody to call an ambulance. We need to get her away from here, so the word doesn't get out that we're violent, Mary decided."

Mary wrapped a clean tee shirt around Kitten's chest and put a dress over her head. They got an old shopping cart and picked Kitten up and put her in it. It looked ridiculous with Kitten's legs hanging out of the side of the cart and two men pushing it with Mary walking beside it. When they got as far as the edge of the park where there was a paved path, Mary pushed the cart by herself and waited and watched until she saw a bus stopped in the distance. She pushed the cart to the side of the bus stop and ran and hid in the bush to see what would happen when the bus stopped.

The bus stopped and the driver opened the doors. He opened the bus doors, looked out and saw the shopping cart and stood on the bus steps. He came out and looked at Kitten and thought she was dead but then she moaned, and he jumped back. He got back in the bus's driver seat and called 911. Soon the police and an ambulance arrived. They put Kitten on a stretcher and just as they were about to lift her into the ambulance, Larry Joe came running out of the trees and started screaming that he was sorry and didn't mean to hurt her and the cops subdued him and put him in a squad car. Mary watched as the ambulance drove away with Kitten, she felt badly but was happy Kitten was going to get the medical attention she needed. She never thought Larry Joe was crazy enough to harm Kitten.

Mary took the shopping cart and pushed it back to camp. It was a mess with blood, but she would wait until late evening when all the visitors to the park were gone then she would take it to the park restroom and wash it down. She pushed it back to camp and told the rest of the group what happened.

Life went on as usual, and Max went back to their tent to work. Material for his book was building up and he had to get it to Ellie so she could get it transcribed into the computer. He set up a time to meet her at their usual place and Ellie brought food and the recorder. Max bought the small tape and gave it to Ellie.

[Chapter 28]

Several days later Kitten came back to camp. Her face was a mess, and she had a huge bandage around her chest. When they asked why she was there she said she signed out against medical advice because she could take care of herself. When Lenny asked her what happened that she was back so fast she told him, "They arrested Larry Joe, but I wasn't gonna press charges, so they had to let him go. I'm waitin for him to come and collect me, but he had to meet some people and then he will be here. Lenny asked Kitten if she was sure she wanted to go with Larry Joe and she told him that he was her best friend and she loved him, and they were going someplace to make a new life.

Lenny was glad that Kitten told him they were leaving camp because he was going to ask them to leave if they didn't go on their own. He didn't want anyone who was unstable and caused trouble all the time. Besides he didn't want the cops nosing around every time Kitten and Larry Joe had a fight which was almost daily, and he was sure that would continue to happen.

Kitten waited all that day and all night and the next day. It was in the late afternoon the second day until Larry Joe finally appeared. He and Kitten spend a lot of time in their pup tent and then they packed their things in their backpacks and bundles and left without so much as a thank you to Lenny or any of the people at the camp.

Max went to the Green Street house and the painters were moving all their scaffolds and other materials upstairs to start painting. The plumbers had updated the bathrooms and some rooms needed new windows but most of the rooms were ready to paint. Max decided he would just play it cool and see how the painters progressed although he avoided going upstairs as much as possible.

The architect Ben had been by a few times with plans for the old house, and he seemed as if something was bothering him because he measured all the rooms several times and just shook his head as if he missed something. Max asked if there was a problem and if there was anything he could do to help him. He answered by telling him that the square footage of the house and his measurements didn't match, they were in fact, not even close. Max heard him talking to someone on the phone about the problem and whoever it was encouraged him to re-measure the square footage of the house again because he probably made a mistake. The old plan was probably not as accurate as it should be, and the measurements were off because of that. Ben put down the phone and for the next 3 hours went to every room and re-measured every inch, again. Still the figures he originally had were the same or off by a few inches but nothing like he expected. Frustrated and not knowing what his next move should be he asked Max if he wanted to walk to the diner and get some lunch. Max agreed. Seated at the counter Ben started talking and began going over his problem with the house. Max let him ramble on. Max was trying to figure out a way to tell Ben about the secret room but didn't want to let him know that he knew about it. Immediately upon finding the secret room and the corpse the cops would be called and that was the last thing in the world Max wanted was to have a bunch of cops searching the house and questioning everybody who worked there.

When Ben finally stopped complaining and he turned to Max and said, "Max what about you? I have been yacking since we got here, and you haven't said a word. What do you do in your spare time?"

"I haven't done much since Hog left. We used to hang around and get a pizza or have a few beers, but I just relax now. Or I go to the library I like finding out things about everyday life."

"What do you mean?" asked Ben.

"Well take this old house we're working on for example. I was curious about it when we first started coming here and I looked it up at the library. It was famous once and there are some pictures of it in old newspapers because it was the fanciest house in town and important people lived there. The richest and most prominent politicians and celebrities of the time visited and there were pictures in the local newspaper of it. In fact, it was built to look like the famous Green Street House in London."

"It that right," Ben answered surprised, I can't believe you found out so much about the house."

"Yeah, and I don't think anybody knows about that." Max replied playing as if that was the biggest secret in the world.

"That's very interesting Max how did you find out about that?"

"Well, I can't really take credit for finding out everything but the librarian who has worked in this town all her life and I were talking one day, and she asked me where I was working, and she told me she knew some things about the house. She got out the archived newspapers and books and told me about the house and that it was a legend in her school days and was supposed to be haunted. It was also "The place," to be in society back in the day."

"Wow that's quite a story Max and it has given me some new ideas." Ben said.

Max and Ben finished their food and went back to the house. Ben got on his computer and began researching the Green Street house. In a short time, Ben let out a loud, "Oh My God!" and got up and went to where Max was working.

"Max, I found it just as you said there is a lot of history here and it may be the answer to my problem. I have been bewildered about the discrepancy between my figures and the square footage on the original plan of this house and I think I know why," Ben exclaimed excitedly.

"Why?" asked Max trying to look as innocent as possible.

"The footage that makes up the difference between my figures and those on the plans are probably a secret room somewhere in this place. It was one of the things people did back then and if this was really patterned after the original Green House it would have a secret room too, maybe even two," Ben answered.

"That is so interesting," Max said, "Are you going to look for a secret room?"

"I sure am, and I hope I find it soon," Ben heaved out excitedly. "Will you be able to help me find it?" asked Ben.

"I, I guess so I'm not sure what would I have to do?"

"Nothing drastic just hold the tape for me when I measure the rooms again and then we would try and find a hollow sounding wall by pounding on it with a small hammer or tool to see if the walls were not as solid between each room."

"You would have to check it out with my boss he's the one who hired Hog and me in the first place, he might get upset."

"No worries I will talk to him and see if he will let you do it."

"Ok," Max responded, "I'll do whatever."

Walking back to camp Max questioned if he did the right thing by directing Ben to the secret room. He was certain they would have found it anyway; it was just a question of time. Then all Hell will break loose, and I would have to find a way to be away from the house for a while until they were done with their investigation maybe he would just tell them he was sick and couldn't come to the house.

Ben was as excited as a kid on a treasure hunt but after two days, they found nothing. They spent most of their time at the back of the house on the main floor, and Max knew they were not going to find anything. One the third day they went upstairs, and Ben was sure they would find the room. They did find a small closet which had a chest and shelves that probably once held guns and ammunition but not the main room. Ben had given up looking at plans and was using his hands and a small hammer to check out the long hall along the main bedrooms. Suddenly Max heard a muffled call for help and knew exactly where it was coming from. He rushed to the wall and started to bang on it with his fists. Ben heard and pounded and yelled back. The door gave way suddenly and Max went tumbling in just as he had before. This time Ben was already there and had a powerful flashlight.

"Look at this," Ben said to Max, in awe of the condition of the room and its furnishings. Wait till he sees the body thought Max then we'll see just how surprised he is. As Ben shined the light around and on to the overstuffed chair there was no body. NO BODY! Max said over and over in his mind, astonished. What happened to the body had he been hallucinating? Was there ever a real body? Max controlled his reaction and said nothing. Ben began searching the room and went on and on about how unique the room was and how it looked as if no one had been in there for years he never saw the concern on Max's face, because the room was very dark, Max was very troubled because now he knew the killer had been in this house.

After they left the room Max sat and thought about the body. It must have been later that night when Ali had been there with the property manager, and they went upstairs. Ali must have come later that night when no one was there and moved the body. That must have been the day Max had come to the house and the back door and the upstairs window were open. There had been no choice really, Max knew with all the renovations someone was bound to find the body and then not only would the project be stopped but there would be a huge investigation and he did not want to be a part of that. No matter how Ali got rid of the body Max now knew two things for sure, one that it was good for him that the body was taken away and not found in the house and two that Ali was the serial killer. Finding the body would have only added to the list of victims they were accusing him of killing now they would say he was in the house almost every day, and he had no alibi. But now things have changed since the body disappeared, Ali didn't know it, but he saved Max's ass this time himself. Max worried now how he would get evidence on Ali and clear his own name. It seemed as if things were getting more complicated and his odds of being cleared were getting slimmer and slimmer.

[Chapter 29]

Thomas was having a hard time getting information on Ali. He thought Max was right in thinking that somehow Ali was connected to Marlene or else why would she be with him when they visited the house. He looked into Daniel Turner Marshall AKA Ali's background and found that he was a loyal employee to Marlene's father's company and had stayed with the company after he passed away. Marlene had taken her father's death badly and Ali had stepped in to help in every way possible. He had literally run the company while she was incapacitated after her father's death and was her right arm man since she had returned as the president and took over the company.

Ali was married when he was in college but that lasted only a short time when he left the small town for college his wife began seeing other men. They divorced shortly after he finished his first year. He started out in the business world by taking a job as a part-time administrative assistant in his junior year at college. He stayed with the company and was offered a job as a very junior officer after he graduated from college. He continued and got his master's degree with the company paying for half the cost with an agreement he would stay with them 5 years after getting the degree. Marlene's father took a liking to him and kept promoting him until he became the father's assistant and was making more money than he ever dreamed of and that made it hard to leave.

Everything in his background sounded like a fairy tale and his record was as clean as a whistle. There was no reason in the world to suspect him, but Thomas wondered what the relationship between Daniel and Marlene really was. They both maintained private residences and personal lives.

The editor was pushing for a story, but Thomas did not have much to go on and the evidence that the police had given him was superficial at best. In the meantime, he searched the arrest sheets and all the cases that happened in that county in the last 6 months to see if he could find any connections.

Thomas came across several cases of assault that were defended by the same attorney and wondered if that was anything he should take a closer look at. The cases were all adult abuse charges that were dropped by the people who were assaulted, and all seemed to be in long term relationships. This was a red flag and just out of curiosity he made notes of the victims and the people who committed the assaults to see what their records looked like. It seemed like nothing at first but as he looked at their records in depth it seemed these abusers had been arrested several times before and always the charges were dropped, with no jail time. This guy must be a Hell of a lawyer, Thomas thought to himself to be able to get so many people off. He put his notes away and went on another idea when the police called to say they had another victim. The murder turned out to be a witnessed argument between two guys at a bar and had nothing to do with the other murder cases.

Thomas went back to the police station hoping to get something more for his story and saw that Detective Finley was there, but he didn't see Thomas. He was talking with some fellow officers and stepped away when his phone rang. He walked over to a corner of the room to talk more privately close to where Thomas was sitting. Thomas's back was to him, and he tried hard to hear what the detective was saying but only heard small bits of the conversation but clearly heard the conversation end with the detective saying don't worry I have a few cases lined up for you.

That sounded odd to Thomas, and he wondered for a minute if Detective Finley often gets people to lie when making sworn statements. What else could he get them to do. This might be a huge coincidence, but it has my curiosity aroused thought Thomas. I have to go back to the office and do some more digging. After reading all the cases assigned to Detective Finley in depth Thomas decided he should check to see who the lawyer assigned to the case was. Surprisingly it was the same lawyer in all the cases. Whoa! His name was Dean Davis. Thomas dug around and found some information on Mr. Davis. He found out that Dean had not been too great in school, and it took him 2 extra years to finish college. When he finally passed the bar after the third try, he was working with a firm that did insurance fraud. He had only been doing assault cases for the last year. When Thomas looked at the records more closely, he found that the leading police officer on all the cases Dean got had been Finley. Instinctively Thomas's gut told him there was something that just didn't smell right about all this.

The next thing he would have to do was to watch to see what new cases were coming up. Finley said he had a few cases for whoever he was talking to so if it was Davis that he had been talking to then that would not be a coincidence if Davis filed as attorney for the new cases.

The following week two new cases were registered with the attorney Davis. They Were both assault cases investigated by Finley. One was a man home from a merchant marine trip who got drunk and beat his wife, the other was a guy who slapped his wife around for leaving their kids alone at night while she went out. Thomas was fairly sure that Davis was the person Finley was talking to, but Thomas didn't see anything in those cases that raised a red flag. Maybe I just got carried away with my so call theory and there is really nothing to this. I will keep an eye out for other cases to see if it might be something or not. Within two days Thomas got his answer, the president of the Mayor's Council had been brought in for assaulting his wife. It was kept hush, hush and assigned to Detective Finley. The next thing you know Attorney Davis was documented as his council. Instead of waiting weeks to see what was going to happen, within 24 hours the charges were dropped, and the president of the mayor's counsel was set free.

Now Thomas knew he had to get to the in-depth histories of both Davis and Finley and see what the real connection was and how it tied in with Max. It all seemed as if there was no way any of the facts fit but somehow, somehow there were facts out there that would connect them, and Thomas had to find them. This was all very interesting but how could it help Max? Thomas was sure there was a connection because Finley was such a crooked cop. But if he was to save Max from being scapegoated, he needed much more than to get the detective arrested. He had people in the office working on getting background info on both Attorney Davis and Detective Finley, but it would take time.

One night when Thomas was at the station two police officers were arguing. The verbal assault was getting loud, and the station master told both cops to cool their jets. They quieted down but still argued. The argument was about the exam to get promotion to detective and if it was fixed or not. The one cop told the other that when he saw that Finley had been promoted to detective, he knew the election was a fake because he was the worse cop in the whole precinct. One cop left and the other sat on the bench holding his head. Thomas decided he would see if he could get this guy to spill his guts so he went over to him and asked if he could sit down. Thomas began talking to the cop and asked if he needed a drink. They went to a quiet bar around the corner and the officer told Thomas how Finley stole the exam from him because he was in court testifying and no one knew the exam time had been changed. He missed the exam and Finley got promoted instead.

When Thomas asked about Max's case the officer told him about new evidence that had been found at the murder scene. Finley was so anxious to pin the murder on Max he had the entire area dug up and the debris sieved, and small pieces of Max's driver's license and passport had been found in a place where they suspected he had a shelter. The story was going to be that Max was a pervert and lured men to the shelter, drugged them and after he had his way with them, he killed them so that they would not be able to ever identify him. Thomas was floored when he heard that.

"I can't believe that" Thomas declared, "Why is Finley so gung-ho on this case? Do you know?"

"No and nobody else seems to know either but ever since Finley got the mayor's right-hand man off the hook, he can do no wrong. The mayor is making the captain go along with everything Finley wants to do. Most of the guys are disgusted about it. Just remember that anything you heard tonight you didn't hear from me. I have to go home I'm exhausted."

Thomas sat and had another drink and tried to figure if there were other dirty things the detective did and why Finley had the captain's ear. That was probably another story for now he would not be able to tell Max what he knew about additional evidence it would crush his spirit.

[Chapter 30]

Ellie and Max met in their usual spot and had sandwiches and beer and he gave her two more tapes. Max was telling her about Hog leaving and how much he missed him, and thought he wanted to come back to his old life now more than ever, but he wouldn't be able to do that until his name was cleared and he wondered if that would ever happen.

"Maybe I should start to look for a place outside the US where I can go and live a normal life. It is so hard to live on the street and see and hear all the agony around me. Granted some of the people do not seem to mind living on the street and seem content to live the way they do. I know for certain though that is not true for all of them. There are some bad people out here no doubt, but some are just tired of living and feel as if the world hates them and more importantly that not a living soul cares about them."

"Max, I know you are down and very frustrated but there is not a lot more we could do. I don't even know if I should tell you this, the police were at the office again, the detectives. That same one who has been there before it's almost like he is harassing people by continuing to come around."

"I think you are referring to Detective Finley, right?"

"Yeah, that's the one. He seems pretty obnoxious, and he was asking the editor about all your past assignments and where you traveled to and how long you were gone and all that."

"I wonder why he's doing that?"

"Well, they told the editor that they would have to go back and look at the assignments and travel expense and all that before they could give him any answers. The editor was disgusted with him also and asked why he was doing all this again and he just said they had some new evidence and were trying to check it out."

"Hmm new evidence I wonder if that was just an excuse to ask more questions or if it was the truth that they found something. But what? There is no evidence about me because I didn't kill anybody. No matter it is all unnerving to know that all this is going on when I didn't do anything and worse can't do a thing to defend myself."

"The boss was so pissed he told the receptionist that if they showed up again, they should say he was in a meeting or not available or whatever because he didn't want to talk to them again," Ellie intoned disgustedly.

"Max, have you heard from Hog lately? How's he doing?"

"Yup, he sends me post cards at the green house where we worked last together, and he says it's ok but If I read between the lines correctly I pretty sure he is not really happy. I think he misses the group at the camp and maybe me I hope I thought we had a fairly good relationship. I can say that I really miss him." "Why don't you go and see him for a visit and see where he works and all?" Ellie asked "I can't travel not with my face still plastered all around and besides I don't have any ID. You know it's hard to do anything these days without someone asking for ID."

"You have a point there it is almost certain that in the future we will all have to have chips under our skins like animals," Ellie said, and they both laughed at that. "Anyway, Ellie I wanted to tell you this story myself without putting it on tape because I think it's good to hear a success story every once in a while. There was this couple Sally and Joel that were at the camp long before I ever got there, and they both had jobs but didn't make enough money to have a house or apartment. They seemed to lead a normal life or as normal as it can get when your permanent home is a tent. Sally worked at the Good Will Super Store and Joel washed dishes in a local restaurant. They saved every penny they made, and Joel got promoted to waiter. He was talking about Sally, and they asked him if she would like a waitress job which paid almost twice as much as she was making at the store, so she jumped at the chance," Max recited.

"That sounds great for them," Ellie replied.

"There's more, one evening an art publisher came in and noticed the picture of a robin on the wall and asked to talk to the manager about it. The manager told him that one of the waitresses did sketching when she had time and asked if they would hang it in the restaurant. The man asked to talk with her. When she came out, he asked her about the sketch and asked if she could do one for him. Sally agreed and did another quickly on a napkin, this time it was a cardinal. She gave it to him, and he asked her how much she wanted for it. Sally laughed and told him she only did the sketching because it was sort of her hobby, and he could have it. She had been doing it since she was a kid. The man thanked her and said he would be back. He was back the next day with an artist friend, and they asked to see Sally. They asked if she could do a sketch for them. Sally took the sketch pad they brought and looked around the restaurant. She saw a picture of a parrot at the bar advertising a cocktail and made a quick sketch of it. She gave it to the man. They both looked at the sketch and then at her and offered her $200 for the sketch and asked if she would do more for them. Sally laughed and asked if this was a joke her husband had them playing on her. They assured her it was not a joke. She told them to wait a minute. She went in the back and brought out a cardboard box full of sketches of rabbits, dogs, birds, all kinds of creatures. The man and the artist drooled over the papers and offered to buy them all and put them in a book. The rest is history. Sally is now a published artist and she and Joel have enough money for a house and got their 3 kids back from her sisters and they are a family again."

"Oh my God what a wonderful story. You have to have that in your book Max, it's a must. What a story book ending."

"I just wanted to run it by you in person to see your reaction and I think you are correct it is so good that every once in a while, there is a good story out here."

[Chapter 31]

Marlene and Daniel (Ali), Ben and Deidre and several others came to the house for a tour of what had been done so far. Ben had told them about the secret room, and they were anxious to see it. Ben led the way, and they were astounded that this room existed and the way everything had been preserved. As Marlene looked around, she was so excited about this room she decided that it would be a good idea to keep the room just as it was found except of course cleaning it up and adding new rugs etc. Marlene told the party that she had been a guest in the house when she was a little girl with her mother and father. She didn't remember much of the visit but knew that a visit there was considered important. She was quite happy with the renovations.

Max was happy they were mostly upstairs, and he sat on a bench in the center of the house where you could hear almost every conversation whether it was upstairs or downstairs as there were few furnishings and the hollow sound echoed everywhere. Mostly Max wanted to stay out of the line of sight of Ali and not tour the house with the group.

Ali and Ben came downstairs and went into the room off the dining room and Ali began telling Ben that he wanted to add an elevator to the house so it would be easy for Marlene to get up and down the steps.

Ben responded, "You know Daniel you never bring your friend Sam here; he always had some good ideas. Where did he go anyway? It seemed he was always at Marlene's side every time I saw her and then poof he was gone."

"Never mention that man's name to me," Ali said vehemently. He was poison to her, and I say I hope he never comes back."

"Sorry I didn't mean to bring up a problem, but I thought he was your friend not hers? She mentioned him one day and called him by another name."

"Yes, she called him Snooky. He was so pushy with Marlene and in her weakened condition she was having a hard time keeping him at bay. So, I would say he's gone for good now and I hope he never returns.!!!

"I won't mention it again," Ben promised.

Max's ears were twitching when he heard the name Snooky. That's what Ali said just before he murdered Joe, Max was as still as a statue and tried to calm himself by thinking of other things.

Most of the work that he and Hog had done was completed and the house was almost ready to move in. Once that happened Max would be looking for some other thing to occupy himself and probably never set foot in this house again. Max followed the touring group at a distance and listened as they roamed the house and heard Marlene say that it was a shame that the custom furniture, she ordered would not be ready for several more months so the move would not take place for a while. Meantime the gardener would be doing some planting and re-designing the grounds. The very sound of Ali's voice was so unnerving to Max that he stopped following them and went outside and sat in the tool shed until the tour was over, and the house was quiet again. The painter's boss saw him and asked if anything was wrong.

"No not really, the group was taking a tour of the house, and I thought I would be in the way, so I decided to come out here till they left.

They are going to be moving in, in a few more months so they won't need anything after that."

"I don't know about that. The furniture is not ready yet and I think there will still be a lot of work here Max, I mean they plan on doing a lot to the front entrance, and lot of landscaping."

"I don't know that I'm really up for digging in the dirt and planting stuff," Max said so once the furniture gets here that will probably be it for me."

"We will keep you in mind for our other jobs it's good to know who you work with and can trust so we will want you for other jobs."

"Thanks, I appreciate that," Max said.

"I'll talk with the guy who got the landscape job and see if he could use an extra hand. There will be a need for unloading supplies and stuff like that and I will put in a good word for you."

"I appreciate you doing that for me," Max replied.

When the tour was over and Marlene and the others left, Deidre stayed back and came to find Max. She invited him out to come to a picnic with her later that afternoon to celebrate the house being finished. Max was in such a state he would have agreed to do anything just to get that voice and that name out of his head. Max and Deidre walked a block down from the house and she brought a basket with lunch. Max brought a bottle of wine that the owner of the paint company had given to the employees for doing a good job on the house. After a few glasses of wine Deidre began talking about her life and told Max that she liked him because he didn't make any judgements on her like the other men she had met. Max was surprised to hear her say this as he never had given her much thought let alone judging her character.

Deidre told him about her punishing father who misunderstood her and that no matter what she did it was never good enough for him and would never measure up to what her brother had accomplished.

"The truth is Max he is a two-bit lawyer and really has not made a success of his life. That doesn't matter to my father, he thinks he is setting the world on fire just because he can say he's a lawyer."

Max commiserated with Deidre about fathers and how much they expect from their children. He told her how much his father wanted him to go into his business even though Max never wanted to.

"Money is all that my father measures success by. I promised him that one day I would show him that I would make more money than my brother and I'm working on that. What's so funny about the whole situation is that I'm now working with my brother, and I think we are building a good business. What he doesn't know is that I will be getting the lion's share of the proceeds even though he thinks he is the star. Max you're so easy to talk to," Deidre said, "I love that in a man."

Deidre laid down on their blanket and dozed off. Max dozed off too. Sunset was starting when they awoke, and they picked up the basket and walked back to the house. It was quiet and still all the workers were gone for the day. Deidre turned to Max and kissed him, and it took him by surprise. Max enjoyed the kiss but knew he could not get involved with this woman nor any woman right now. He was on the street. Deidre was surprised that Max didn't seem to be as responsive as she wanted.

"Is there anything wrong Max? Are you upset with me for some reason?"

"No, no nothing like that it's just my situation right now is not exactly where I want to be so I'm reluctant to start a relationship with a woman."

"I see and what is that are you married?"

"No nothing like that it's just I'm between jobs and not stable at the moment. I don't have much to offer anyone."

"Oh, I see I'm sorry I came on so strong then I didn't mean to upset you."

"I'm not upset by you just by some other circumstances. If that changes, I would be more than happy to have us get to know one another much better."

"I'm happy to hear that. I know this is sort of awkward, but it was fun anyway I like you."

"I like you to."

Deidre gave Max a peck on the cheek and picked up her stuff and was gone. Max walked to the camp slowly thinking about the events of the day.

Deidre began thinking what a nice person Max was and he was handsome too. I have to stop this kind of thinking Max can't do anything for me. My boyfriend is a man of ambition and knows what he wants I would have been with him tonight if he wasn't always tied to his job. But I shouldn't complain he does what I want him to and understands me. I have to be a success and show my father I'm not the loser he thinks I am.

[Chapter 32]

Ali AKA Daniel Herbert Marshall was a ruthless man, and there was only one person he trusted with his darkest thoughts and secrets, that was he assistant Herbert. As they sat and had a few drinks in Ali's apartment the alcohol loosened Ali's tongue and he began talking.

"I probably should get an award. No, I deserve a prize for all my service to Marlene's father and the company. I almost made the mistake of trusting Snooky with my plans and with Marlene. I brought him here to keep her entertained while I got the company set up the way I wanted, but she went and fell in love with the sap. The sneaky bastard thought he had her affections under control, and he was about to move in. I had to do something to keep that from happening. There was no other way, I had to get rid of him but not before I needed to tell him how angry I was that he had double crossed me. Snooky was the cutesy name she gave him, and it sends arrows shooting through my body every time she called him that name. Everything would have been fine if that stupid homeless prick hadn't seen me do what I did. It has interfered with my plans and now I must find the bum who saw the whole thing or forever be worried that one day he will pop up and demand millions of my fortune to keep his mouth shut."

"Don't worry boss you will come up with something you always do," Herbert said with a confident grin.

The only one I could ask to help me get out of this jam was Detective Finley. It seems that he was instrumental in getting Ross Collins, the mayor's main man, off the hook for slapping his wife around and controlled the situation so that the press was ever able to find out about her ER visit or surgery. He thinks he is as clever as any criminal you could meet and hides behind his badge to make himself look like he is a dedicated public servant. But if it wasn't that I have something on him he would not help me at all. The mayor threatened to stop my new building project from moving ahead if I had to go to the president of the police board to get Finley promoted to ensure I could keep him in my pocket. That cost me a bundle but as it turns out it was well worth it because that very guy is going to save my ass. I had the power to get Finley promoted by making the largest donation from Marlene's company to the police benevolent association and allowing the President of the building permit board to take the credit. He courted me, and was like a dog with a bone, until I donated the money in his name, but so be it.

Now I have the freedom not to worry about being convicted of murder because he is going to find how to get me off. Then I might let him off the hook. What he does on the side with that ambulance chasing lawyer Dean Davis is no business of mine except that I don't want him to get caught and have his credibility questioned, at least for a long time. I know that the captain had to kowtow to him now for getting the mayor's secretary off. I wouldn't stand for that I would whack him, or have it done and not feel one minute of remorse because if I can bribe him there is no telling how many people he has been extorting."

Is there anything you want me to do to help you out?" Herbert inquired as he sat back and watched and listened as Ali got more and more drunk. The drunker he got the faster his tongue wagged.

"My plan was to have Marlene moved into a splendid house and with new communication devices all over the house so that I would be aware of her every move and conversation both business and personal. When I'm sure she is at her most vulnerable I will swoop in as the hero and asked her to marry me and be in total control of all she owns, both business and personal. Then she may or may not have an accident or become very depressed again and I will become the richest and smartest businessmen in the world. The world will be my oyster, and I will have anything I desire woman, men, money, I will have it all. But I couldn't stand her sniveling and whining so I stupidly brought Snooky into the picture. After I introduced Marlene to him, they instantly became inseparable. He knew exactly what he was doing, and I had to stop him. It would have all worked out just fine if it wasn't for that disgusting street dweller. As Ali got more inebriated, he began to tell the story over and over.

"I tried to find him on my own several times, but he is a street rat and knows every rat hole and place to hide there is in the city and I wasn't successful in finding him. Then by some stroke of luck, some crazy serial killer decides to show his raisins and start taking people out and it's the perfect way for me to blame the killing I did on him. Snooky, Snooky, Snooky how I hate that name!"

The entire police force has not been able to find the killer and they have no clue that I killed Snooky and left him in the alley. They just lumped all the murders together and will pinpoint one person for them all. I almost wish there was someone else I wanted to kill at this minute (not counting Detective Finley) but I can't get rid of him yet, he has to do my bidding and get the street rat either sent to jail for life or get the death penalty first.

The house on Green Street turned out to be a good deal because it kept Marlene occupied for the majority of the time without her looking over my shoulder always. It also kept her mind off "Dear old Snooky," so that she could even feel free to cry on my shoulder about him and how she misses him. It makes me almost nauseated to listen, but I must endure and keep a compassionate tone because I would never want her to suspect anything.

So far, I have been able to transfer about 65% of the business assets into my name without looking too suspicious but I must be careful because if Marlene ever gets a bug up her ass to really check the books, she will surely find all that I have done. She has been so trusting that she allows me to control her check book and stock and bond portfolios which is to say out of sight. Her old man started accounts for her the day she was born, and they have grown enormously. I dare say she is one of the richest women in the state but doesn't know it. She also told me she did not have the heart to look into all that her father left her some of which was in gold coins. Collecting coins was his hobby as a boy and some of them are very old. I should start reading up on coins but right now I have all I can content with to keep Marlene out of the business.

"I can do some research on coins Boss I will start tomorrow now I got to get outta here my old lady will be looking for me," Herbert declared. Herbert got up and left. Ali had two more drinks and then fell into an alcoholic stupor.

[Chapter 33]

Max was having a hard time getting to sleep and he kept thinking about what could have happened to the body that was in the secret room, where it could be now and most of all who took it. After tossing about for quite some time he finally got up and when he looked at the cheap second hand watch he got at the pawn shop it was only 11:00 PM. I wonder if it's too late to call Thomas, Max thought. He thought it over for a minute and decided he would give it a try and if it only rang twice and he didn't pick up Max would hang up. He punched in the number. Within seconds of the first ring Thomas picked up.

"Hey Max, I was just thinking about you glad you called."

"I hoped it wasn't too late I didn't want to wake you," Max blew out.

"I don't have a lot of news, most of it is not good," Thomas said, glad Max called.

"No matter, it's news spill it," Max intoned.

"It just so happens that I have encountered Detective Finley on two occasions now. One was at our old hang out that bar called The Winning Circle, and once at the police station."

"How did that go?" Max asked curiously.

"Well, it really wasn't and encounter with him I just eavesdropped and listened to him talk and I can tell you I did not like what I heard?" Thomas said thinking of the cop harassing the woman in the group.

"What happened?" asked Max.

"Well at the bar he was about shy of a quarter inch from harassing Doris, you know the woman who always comes in there and complaints about her job."

"Yeah, I know who you mean," Max replied.

The detective questioned her about you again, until she finally agreed to give them a sworn statement that you were not at the bar the night of the murder."

"Poor Doris she can be so easily swayed on most controversies if you press her hard enough," Max stated, "She is a sweet lady, but she has a tendency to become dramatic."

"Well, she was so dramatic she agreed to sign off on a statement that is not the truth."

"Who else was there?" Max inquired.

Amico, Johnny V, Larry, Richard and Frank and they would not budge on what they said before and refused to sign a statement changing their stance." Thomas emphasized.

"On another night I was at the police station, and I heard Finley talking to some lawyer telling him he was going to meet him at the Bull and that he had another case for him. I don't think that's what detectives are supposed to do, is it? I really wasn't going to tell you any of this because I didn't want you to get depressed but on second thought maybe you can see if there is anything else you remember or can think about to help us get to the bottom of all this. The good news is that we know for sure now that Finley is a rat and out to get you, so forewarned is a bonus for us.

A few days ago, Ali, Marlene and their architect came to the Green Street house where I'm working. At first it scared the shit out of me because

I thought they were on to something and I wanted to stay as far away from them as I could, but if they come again, I will try and listen to the conversation to see what they talk about. I doubt if Ali would say anything especially if Marlene was there but sometimes, they walked in different rooms, and he says things to the architect," Max said.

"If you think that might help it's ok but just don't get in his way and by God don't let him, see you. Although he might not remember your face, he might put two and two together and think you were stalking him and then we would have real trouble," Thomas declared.

"It's so frustrating that my hands are tied, and I can't even walk about freely for fear someone will recognize me, and then the cops would come and get me. It's really like a nightmare come true," Max sighed.

"You just hang in there fella and I will do my best for you. I have a few favors I can call in if I need to but I'm holding out until I know which direction this is going to go," Thomas promised.

Sometime during the night Max thought he heard some noise, but he had wandered around the camp till about 1:00 AM and then had some wine with Lenny so he was in a sound sleep and chalked it up to a dream.

In the morning Max woke up and saw someone sleeping on Hog's cot and got really pissed. He went over to the cot and pulled the blanket down and began yelling at the person to get up and get the Hell out of there. Suddenly he stopped in his tracks. The man pulled the hat off his face and called out, "Hold up it's me!"

"Oh my God Hog what are you doing here? I mean when did you get back. I didn't know you were coming back, I'm so surprised. It great to see you Hog I missed you a lot," Max almost screamed with joy.

"Max it's good to see you too, I got in late last night and about fell out. You were three sheets to the wind, so I just let you be," Hog said cheerfully.

"How come you decided to come back? Are you here for good?" Max questioned.

"Hold on now let me get myself together and I'll answer all your questions. What's say we go down to Dunkin Donut and have a good cup of java and a few donuts?"

"That works for me," Max replied happily.

After two cups of coffee, an egg and bacon sandwich and a muffin Hog began to talk. "Ya knows Max it's kind of like somethin you dream of when ya think of the best job in the whole world, and you're so good at it and have folk's tellin you what a good job you're doing. That's what it was like with Duke and the boys. It was all there but somethin was missin. If I had found that job years ago when I had a family and could feel as if I was a success and made good money it would have been like I was in heaven. But it was not all what I thought it could be. Oh, at first, I was in pig heaven great gig, beautiful bikes, best tools and clean repair shop, best boss I ever had. No used parts no chasing money everybody paid whatever I asked. I could work as fast as I wanted to, for as long as I wanted to with no boss looking down his nose at me. But then at the end of the day there was nobody to go home to, nobody to talk to or nobody to help if they needed it. Sometimes I hung out with Duke and the boys, but they had lives of their own. I had a nice room all to myself and all the food I wanted. It sounds great, don't it? Duke and them asked me to go with them when they had family gatherings, and we did plenty of partyin, but then Duke found a girl he fell for and he wanted to spend most of his time with her and I don't blame him, when we went out, I felt alone even if was crowded. I didn't like it. Ya knows my hands were getting to be a big problem I exercised them but the scar tissue from the surgeries was not gettin any better. My days got longer and there was less I could do. I couldn't do the work like I used to.

"Did Duke say something about your work? Asked Max."

"No never, I told Duke how much what he did for me meant to me, but I just couldn't do it any longer. As they say I was a day late and a dollar short, but truth is I'm past my prime. There was only one thing to do,

I hitched a ride back here hoping you would still be around," Hog said, "that's my story and here I am."

"Hog I'm so happy to see you. The place hasn't been the same without you. Everybody will be thrilled to have you back. Let me catch you up on what's been going on here," Max stated.

They talked and Max told Hog about all the things that were going on at the camp. Hog wanted to know if he was still working at the Green Street house and was surprised that it was almost done, and they had asked Max to work in the gardens.

"Sounds like they have taken a likin to you, and decide to keep you around," Hog teased.

"Yup, the boss told me he liked that I just did my work and kept my mouth shut, I guess that's a compliment."

"We have a bunch of money coming from the antique shop because they were able to sell some of the pieces we brought in," Max told Hog.

"What ya mean we that's for the work you did when I wasn't there." Hog said.

"No that's from the stuff we brought in together in the beginning, I only had a few things after you left, and I told you we would split it 50/50 and I meant it," Max exclaimed.

After catching up on what each of them had been doing while they were apart, Max told Hog that the police had been there looking for him but the picture they showed them did not look like Hog at all. It looked like a much younger you, "No one recognized it when they showed it around," Max declared.

"I think that's because the only picture that Janey had of me was when I graduated high school, and that was a lifetime ago, so that's good," Hog replied.

"How's the old house shaping up? Dang, I miss going there doin our little scavenger hunt with all that stuff that was left, that turned out to be fun."

"I enjoyed that too. We should go there this afternoon so you could see how it looks now all gussied up with new paint and windows and all that," it's almost ready to move in except they are waiting on some specially made furniture they are having made and it's not ready yet," Max professed.

"Ok let's go talk with Lenny and the others and let them know I'm back and then we'll go to the Green Street house and after get a pizza and beer," Hog suggested.

They went back to Green Street house and the painters were there, they were happy to see Hog and told him they were glad to have him back.

"Hey Hog, are you gonna come back with Max here and work on the landscaping and garden? I hope so cuz we like working with people we can trust," Stanley one of the painters said.

"Well, I guess, I'm not much on digging and weed pullin though," Hog confessed.

"It's not all that they hired a bunch of laborers to do the digging, it would mostly be waiting on deliveries and makin sure the right stuff was delivered and old Max there is good at that. By the time the landscaping is done we will probably have another job for ya all," Stanley said with a grin and slapped Hog on the back and let out a laugh.

"How about that Hog you're not back ten minutes and already you have another job lined up," Max said and grinned.

"That's the cat's meow, now I guess I didn't know what I was missin," Hog replied, and they all laughed this time.

For the next few days Hog hung out at the camp and got reacquainted with all the folks and met the new ones. Hog and Max went to the diner on Sunday evening for supper and were looking forward to starting at the house on Green Street the next day with the landscape crew.

Monday Max and Hog went to the house and talked with the head landscape guy, and he was glad to have them. He said they we recommended by the paint crew and that they might still need some help if there was touch up work and such in the house, in the meantime you all will be working out here with us That morning some deliveries were made and around noon Deidre showed up.

"Hi Max, oh and I see Hog is back that's great cuz I might need help put up some window dressings, at least someone to hold the ladder for me," Deidre said.

"Sure, we can do that Max." agreed.

Deidre was on the ladder and Max would hand her the curtain material. Deidre would then begin to drape it on the rod and work with the folds. It was not going well and each time she started over she did not achieve the effect she was looking for. They had been at it for several hours and had only done one complete window. Deidre was on the ladder when her cell rang. It rang a few times and then stopped. After a few minutes later it began ringing again and Deidre became annoyed.

"Max go get my phone there in the outside pocket of my purse and answer that call. The ringing is driving me nuts!" Deidre declared.

Max did as she instructed and said into the cell, "Hi this is Max I'm answering for Deidre who is on a ladder and can't come to the phone right now can I take a message?"

"Who is this? Demanded the caller?"

"My name is Max, and we are at work, and she can't come to the phone right now."

"What is she doing that's more important than me? "Never mind," said Dean, "she has my number. I will put off going to the Golden Bull restaurant and be at her beck and call as usual. Tell her to call me when she's ready, and I'll meet her there."

"Got it," Max told him I will tell her what you said.

The phone had been on speaker and Deidre heard the entire conversation. Deidre began mumbling about what an ingrate he was and how she would take her good old time and he could meet her when she was good and ready even if it was midnight.

"I didn't want to get in the middle of a lover's quarrel," Max stated. "It's not a lover's quarrel Dean is my brother. He should just be grateful for all that I have done, and I'm still doing for him, instead of being pissed that I'm going to be late. I'm sorry he was so rude to you Max; I will make sure he hears about it." It's ok don't worry about it," Max said.

Deidre and Max finished a second window and Hog came and sat and watched as they worked. When they were done Deidre asked if she could drop them off somewhere and Max quickly said, "No we're good we don't have far to go." Max and Hog walked to the diner and then back to camp. Hog said as they walked, "That gal sure is bossy ain't she?"

"I know, I think she was concentrating on her work. She told me she had never messed with window dressing much and didn't realize how hard it was."

Deidre met her brother for dinner and told him about her disappointment in his phone call. She reminded him how she had sent so much business his way and that now he was doing real work for a change. He agreed he had been abrupt and told her it was because he was, as she said, really busy now and was working hard. Looking to change the subject quickly he said, "Do you have a date tonight?" He asked.

"No, I'm not going out tonight with my friend, he is busy with a case of his own. I am very anxious about finishing up the window treatments I'm working on. I hope my client will like them. Usually, I tell myself if you can't make it, fake it but this time my work is right there hanging on the windows for everybody that walks in the house to see, and I need it to be right. The following week Deidre tried again but just didn't have enough experience to get it right. She ended up hiring a drapery company to come and do the work on the weekend so no one would suspect that she couldn't do the work.

As they walked home Max was unusually quiet. Hog asked him if anything was wrong, and Max said he was just tired.

[Chapter 34]

Max contacted Ellie to ask her if she could meet him. They met in the same place and Ellie told Max that she had started to put all he gave her into her computer and that the information was piling up.

"I know I have quite a bit of material but I'm still not free to really come home and legitimately work and write a book. I would have to have a completely new identity and change my whole life. That makes me very unhappy. The thing that makes me even more unhappy is that I am still wanted for murder. I'm not sure this will ever end I'm very discouraged."

"I wish I had some good news for you Max but nothing I know of has changed. Every few days the detective comes back to the office, but everybody tries to ignore hm he has become so obnoxious."

"What do you mean?"

"He just walks into the office unannounced. He doesn't stop by the receptionist and walks into various offices and starts questioning people. The editor is sick of it, and he called the mayor's office, and they told him there was nothing they could do about it and he would have to put a complaint in writing."

"I wonder what motivates this guy he seems to think he is able to do whatever he wants, and nobody can stop him."

"I sure don't know but it surely gets under my skin," Ellis responded with a scowl.

They discussed some things about the data Ellie was putting on her computer and in what order it would go. After a long talk about it Max told Ellie that it really didn't matter because after he read through the material, he moved it around not just once but quite a few times.

Monday morning Max and Hog went to the Green Street house. Hog was directing traffic so the big delivery truck could park near the house and Max was checking in the supplies as they arrived. Later that afternoon a lowboy transport truck brought a small backhoe. All this activity had taken a lot of time and before they knew it the day was over.

The next day the landscapers began digging up the old uncared-for flower beds. There were two old tree stumps that had to go. They were deep, so they had the backhoe dig around the base of the trees to loosen the ground before they would try and excavate them. All was going well when suddenly there was a lot of noise and shouts for the backhoe operator to stop. Max and Hog went out back to see what the problem was.

"What's goin on here," asked Hog.

"We got big trouble," the lead gardener said, "they just dug up a body."

"A body?" Max almost shouted.

"That's what I said, that means that our operation will be shut down now until they get the cops and the body snatcher out here and it will depend on a lot of things whether or not they let us keep on working."

"W, what did it look like?" asked Max.

"It's hard to tell because the backhoe bucket sort of cut it in two, but from what I could see it had on pants and looked like it was a man."

Max said to Hog, "I feel sick I'm going inside and sit down and have some water."

It was true Max was feeling sick to his stomach because he was also afraid that the dead body would bring Detective Finley here to investigate the crime scene.

Once inside Max began to think about the day he fell into the secret room. At least I know that I'm not crazy and didn't dream I saw a dead body that day but how did it get removed and planted in the back yard? I guess it can only mean one thing, that someone who had access to this house knew about the body and buried it out there. Maybe, maybe not, if it was outside, it could have been anyone the point is that no one will know that the body had once been in the secret room except me and the killer. That is not a comforting thought. It could be that the body was here before the renovations began and the house was used by someone who was not supposed to be here, maybe a gang or something. Right, that was a good theory thought Max but when we first came here everything seemed to be intact and not touched for a very long time. The house was locked up and the windows and doors were boarded up. The workmen that were here never made mention of anything out of place or any messes. What was the difference if the body was found in the secret room or buried outside? I guess the chances of it being found would be better if it were outside than in the secret room because that would enlarge the suspect pool knowing that the house was intact and only a few people had access. Hold It! That means that Hog and I will immediately become suspects. How could I be so dumb not to have thought about that first. I have to get Hog and we have to get out of here as fast as possible. But then on the other hand if we run away, it would make us look more suspicious. Another dilemma. I have to go and talk to Hog. He will know what to do.

Max went outside to find Hog. Max pulled him aside and told him he was afraid they would suspect them.

"Wait, cut some slack here Max." Think that the real estate guys and the painters were the first guys here and they brought us here. Then the stiff was outside so anybody could have buried it there and right now they don't know how long the body was in the ground. It won't look right if we don't go along with everybody else and ask questions like everybody else. It jacked my jaw when I heard about all this fuss myself, but we gotta hang tight for now."

"Ok, ok that sounds good," Max agreed.

After the cops arrived, they cordoned off the area with the famous yellow tape outsider Max and Hog went into the house with the lawn crew. The police gave them a clipboard and told them to write down everybody's name that worked there and they would question them later and they were not to leave.

Hog asked Max if he had any ID. Max told him he got a driver's license but that was all. Lenny told Max where to go to get a bogus Driver's License a few weeks back and he was happy he had it.

"The cops will want to see ID. We need to show that we have a fixed address, I have a driver's card too," Hog said.

"I'm worried look how we're dressed," Max lamented.

"Look at the others do they look any better," Hog asked.

"I guess I'm just nervous," Max declared.

"Sit tight and don't get all up in anybody's face, we are day laborers stick to that Story," Hog recommended.

Luckily only one of the cops questioned all the workers. He asked a few questions about how long they had been working at the house and wanted to see ID. Max's dreaded fear that the detective would come here and question him was over now and everything had gone ok.

A few days later Hog and Max were back at the Green Street house, still doing odd jobs to get ready for the grand opening.

Strangely enough Marlene wanted the secret room preserved as it was but wanted it cleaned up. The carpenters made a place for a switch on the wall to open the door and it would be painted and cleaned up and then put back together. The painters took several pictures of the room in its present state, and they wanted Max and Hog to move the furniture over to one side while they painted.

They were working upstairs in the secret room with two painters when Hog looked out the window and saw the cop car pull up. He motioned Max over so he could look out too. The window was cracked, and they heard the other police who were there say that Detective Finley was here. Max closed his eyes and prayed. The painters paid no mind and Hog and Max closed the door to the secret room and never said a word as the police officers and detective searched the house. They missed the secret room completely and Max started breathing again. The police were about to leave when Ali, Marlene, Ben, and a few others showed up. There were many people in the house working on setting it up and as predicted the landscaping section was completely shut down.

Ali saw Detective Finley just as he was about to step out of the house and motioned for him to come over to meet Marlene. After a few polite words were exchanged Ali told Finley he wanted to show him something upstairs. They came up and walked down the hall until they came to the entrance to the secret room. Ali made a big deal of the room and how it was so hard to find, and they speculated for a few minutes about what it might have been used for. Then Ali hit the switch and the door to the secret room opened. There were Hog and Max with cans of paint and a bucket with tubes a caulk surprised when the door opened. The painters stopped and acknowledged the visitors and the detective asked who they all were. Stanley, one of the painters pointed at Hog and Max and the other painter and said they are "my crew," and have been with me a long time now. That seemed to satisfy Finley and they stepped out of the room but did not close the door completely.

They talked Ali said, "Marlene is going to visit a friend in the mountains for the weekend. Let's have dinner Saturday and bring that pretty girlfriend you have with you to the Bull, she sure is eye candy, and if she has a friend bring her too. I also wanted that lawyer you are using because I want him to do some work for me on some properties I have purchased. We'll talk then, let's go back to join the others."

[Chapter 35]

There was no work for the next few days at the Green Street house and Max wanted to do some research at the library. He was dressed in his shirt and tie and sports jacket and was there when the place opened. He stopped and got Agnes the librarian a coffee and donut and she was really flattered at that. Max began by looking up information on Detective Finley. He wanted to find out all he could about him when his phone rang. He went outside and took the call, and it was Thomas.

"Hey buddy, I read about the body they found at the Green Street house. I was worried that the police would question everybody, and you might get recognized."

"You better believe I was scared out of my mind, but it seemed to go ok so far, and we still have some work to do there. I'm really glad you called I wondered if you could do me a favor."

"What's that?" inquired Thomas.

"It just so happened that our friend Detective Finley showed up at the crime scene and talked with Ali. They are planning to go out to dinner together to the Bull with their girlfriends and I thought it might be a good idea if we got some pictures of the event and maybe even, if possible, hear a little of what they talk about? I don't know for sure, but I get the feeling that they are trying to close in on getting these murders solved and will say that the body found at the house was another victim of the serial killer. That would keep the fires burning so to speak so that the serial killer thing could be brought up to the public again and they might come up with some circumstantial evidence they find will yield a serial killer."

"Whoa boy, you're kidding me. Why do you think that?"

"Because Marlene is very anxious to get in the house. They need to solve the crime of who killed the victim found here so the landscaper can come back and get the place finished. Once she is moved in Ali is going to ask her to marry him so he can have access to the rest of her money, and he is getting anxious to do that."

"Jesus how do you know all this stuff?"

"I have befriended the librarian here at the library and her father is the head of the planning commission. They are getting ready to declare some old houses down near the water as condemned so a new city center can be built. Ali has bids on all that property so he will make a fortune when it is developed."

"I have to say you are doing your homework. That would mean they will stop looking for you."

"I'm not too sure of that. I say that because when I talked to the painter's boss, he told me the police came back and have asked him to provide them with all the employees and their social security numbers etc. etc. that means that he has to come up with bogus paperwork for Hog and me or be in big trouble for paying us under the table. They are great to work for but I'm pretty sure they will not step on their own dicks to save me and Hog."

"You have a point there. So, what's the plan?"

"The plan is to build a case against Finley as a dirty cop and maybe get Ali in jail as a murderer," Max said.

"Just how are you going to do that?" asked Thomas.

"I will testify against him as an eyewitness to a murder."

"Max, have you lost your mind? Why would they believe you?"

"Well for one thing Finley had his men go back to the site where Ali did the murder and found bits of my driver's license and passport which proved I was there. I also found out that he hated Joe, the guy he killed, and many people knew that but would not step forward."

"My God Max you would be taking a big chance and if it doesn't go like you want you will either be sentenced to death or be in prison the rest of your life."

"I know Thomas, I struggle with this every day. Ali is a very evil man, and he won't stop until he has everything he wants. He is using Marlene to get her and her father's money so he can do whatever he wants with it."

"Man, I'm doing everything I can to help you, but I don't know if all this will work. You have someone who has money to use against you and a detective who has the inside police information and Joe was Marlene's lover. With all that they might be able to get public sympathy. That might be enough to convict you as a serial killer. I'm on your side but you have a chance like a snowball in Hell guy."

"Here's the thing I have two choices, I can try my best to clear my name. If I can't, I will have to assume another identity and at some point, leave the country and find a new life somewhere else providing I'm not in jail. Not two really good choices because I would be on the run all my life if I don't get out the real truth and convince all others of it."

"Let me see if I can get something on this mess and I will get back to you. Call me if you have any more ideas or things, I can check out for you."

"There is something else you can do, keep your eye on the lawyer and Finley's interactions, if nothing else I think we can at least get an ethics charge going for Finley. And maybe just maybe we should check out Finley's credentials. Did he really pass that test and what was his score.

What other things might he be into, we know his fellow police don't like or trust him so many there's more."

"Did they ever find out who the corpse was and how long he has been dead?"

"The body was an older male they are still waiting on DNA Identification, and he was probably killed 1-2 years ago long before the house renovations started."

"That's interesting it must have been someone who knew the house had been closed for a long time. Ok I'm on finding out more info."

[Chapter 36]

Thomas had to be really careful because Finley knew his face and they he had been poking around the serial killer cases, so he got to the restaurant super early and talked to the hostess as if he were interested in her until she got called away from the podium where the reservation book was. He quickly perused it and saw that Ali's name was penciled in for 7:30 for a private booth. Thomas walked around the dining room looking for a good place to sit so that he could hear the conversation at Ali's table. When he found a place that looked good, he told the receptionist that was where he had to sit and when the waiter's back was turned, he pulled a potted palm close to where he would sit so his face was obscured.

At 7:35 the party arrived and there were only four guests. They ordered drinks and then Ali said, "You look lovely tonight Deidre I'm so happy to meet you. Our friend John here has kept you hidden long enough."

"Thank you so much we don't get out as often as we should as we both are busy with our jobs."

"They ordered drinks and began looking at the menu. They ordered appetizers and another round of drinks. Diedre had a martini at the bar while they were waiting for Ali to show up and then had two more at the table. When she began to talk, she had a twang in her voice that was not there before. Ali picked up on that as Deidre became very talkative. They ordered dinner and afterwards began to talk business. Ali had some legal business that he wanted Dean to do, and they agreed to meet later in the week to discuss it at length. Ali excused himself and went to the men's room. Deidre's phone rang. She answered it thinking it might be Joseph as he was in town again.

"Hello," she said, who is this. There was silence and the line went dead.

When Ali came back, they ordered dessert and discussed the body found at the Green Street house.

"Did they ever find out who the body was that they found in the backyard of Marlene's house," he asked Finley.

"Yeah, they did it was an old man that was in a nursing home no one seems to know how he got out of the home as it is a secure place. He was shot and since the serial killer has used other method to kill. they are not the was the same killer." Ali asked, "do they have any motives or suspects?"

"Not so far but we are still looking."

"Maybe someone wanted to steal his money?"

"No that doesn't seem to be the case as he had all his money designated in a trust that the retire home kept for him, so it's not the money."

Just then Deidre's phone rang again, "I'm sorry she said as she got up and walked a few steps from the table. Thomas heard her say that she was interested but could not talk please leave me a number and name on the phone number I'm about to give you and I will answer as soon as I can." Then she hung up.

Back at the table, "Sorry I had to take that my employer is in town and needs some things done ASAP, so I need to be on duty 24/7, so to speak for the next days until he is settled."

"Ok it's too bad we all have to work but we can do this another time." They all said their goodbyes and were gone.

They left the restaurant and Thomas was disappointed. He thought they might get into talking about money and the cases of the serial killer, but they did not. He did get the phone number that Deidre gave the caller, and he would have someone he trusted to see what they could find. Thomas suspected that Deidre's phone calls were from her side job as an escort. She had not given it up because the money was so good and tax free too, and who knows she might blow the interior decorating gig because it was becoming very challenging. If John knew about her extracurricular activity he probably wouldn't be pleased.

Thomas waited until they were completely gone before exiting the restaurant himself. He called Max and told him what he heard. They were both disappointed that all that effort did not yield much. Maybe we will find another way Thomas hoped because he really felt sorry for Max.

Max and Hog were still going to work at the house. The next day Stanley approached them and told them that the police were coming that afternoon and wanted the company paperwork.

"I'm telling you this because it probably would be best for you and us if the two of you were not here when the cops showed up. We feel bad that we can't help but you just don't check out and they will know that soon enough."

Hog and Max knew that was true, so they left and went back to camp and tried to figure out what to do. They felt they were safe for a while because the IDs they had showed had bogus addresses on them and neither Max nor Hog had shared with anyone where they actually lived. What to do in the long run was the bigger problem. If they stayed until they were discovered, they would put the camp in jeopardy in that the police would begin to harass the rest of the people there for hiding them.

Max asked Hog if they should tell Lenny what happened and see what he wanted them to do. They decided that they had to tell him.

After they told Lenny what happened he said he understood.

"Hell, ya all didn't know a body was planted where you were working. Let's see what happens and if anyone comes around or anything suspicious goes on then we'll talk it over again."

Though Hog and Max were very pleased with Lenny's response they knew it would only be a question of time when someone would figure out who to ask about them and their cover would be blown.

[Chapter 37]

The day had been going really well for Deidre then suddenly things changed drastically when her phone rang. It was not the cell number she gave to friends and family; it was the phone she kept for her other job. The voice said I know who you are, and I'm surprised. I'm wondering if your boyfriend knows about your alternate career. By the way I think you owe me some money as our arrangement was not fulfilled. We will settle up soon. Deidre was shaken up. How did this guy know it was me? I'm always so careful and now this.

"Who is this and how did you get this number?"

"Don't be coy with me you know exactly who I am and now I know exactly who you are. I have your number because you answered your phone at the restaurant remember?"

"Yes, I do. What do you want?"

"What I want is to for you to meet me so we can talk privately."

"I can't talk now I'm busy so call some other time and we can get together,"

"Fair enough I will take you up on that."

Now he has seen me but there is no help for it. I will just try and avoid him as long as I can while I think about what to do about him. There's nothing I can do about that now I will just have to be very careful. Obviously, he is not going to do anything about it so for the minute I will not worry about it.

Max and Hog had been thinking of other things they could do because doing nothing all day was getting on both their nerves. At about 10 that morning they heard sirens and then two police cruisers came up the dirt road and 5 police officers got out and walked to the camp. Lenny and a few others were standing at the entrance waiting for them.

The first police officer approached Lenny and asked for all the males to come out so that could see who all had been staying there. Lenny told one of the other men to ask the men to come to the front. A group of men walked to the front and of course Hog and Max did not accompany them. The officers held up a picture they had and asked them to look at it. After a few minutes the cops agreed he was not among them.

"Is there anybody else staying in this camp the Sargent asked in a firm voice?"

Before you answer I'm going to tell you that if we find that you are hiding this person we will take in the entire camp and make sure it is destroyed."

Before Lenny could answer Max and Hog came walking up to the entrance. They had talked about what they would do if it came to this, and Max told Hog he would give himself up before he would allow anything to happen to the camp. Now it was time to act.

Max stepped in front of Hog and said, "Can we help you officers?"

The Sargent looked at the picture and then went over to where Max and Hog were standing and said to one of the cops, "Take him into custody." Max stood his ground and waited for the police to come to get him. But a strange thing happened. They came and walked behind Max and Hog and then told Hog to put his hands behind his back and put handcuffs on him. Max was taken aback. What the Hell was happening here? Why were they arresting Hog and not me? I'm the one they think is the serial killer not Hog. Something is not right.

Getting his wits back Max said, "Whoa officer what are you doing? Why are you arresting him? He has been here and not done anything against the law why do you want to take him away." He almost added I'm the one you want but held his tongue.

"We have an old outstanding warrant for this man's arrest for vehicular homicide and an array of charges."

"Vehicular homicide the man doesn't even own a car, how can that be?" Max shouted.

"We have been working on cleaning up outstanding warrants and when we put the picture, we had of him in the computer and did and age progression study on it we got this." He held out a picture of Hog. You could have knocked Max over with a feather because it looked very much like Hog.

"Wait, wait a minute are you sure maybe…." Max tried to say but Hog cut him off. Hog said, "I guess you got me, Max stay here."

The cops took Hog and put him in a squad car and drove away.

The entire camp was in a tizzy. Lenny and the others could not believe that the likeness was so much like Hog. Lenny knew about Hog's past but was shocked that an incident that happened years ago was going to ruin a man's life again.

"What are we going to do Max," Lenny asked, "we can't just let him be thrown to the dogs."

"I'm going to call a friend of mine and see if we can get a lawyer to at least get him out of jail. Then the only thing we can do is get to the truth of what happened and see if we can get the charges dropped for good."

"That will cost a lot of scratch Max where will we get the money?"

"I don't know right now. I just know we have to get Hog out of jail and back here before he goes crazy," Max said worriedly.

Back in the tent Max called Thomas and told him the story. "Thomas, I want to defend this guy he literally saved me out here on the street. I have money but I can't get to it without coming out of hiding. If you will get the ball rolling by getting him a lawyer and spring him, I will owe you big time and will pay you back every penny."

"I can get him a lawyer for sure, but this could become a long-drawn-out affair and cost big bucks."

"I don't care I will make it good I need this to happen now," Max begged.

"Ok I will go down to the jail and see if I can bail him out then I will look for a good lawyer. I trust your judgement about people Max."

In the next two days Thomas was able to get Hog out on bail and get him a lawyer. Hog came back to camp but was worried about what would happen to him in the future.

"Max, I sure appreciate your doin all this for me, but I don't have any money to pay a lawyer. Someone came and got me out on bail. He also got me a lawyer. Now he wants to meet with him and get me out of camp. He says that I need a decent apartment and a job to show that I'm a responsible citizen in order to get me off. I can't do that, it's too much. Besides I don't want to leave the camp nobody else out there cares about me. I ain't hurt nobody. I really don't care what happens to me. If they throw me in jail, it's no big thing."

"No, Hog you can't think about it like that. You don't deserve to be in jail for something you didn't do. You have already paid the highest price there is by losing your life and your family. I have never told you my whole story and I can't start now. I will someday but believe me I can get my friends to help you and I want to do this for you. Will you accept it? You saved me and I wouldn't have survived out here on the street if it weren't for you. I want to do this for you now."

"I guess I don't have a choice cuz I sure don't want to go to jail and lose my freedom. I will trust you Max I hope you know what you're doin."

[Chapter 38]

Since Max could not visit Hog, he tried to help in other ways. He asked Ellie to visit Hog and then she would call him and give him a report on how Hog was holding up. Ellie did this and she and Hog became good friends.

When Hog's trial was about to start Hog told Ellie that his attorney said he did not have much evidence to go on and that Hog didn't have much of a chance to win the case. Hog's lawyer had asked Hog if he could put his wife on the stand and Hog would not hear of it. He told the lawyer that if he had to go to jail that was alright as long as he did not cause any more pain for his family.

Max was quite distraught when Ellie told him about Hog refusing to put his wife on the stand. He wondered if Hog had even told the whole story about the crash to his lawyer. Max called Thomas and talked to him about Hog not defending himself and asked if Thomas could talk to Hog's lawyer to see if he could get the trial postponed for a few days at least while they waited for additional evidence. Thomas agreed. Max had wrestled with the idea of revealing what Hog made him promise not to do, but this was a matter of life and death if Hog would not say anything to help his case.

Deciding it was necessary, Max told Thomas the whole story of Hog's life and asked him to dig into the files and find the investigation of the accident and Hogs old medical records which would tell how many surgeries he had and how he has so much trouble with his hands to this day.

Thomas was willing to help Hog, so he worked with Hog's lawyer and found there was a lot written about the accident in the small-town paper because of the two deaths. The charges of vehicular manslaughter were never dropped because no one came up with the real way the accident happened, and no one could say why the car had driven off the road. The investigation was only what the police saw long after the accident happened and then everybody was concentrating on saving the victims' lives. The report said that the motorcycle driver forced the car off the road and made it crash resulting in the deaths of two people. There were no witnesses except Hog's wife who would not talk to anybody. It was much more than the lawyer had before, but he was not certain it would be enough without any more facts and because the driver of the car could not be interviewed. One other thing that would be in Hog's favor is that when the insurance company wanted to settle the claim with a large monetary settlement, because the car had a recall on it when the crash happened, Hog told them that all the money belonged to his wife and son, and he did not want any of it. That would be looked at favorably by the jury.

The jury was selected, and the trial began. Max was nearly crazy with fact that he couldn't be there for Hog, but it was too big a risk for him to take. Hog told Ellie that he wanted Max to stay away and not come to the trial. After the first few days of court procedures, it was the prosecution's turn, and it was not going well.

Ellie called Max the afternoon after the prosecution's presentation and gave Max the bad news that it looked as if Hog was going to lose. She told Max that the picture they painted of Hog was a member of a biker's gang that drank and used drugs and had robbed several banks. That he is now a despicable man who sucks off society and lives on the street because he didn't care about anything or anybody. That he dropped out of a regular life because he was worthless, lazy, and shiftless and most of all guilty that he had killed people because he was in a drunken stupor.

Max was terribly disheartened when he heard all that was said about Hog. He sat and thought about what he could do. Then it came to him like a bolt of lightning. He called Thomas and asked if he would call Hog's lawyer and get a recess for the rest of the week because he had an idea, that he would tell Ellie what he was going to do, and she would pass that on to the lawyer to see if it would fly.

The following Monday the trail began anew, and Hog's lawyer stated he had some new witnesses. The place was a buzz because no one knew who the witnesses were. The first witness they called was Angie. Angie took the stand and began to tell her story of how she would have died at least twice if it hadn't been for Hog who came to her rescue and left her with not only her life but her pride and dignity.

The second witness came forth with help from Lenny who was at his side. Lenny stood close to David as he took the stand and began to explain that David didn't talk very much but he wanted Lenny to tell his story. Lenny went on to say how David was very deeply depresses after James passed away and tried to commit suicide twice. If it wasn't for Hog, he would have been successful and how after Hog treated him like a son and watched over him. As they walked from the witness stand David veered off and went over to the table where Hog was sitting and gave him a hug and kissed him on the cheek. At that point there was not a dry eye in the courtroom. The jury was very impressed, but would it be enough to sway the verdict? Hog's lawyer was not certain and did a bit of digging and came up with a witness of his own.

The next witness requested anonymity and the court was prepared with a screen so that the witnesses could testify and not be seen. The courtroom door at the side opened and the vailed witness entered. Hog's lawyer escorted her to the witness stand and she sat down. As soon as she began to tell her story, though her voice was garbled, Janey told them how much she missed her son and her mother and said that James was a hardworking man who loved his family. Immediately Hog knew who it was. No one else had called him James his entire life. Then she began to cry and said, "Sally Sue Evers had very poor eyesight and had to drive because I couldn't. My two sons both had high fevers and were very sick. Jacob began having a seizure and I had to try and keep him breathing. The driver had very bad eyesight and didn't see the stump near the road's edge and the car ran over it and she lost control. James was nowhere near us when that happened. He rode his bike down that ravine to come to help us and crashed into the car and they both burst into flames. I know in my heart after hearing how he helped other people that he was trying to help us, but there was nothing he could have done to change any of the outcome."

Hog was sitting at the table with his head in his hands crying also no doubt remembering that horrible night.

After a few questions by the prosecution, Janey got up and left the courtroom the same way she arrived, and the doors closed.

It did not take long before the jury came in with a not guilty verdict and Hog was a free man. He left the apartment and came back to the camp and told Max he was pissed at him at first but at least his story was told, and he didn't have to go to jail. Their relationship changed somewhat but Max was sure in time Hog would forgive him for breaking his word.

Several weeks later Ellie called and told Max that Janey had contacted Hog's lawyer and wanted to know if he would be interested in meeting her to talk. Hog agreed. Hog came back after meeting with Janey and looked happy.

"How did it go Hog?" asked Max.

"Well, we didn't set the world on fire but we're gonna talk again so I gotta hold on and cool my jets and see what might happen. But it was mighty cool."

"Hog if you don't want to answer you don't have to but what made Janey agree to testify for you?"

Hog looked at him in a strange way and said, "it was you Max."

"Me? It couldn't have been I have never met the woman ever."

"As I understand it from Angie you came to her and asked her to testify for me right?"

"Well once my lawyer heard Angie's testimony, he decided to ask Janey to testify for you to."

"Well yeah but what changed Janey's mind?"

My lawyer took Angie out to visit with Janey and when she heard her story, she knew she made a mistake in blaming you and she wanted to help you."

"Oh Hog, I'm so glad that it all worked out so well," Max said with a sigh, I have one more question.

"I know what you are going to ask. No, my son did not come to the meeting. Janey tried to explain to him why she wanted to keep me away but now he is as pissed at her as he is at me. We decided that we would let it alone for a bit and let things settle then see what happens."

"Ok all I know is I'm happy that you're not in jail, and you are talking to Janey that's more than I ever expected," that is a bonus.

Chapter 39

Detective Finley sat in his office and was pondering all his open cases. I'm doing my best to find that fucking homeless man for Ali, but it seemed that he disappeared into thin air. I'm getting more and more frustrated because Ali is on my back day and night about finding the killer. Ali wants to get Marlene to move into the Green Street house and then when she was all settled in, he is going to spring the idea of marriage on her. He wanted the murder case cleared up before he did that. It just seemed that, that piece of shit house is a never-ending project with changing this and moving that and then finding that body in the garden was the last straw. There was not much to get from the body except for one little piece of DNA testing that is not back yet.

    I thought after we release the backyard area, they would be able to move in but the last thing they are waiting for was the specially made furniture Marlene ordered and it should be coming in a few weeks. It seems as if covid fucked up everything especially the furniture making business and shipping. Stuff that was easy to get in a few days or tops one week now takes about 3-4 months. The garden and lawn are not complete, but they could probably live with that for now. The main thing was to get this killer thing squared away and then Ali would get off my back. Since the murder of Joe,

Ali has spent a lot of time with me, and I had gotten to know him. From the things he said about Joe, I got the drift that he didn't like him very much and didn't want him around. So why is Ali so Hell bent on finding the guy who killed Joe. Ali was happy he was dead and no longer a thorn in his side. After all, now he could marry Marlene and use her father's fortune anyway he wanted. I'm trying to get all the recent homicides pinned on the same killer that took out Joe, but I don't know if that is true. So far nothing is adding up as a serial killer story and there is only circumstantial evidence in all the cases. I have tried to tell Ali that, but he wants me to stick to the serial killer theory and I don't have the evidence. I got so desperate I went so far as to ask others to help me, but they didn't turn up anything either. I'm going to go over all the evidence again to see if there was something I missed. I hope I find something.

I'm worried about Deidre. She seems so distant lately and she's always so busy. She is so concentrated about becoming an interior decorator and finding clients, that's all she thinks of lately. She must know by now that I want her in my life. I even prop up that loser brother of her's by feeding him cases. If someone picks up on that it will make me look terrible and I will probably have to face the Ethics Committee. If I need to, I can probably take care of that too, all I have to do is get a few more politicians and people in high official jobs in my pocket and then I will be able to do no wrong. I don't know how I got into all this shit. I only thought I would be doing a good thing by being a detective. I never wanted to see so many people in trouble. I have tried to be nice to the guy who missed the exam, but he thinks I'm rubbing it in his face. What a mess. How can I ever get out of this? I have been really good about staying away from the real reason I got in so much trouble myself.

Finley stops and comes out of his pensive mood and looks at his vibrating cell phone. It's Ali. What does this fucking guy want now?

"Detective Finley how can I help you?"

"Finley, I want to get together with you tonight and go over a problem I have with the city and parking. Meet me for dinner tonight and bring your girlfriend, she is good company, same place 7:30. See you then.

At dinner that evening they chatted about everything from the latest new movie coming out, to elections in the city that were fast approaching. Then Ali got to the reason for the meeting.

"Marlene's company has received a notice from the city stating that the landscape company that is working on the Green Street house has been violating the city codes. It seems they have been parking their trucks in front of the water hydrant and have been using water from the hydrant on the project. They have issued fines of ten thousand dollars and are threatening to shut down the project," Ali explained.

"Look there's not much I can do about that, that's the parking enforcement department not the criminal investigation section," Finley responded in an annoyed voice.

"You mean to tell me you are not all one big happy family?" Ali joked. I know the structure of the police department, my dear boy. My point is didn't you save the mayor's trusted assistant's ass several weeks ago?"

"Yes, but that was for a different reason it was an arrest that fell within my department."

"I think the mayor's office owes you a favor or two and I want you to get them to take the charges back and make the fine a more reasonable one say one thousand dollars and no question about closing down the job. If that happens it would be weeks before we could find another contractor and Marlene won't be able to move into the house," Ali insisted.

"I don't see why you couldn't move into the house," Finley said adamantly, "It's only the outside landscaping."

"Marlene is planning a huge housewarming party, and she wants everything to be perfect and some outside stuff to, that means everything including the outside." Seeing that both Finley and Ali were getting hot Deidre jumped into the conversation.

"Boys, Boys let's hold it down for a minute. There is no need to get upset about something as trivial as a fine. I'm sure John will be able to go and talk with the department heads of the parking division and get things fixed. Let's just see what can be done before getting in each other's faces."

"Ok," John said, "I'm going to the rest room and will be back in a bit." With that he stood up and walked off.

"That was good thinking," Ali said, "he needs to cool off. As for you, I need you to come and see me tomorrow night at my apartment. I'll text you my address and you should be there at 7:45."

When Finley got back to the table, they ordered dessert and coffee, and the topic of the notice never came up again.

[Chapter 40]

Marlene was all excited about the Green Street house and she was certain that if her father were alive, he would be very proud of the way she had restored the place. Once they had shown her the secret room, she was intrigued by what went on in that room. She wished he was alive now so she could ask him about it. One thing she did was to reread the letter her father had left her when she was upset about something. No one else knew that her father had left her a letter to be read after his death and she kept it with her always. No reason that snoop Daniel had to know about the letter.

Marlene had not read the letter for a long time after her father's death because she was so distraught by his death and was really not in any frame of mind to read or understand it. Her personal lawyer Ashton had held it in his possession waiting for the right time when she was her old self, and her grieving period was over.

Once the letter was in her possession Marlene had read it more than a few times. He did not exactly point out what she should do but offered advice about the people she surrounded herself with. Her father told her that he wished she found the right man and have a family but that it was a very difficult thing to find someone who was not interested in social climbing, wanting her money or notoriety.

"My sweetest darling daughter,

Always remember that finding true love is one of the most difficult jobs in the world." There were specific people he talked about, and Daniel Herbert Marshall (Ali)was one of them. He told her that Ali was a patient man and was a good assistant but that, "I sometimes questioned his motives to be second fiddle." There were several instances when he signed documents in my name without my permission. They were quite trivial but all the same it was a devious move on his part. I never told him that I knew about them but watched all documents going forward so that would never happen again. Don't trust him. One thing I know he resented was that I was planning on turning over the business to you. His views on a woman running the business were archaic and outmoded. He questioned if that was the right thing to do on my part. At one time after I recovered from my heart attack, he suggested that it might be good if you and he would one day get together to keep the business in the family. I did not like that at all. You are quite capable of running the business and smarter than any of those other young sprouts that the board keeps pushing to join our group. I know this is a lot to digest and I hope you are not grieving too much, always know I'm with you watching over your shoulder and will always be in your corner in the long run.

Your loving father.

Privately Marlene planned to move into the Green Street house and make it her own. Slowly she would get back into the business and take over as President and CEO herself and if Ali always had her back and supported her decisions then maybe they might consider being together in business. When she was ready to be back and fully installed in the business things would be different. She realized she did owe him a debt of gratitude, but she was certain he was very well compensated for everything he did. She would check that out next week when she went to the office and began checking the books. She had not told Ali of her decision to do this because something in her father's letter had put a feeling in her gut, and she needed to check all the past transactions that took place when she was still mourning, by herself.

Marlene waited until Ali went on a business trip and then she went into the office. She asked to see all the transactions that had taken place since her father stopped coming to the office. After several days of this review Marlene felt she had a good feel for the pace and flow of the business and where the profits and losses were. She could go from there to build on what she now knew, and she began making business decisions on her own. Since it was getting close to the completion of the house, Marlene took a trip to see the house. She met Deidre for the first time in person. They discussed various things about the house and Marlene got the distinct feeling that Deidre did not know as much about interior decorating as she did. Marlene also got upset at the condescending attitude that Deidre had toward her as if she were not capable of making decisions about the house or that she needed to seek approval from Ali, though she said nothing that would indicate that. Deidre on the other hand was quite surprised that Marlene had shown up at the house alone without the usual assemblage of lawyers, assistants, architects and to say the least without Ali. She made a mental note to say, "that you need to watch yourself here Deidre and step lightly the chick is stepping out of her shell."

Ali continued to call Deidre and demanded that they meet. She kept putting him off and told him how busy she was and spit out whatever lie came to her lips to avoid seeing him. She bought a new phone and had a new number so at least the calls stopped. Then one day he just showed up at the Green Street house and there was no getting away from that. She told him she didn't want anyone to overhear their conversation so they should walk down to the park. Once at the park they sat on a bench and Ali began asking her about her "other" job activity and told her that he knew all her secrets.

"Deidre, I wanted to get together with you to talk to you in person and since you were not answering my phone calls, I decided to come to you. I want to know about the other projects that you have when you are not working at your, "a hum, decorating," he said with a sarcastic lilt in his voice.

"I'm not sure what you mean." She responded playing dumb.

"Oh, don't play that game with me you know I have your special number and that you use it to make yourself a small bundle on the side. But isn't that side stuff you do against the law?"

"What do you mean going out with gentlemen who need a plus one so that they look good at a dinner party or a special occasion. So, what, that's no big deal."

"How about John? Does he know about you little charade?"

"That doesn't matter we are not married, and he can't tell me what to do." Deidre answered tartly.

"No, that's true but how would he feel if he knew he was not the only man in your life? Wouldn't that make him feel as if he were not enough for you"? And it might stop him from telling you all the things he has going on in his life. Then one has to wonder if his feelings were to change would he keep his arrangement with your brother and keep everyone as happy as clams," Ali spit out.

"He doesn't have to know about all that unless you tell him."

"No that's true but really, what's in it for me? I can keep a secret as well as the next guy, but I need a little incentive, if you know what I mean."

"Like what?"

"Well, I could use a servicing once in a while myself, it would save me all the energy and humiliation of finding someone who could make me feel good and keep their mouth shut at the same time. I'm not that hard to please."

"I guess I could do that for you if you would keep your mouth shut about me," Deidre agreed.

"Ok that sounds like we can work together very well after all. I will call you when I need to see you and you better answer the phone and be on time."

"I'm very punctual and meet my commitments," Deidre in a snarky way.

After she left Ali Deidre walked back to the house and went upstairs and hit the switch to the secret room. She sat in there so that her angry face and hot tears would not be seen by anyone. The fucking nerve of that guy was astounding he is so conceited and brash it makes me sick.

Deidre went downstairs after she calmed down and found Max and asked him to come to lunch with her. She felt that talking to Max always seemed to make her feel better, he was very much a gentleman nothing like John who was a bull in a China shop.

The painters wanted Max to do the punch out list for them and other odd jobs they didn't want to be bogged down with so he was still working at the Green Street house and would be for a while. It was good because he had to say he had a job on the paperwork he filled out for the police investigation of the body. He had put down the wrong date of when he started being a steady worker for the paint company, but no one seemed to notice. The police released the outside areas that had been cordoned off and the landscape company would be back. The final turnkey product of the house being complete was not yet in sight as the corpse they found had placed slowed down progress, but it was coming along.

It was nice to have a meal with a woman and Max enjoyed the outing. They talked about Hog and how he was so lucky not to be spending the rest of his life in jail. They walked back to the house, and each spent the rest of the day in separate parts of the house. Near the end of the day Max was called out to check a delivery of lawn supplies and as he was directing the delivery man where to store the materials, he saw a plain police car drive up and park, he pulled down his hat and turned so that his face could not be seen. The man got out and went into the house. Soon Deidre and the man came out. Deidre waved goodbye as they drove away, but Max did not acknowledge the greeting.

[Chapter 41]

Deidre was feeling depressed. Marlene's visit to the house was much more demanding than she would have guessed. And where was that worm Ali, not available to come with her and lick her ass. Then she remembered that he was back from his trip tonight and expected Deidre to come to his apartment and be with him. The thought of that nauseated Deidre but she had no choice now she could not afford to piss him off because that would mean that her relationship with John Finley would also suffer. She was actually going to see him that night.

That evening she did her best to be pleasant to Ali and when they were finished in the bedroom as usual, he went to his bathroom to take a shower. That made Deidre feel dirty as if he felt contaminated after being with her and needed to be cleaned and scowdered.

She looked around the room and decided she would do something to make him pay for making her feel so shitty. She looked in his jewelry box and saw a small pinky ring and decided that it would look better on her pinky than his. It had a fancy elevated design on top and was heavy, so she thought it was solid gold. She took it. She looked at several other pieces but decided that they would be too obvious if she took one of those. When Ali came out of the shower, he told her he wanted her to help him unpack and then she could go. Deidre was steaming when she came out of the building but felt better when she put her hand in her coat pocket and felt the ring. Aha! how sweet revenge is.

The next day Deidre went to work at the Green Street house. It was really going to be a good day, it seemed that everybody that worked in the house was there that day including Hog and Max. The contractors of each of the services, painting, plumbing, carpentry, and the others had all decided they would get together for a final walk through the house. The old house had regained its old splendor and elegance and was ready for a new tenant. They had lunch catered and it was a party atmosphere. It took a long time coming but was well worth it. Deidre talked with Max and Hog and told them what a great job they did.

"We really didn't do much," Max said, we were only arms and legs, but we had fun doing it didn't we Hog?"

"Yeah, it was nuttin like I ever done before, and I was never in a fancy house like this in my life."

Stanley the painter asked Hog and Max if they could come to a new house, they were going to start next week.

"We would be asking the usual to move stuff from one room to another and wondered if you would be up for it."

"Sure, we will give it a look see," Hog agreed, right Max?"

Max shook his head to agree as he watched Deidre and Detective Finley go up the steps in the grand foyer.

Deidre had talked to Finley and told him she was at the Green Street house.

"That perfect can I come there and see you I want to see something and follow up on the body case as well."

"There is sort of a party going on but I'm sure they wouldn't mind," Deidre answered.

When Finley got there Deidre was waiting for him and they immediately went upstairs, and Finley asked if she would take him to the secret room. We got the coroner's report from the body, and it seems that the body was not in the ground that long. It did not have the necessary insect or vermin information on it that would put it in the ground long. Since this house had many people moving around in it the body if it was stashed inside would have been hidden someplace like in the secret room. I brought my light and some luminal solution to see if there is any blood up there."

They went to the secret room and Finley was amazed. He looked around and wondered where he should start first. He went over to where the fireplace was and sprayed around and shined the light but nothing. They went to a couple more places and did the same without success. After about an hour he said, "let's pull back the carpet near the sitting area and test between the boards. Even if it was cleaned it might have some residue." Deidre held up the rug on its side while Finley sprayed the area.

"Whoops! Sorry honey I didn't mean to spray your hand and I got it on your ring to and he gave it a swipe with the Q-tip to clean it off. Then he turned on the light and got close to the floorboards and got another Q-tip and swabbed between the boards. Only a slight reaction. Then he stopped and paused and said nothing for a few minutes.

"Is that it did you find something?" asked Deidre.

"No nothing."

"Are you ok I thought you got so quiet for a minute."

"Oh, I'm just disappointed. I think we can go now this was not a good idea."

"Ok Deidre," said and they put back everything they had disturbed and left.

[Chapter 42]

Max and Hog didn't have anything to do for a few weeks. Hog went back to his old clients that he did favors for before he met Max. Max would wait for him in the park until he was done.

Max was sitting on a bench waiting for Hog when a lady dressed in two coats and two hats came up to him and told him he could not sit on that bench. Max looked at her strangely and asked her why she said that the bench belonged to her family, and she did not allow anyone to sit on it but her. She was nasty and began to curse and kick at Max and tell him he was not good and not worthy of sitting on her bench. At first Max went along with a good attitude and just ignored the lady and continued to read the book he had with him. That seemed to ignite her flames even more and she began shouting.

"If you don't move from this bench, I will call the police."

Max paid no attention to this screaming lady and continued to sit and read. Just then a police cruiser came by and stopped, and the officers got out to see what the commotion was. The woman told the cops that the man on the bench stole her purse, and he won't give it back to her. When she tried to take it back, he swung at her and hit her on the back.

The police asked Max to stand up. He did so. They searched him and he had no purse. They asked him what happened.

"Officers I was sitting on this bench waiting for a friend reading a book when this lady came up and told me I could not sit here because this bench belonged to her family, and I was not worthy of sitting on it. That's all, I did not strike her or say anything else to her."

The woman started crying saying that her back hurt and that the man on the bench hit her and she is in so much pain.

One officer looked at the other and said we should let somebody with a lot of time sort this out. Let's take both of them to the station house and see what they can do with them.

As Hog was coming back to meet Max, he saw what was happening. He immediately recognized Two Hat Sally and felt bad that he forgot to warn Max about her, but now it was too late, and the cops were guiding Max to a squad car and took him to jail.

Once at the jail they asked for Max's ID, and he gave them the bogus one he bought. When it came back as nonexistent, they decided to fingerprint him and hold him to see if he was wanted for any other crimes.

Two hat Sally was released when one of the cops recognized her as a regular who lived at the halfway house and frequented that park.

Hog went back to camp kicking himself all the way for not warning Max about Two hat Sally. He called the lawyer who had defended him to tell him about Max and asked for his help.

The lawyer called Thomas and they went to the station house. The lawyer told Max he would have to stay there that night and he would be back the next day to see if the judge would accept bail. They got lucky and the next day Thomas would put up the bail and they were about to release him on bond. As they were about to exit the station house a cop came running out and stopped them.

"What's going on here asked the lawyer we're leaving right now, what's wrong with you?"

"He's not going anywhere. We just got his fingerprints back he is the guy who killed the man in the alley. He just might be the serial killer we have been looking for, for months and he is staying with us."

Max couldn't believe it his greatest fear of being sent to jail was now realized. His goose was cooked. Ali would be over the top with the news and Max would be in prison or executed for a crime he did not commit.

The lawyer that helped Hog was now working with Max. He told Max that he was going to ask the court to set bail for him and see if he could be released on his own recognizance. Max thought that was a crazy idea, "Do they really let people accused of murder out on bond? He asked the lawyer.

"The way bail works," the lawyer explained. "If you could put up 10-20% of the bail amount set by the judge and the rest could be covered by personal property, cash, valuables, or other assets that you own, or someone put forward for you. The percentage amount was usually refundable. The judge was not aware of Max's real identity and saw that he had no fixed address when he was arrested and set the bail at $500,000 which he thought would be an unattainable sum for Max to raise. Max talked to Thomas when he came to see him and told him what happened. Thomas heard the story and told Max he would see what he could do to get him out of jail.

After a few days a police officer came to his cell and told him to gather up his stuff and come with him. Max was worried they were transferring him to the state prison and was very upset. The officer told him to get dressed in his civilian clothes and wait till he came back for him. When the officer came back, he took Max to the main station room and Thomas and his lawyer were waiting for him. His lawyer and Thomas greeted Max and told him they made bail for him, and Max was near tears, he was so happy. Then they told him that he would be going with Thomas to his apartment because he could not go back to the camp. He had to have a fixed address and be there if they wanted him back. It was a bittersweet thought, Max, but worth it.

"Not to worry Max," Thomas told him, "We talked to Hog, and he knows where you are and is very happy that you are out of jail. He'll catch up with you soon. Max was thrilled to be in a real apartment and was so grateful to Thomas. He vowed to pay him back.

[Chapter 43]

When Detective Finley broke the news to Ali, he was livid. He ranted and raved and demanded to know how this hobo had enough money to make bail. Finley told him he had to get into the system and see who did this for him. The detective promised he would do all he could and left with Ali still fuming and cursing.

Finley would look for Max's benefactor later now he wanted to call the lab to talk to the tech about his visit to the Green Street house to look for blood and ask the tech if he found anything.

There is evidence of only a very faint trace of blood on both the swabs you gave me. Finley said to the lab tech, "Both the swabs?

"Yeah, both of them."

"Is it possible that something was wrong with the luminol solution? Could it have been too strong? Do you think I should do the test again?

"It's possible but highly unlikely because the solution comes from the same batch, I have used for all the other specimens, and I have been using the same solution and it has given good results.

"I ask because I spilled some solution on my ring, and I thought I saw a glow of light on it when I did the swabs, is that possible."

"I don't really know I would have to see the object to give you a good answer you should bring in the ring and let me take a look at it and see what turns up. Do you have it now?"

"No, I don't wear it all the time, but I will get it to you."

That evening when Deidre and Finley went out for dinner, he looked at her hand and saw she had the same ring on.

"Sweetheart I see you have a new ring it's nice," Finley says, "Where did you get it?"

"Oh, this thing," Deidre said playing it down and stretching out her hand so he could look at it. "I got it at a Flea Market one day when I was in town shopping for the decorative items for the house."

Finley looked at it closely, "It is attractive, but the way this decorative scrolling is set up high it looks as if it could be shiner and maybe needs a good cleaning. You know I busted the strap on my watch and I'm going to the jewelers tomorrow I could get them to clean it up for you. The guys a friend of mine so he could do it while I wait to have my watchband replaced."

"That would be great if you would do that for me," Deidre agreed and took the ring off and gave it to him. Later, Deidre was thinking as she got ready for bed. It was a very sweet gesture that John made in taking my ring to be cleaned. It sounds silly but I'm really glad to get Ali's presence off the ring if that's possible and it goes without saying I will never wear it in Ali's presence, I really hate that man, but I can't do anything about that right now because of his relationship with John. The next day Finley gave the ring to the lab tech and asked him to test it for him. Finley stayed in his office and worked on other cases and several hours later got a call from the lab.

"Detective Finley you were right the luminol test is positive, there is blood on the ring and I'm going to see if there is enough for me to get a good sample and run the DNA then maybe we will see where the blood came from."

"You know I appreciate you doing this for me, but you don't have to go through all that trouble for me. The ring came from a flea market and there is no telling whose blood that might be."

"It's ok detective we are fairly quiet in the lab today and now you have my curiosity up and I am by trade very nosey. I will do the testing and get back to you later today or tomorrow if I can get a good enough sample."

"Thanks that sound good."

Finley went back to work and thought no more of the ring or the testing because he knew he could trust Deidre and it was sort of intriguing to see if the blood was going to match anybody in the system.

He had been successful in diverting Ali's phone calls most of the day but now here he was calling again the man was such a pain in the ass.

"Finley, I need you to put a tail on the man that was released on bail today. I know he must be the one he looks just like those sketches they made from my description, and I don't want him to get away with murder."

"Ali I can't do that. That has to be ordered by the court and paperwork before I can have someone followed. I can't justify following this man when the judge let him out on bail."

"That's not what's going to happen. I want him followed even if we have to hire a private dick. Do you know anyone we can use?"

"No, not off the top I'll have to ask around and see if there is anybody that has been used before, I will have to get back to you."

"Ok but make it soon I don't want him slipping through our fingers."

[Chapter 44]

Ellie was so relieved when she heard Max was out of jail. Maybe they would have some time to go over all the material Max had written and get it organized. She visited him at Thomas's apartment and asked him if he wanted to start reviewing the material he collected.

"Max this would be a great time to start putting your book together and at least get an outline going," Ellie suggested as they were having dinner with Thomas.

"I'm not sure now that I want to go through with it," Max confessed.

Both Thomas and Ellie looking shocked stared at Max and asked, "Why?"

"I started out with such a different picture in my head of what it would be like to live on the street and now that picture is very distorted. Yes, I see the ugly tents and eyesores that dot the city. I agree they should not be there. But Hog and the people at the camp that are not in the mainstream of the city and are not the in-your-face people you see on street corners, they are different. They do not want to be in the public eye and have everybody watch them and criticize them. I wish there was a way for them to get the help they need and the creature comforts that most Americans enjoy. Even the basic stuff like hot and cold running water and toilet facilities and a place to cook a meal. In my heart I also question that because poor souls like Bonnie who are so depressed and don't have the drive to live a normal life and work and cook and even keep herself clean, we need some way to help people like her," Max explained.

"Do you think they have a good life the way they are now?" asked Thomas.

"No, I'm not saying they have a good life the way they live now but what is the alternative. To be in a home or institution? To have everybody have the same meal at the same time and lights out it's bedtime and you will all wear the same clothes because they are easy to launder. That's not life either."

"Do you have an idea of how to help them out?" Quired Ellie.

"I thought I had it all figured out that an army of psychiatrists, social workers and doctors and nurses could come in and attend to all these people and make them better. Make them forget what happened to them in their lives and somehow get them to learn how to cope and adjust and be useful again. But some of them are just lost souls who will never be better and who will never recover from what they had to endure not with all the medicine and therapy in the world. They have given up on life."

"Max, are you ok you seem more upset about all the people on the street and yet you know in your heart that there is no one who has the real answer," Thomas commented, "but for now we need to concentrate on your case."

"I know, I know and believe me if what happened to me had not happened, I would not have this attitude. Look at Hog for instance. He lost everything even his own flesh and blood and the loves of his life, his wife, his bike, his great job that he loved and yet he still found it in his heart to help me."

"I just read a really good article on why people go homeless. It mentioned some of the things you are talking about Max, but the bottom line is that there are people in this world that are not as strong as we expect them to be or at least as strong as we think we would be in a crisis. And they can't cope.

"Sure, we can make them zombies by giving them medication to forget or by making them conform back to the society they dropped out of, but that does not change or make them forget all that happened to them. They are truly unhappy persons who do not have anywhere to go, and their minds cannot be changed," Ellie added to the conversation," and nobody seems to be able to solve this problem."

"This is a topic people have been trying to solve for many, many years. Back when people who were in the war or had loved ones in the war or who were prisoners when they came home people used to refer to them as being, "shell shocked." They tried to get back in society and be with other so call normal people who did not experience any traumatic things but somehow, they never succeeded in being able to tell their story or were afraid if they did, they would have to relive it again. They had to have so many coping crutches that it was not easy to keep up. The anxiety that the traumatic events brought to them were never overcome. And not always but often it's because they have within themselves given up, but their bodies have not. Giving up on life is possible, but you just can't lay down and die it's not that easy."

Thomas, you saw how emotional it was when Hog's wife Janey came to testify. She couldn't even face Hog let alone a whole room of people. She had to relive all that emotion and pain that she experienced so long ago and like Angie said to Hog and me when we found her in the bushes, "Sometimes the demons are kept at bay for a while but they are always there lurking to take a bite of your heart and gnaw at you just because you remember what bad things happened and you can't shake them off."

"Max please we didn't mean to upset you," Thomas said sadly.

"I know that the things I saw and heard I never expected to be so painful and grievous that it's hard to write about it now that I have lived it," Max told them.

"Let's just have a glass of wine and go on to another topic," Ellie suggested.

"It's been such an emotional experience for you Max going to jail, and people find out your real identity and all, it's no wonder you are all pent up and we already know you are passionate about these people. Needless to say, it has been a strain on all of us. Let me fill you in on what I have been able to find out," Thomas declared.

"Good idea let's go there," Max agreed.

"Our friend Daniel Herbert Marshall AKA "Ali" is not as swift on paper as I thought," Thomas told them. It turns out he was a mediocre student and took the job at Marlene's father's firm because he could not find another job. He probably stayed there because he was a yes man and apparently Marlene's father liked that. When she had a bad time after her father's death he swooped in and took charge in her behalf without her really knowing or caring, but you already know that. Now he is anxious to move her into the house on Green Street to keep her occupied and not nosing around the business. Word has it that he is going to propose to her the minute she is in the house and get his name on everything she owns including the business. I hope she doesn't fall for that because he has done some shady deals and made investments in the company name that are being investigated by the feds.

"Is that right Max responded, that's music to my ears. I would be glad to testify that he is also a murderer and should be in jail."

"Let's not jump the gun here, we know that he has Finley in his pocket, but we couldn't find out exactly why. Until the day before yesterday when his private assistant was seen making a large deposit in Finley's bank account. When my guy asked around it seems that Finley has a nasty habit of betting on the ponies. He was in debt for a very large sum. Somehow

Ali found out and offered to pay off the debt if he would find the homeless man who killed his friend. Any way that's how that got started," Thomas informed them.

"Oh my God!" Max said, no wonder why he has been jumping through hoops to get evidence on me. The funny thing is there is none. So, anything they say is a lie." Max said. Wow the worm turns!

[Chapter 45]

Detective Finley didn't have time to think any more because he was called to another murder. He was all excited because this time the murderer got sloppy and left a shell casing. Now it would be a hunt to find the weapon that matched that gun and that was no easy task.

In the middle of the afternoon the lab tech came to Finley's office all excited and told him he had some good news.

"Wow you already found the owner of the gun that the shell came from?" Finley asked hopefully.

"No, but I did find something else. Do you know where you got that ring from that I did the test on?" The tech asked.

"The ring? Oh, the ring, I almost forgot about that. Not exactly it came from a flea market, and I would have to do some tracking to find out where it came from originally," Finley answered.

"I got lucky and found enough blood under the top of the ring to make a match." the lab tech said.

"Well, that's good tell me whose was it?" asked Finley.

"Some of it was the from the body we found in the alley several weeks ago. It's a perfect match."

"A, A, perfect match?" repeated Finley, what do you mean by some of it?"

"Yeah, I couldn't believe it myself. There were two different blood types under that crown thing. I'll send you the written report later I just thought you would want to know right away."

"Yeah sure, thanks, I'll be looking for it," said Finley. "What about the other blood type?"

"I'm still looking for that one, it may take a while."

"Do me a favor when you find the second blood type don't tell anyone, I want to make this case myself and I will see that you are rewarded for that, if you get what I mean."

"I get it, my lips are sealed. I will let you know when I find something."

Finley sat with his head in his hands for a long time. He was in a quandary. What in the Hell was going on here. How could Deidre possibly have a ring that has the blood of the dead guy in the alley. I know she didn't kill him because we were away that weekend, he was killed, and we were together every minute. I wonder if it's possible that she is seeing someone other than me and he gave her that ring and is the killer. This is so screwy I have to think about this slowly and go over all the facts again, just not right now. After I get the preliminary stuff sorted on this latest case, I will dive into this and get a solution.

A few days later and Finley begins thinking about the man in the alley case again and the ring. I hate to do this but the only way I will ever find out the truth would be to follow Deidre and see if she is seeing someone bedsides me. I know it's not right but it's driving me crazy so I'm going to follow her.

This is so pathetic Finley is thinking we just ate dinner together and I wanted to come up to her apartment, but she begged off saying she had a very early morning tomorrow and wanted to get some sleep. So, I left. Now here I am, watching her apartment and within 10 minutes she comes out and gets in her car and drives off. I ran to my car and followed her. She stops at the apartment complex of Ali, and I'm stunned. What could she be doing here? I follow her to the apartment and hide as she knocks, I hear her say it's me and the door opens.

What the fuck is going on here? I ask myself. My first thought is that he is blackmailing her for something like he is doing to me. But what could it be? I wait to see if she is going to come out, but time goes by, and she is still in there after an hour and a half. Finally, she comes out and gets in her car and goes home. I go home to my place very weary now at what I have seen, and I can't seem to stop my imagination from conjuring up the vilest scenes my mind comes up with, but I let it pass.

The next day my mind is awash with ideas and scenarios of what went on in that apartment and why. Days go by and I try and act as normally as possible. I tell Deidre that I have to go out of town on business and continue to follow her. On Tuesday of the next week, she gets in her car and goes to Ali's apartment again. This time I followed her to the apartment and after she went in, I turn around and go back to her apartment. I let myself in and began to search. I found the ring it is in her jewelry box. I find nothing else but as I'm about to leave I hear the door open and the sound of Deidre's voice cursing. She is cursing Ali saying what a horrible person he is and how she hates him. I'm hiding in the hall closet and I can see her through the slotted door. She takes off all her clothes and says she must take a shower and wash all the filth off her body and be clean again and she is crying. She goes into the shower, and I get out of her apartment.

Now I'm sure Ali must be blackmailing her but for what. I can't ask her. I will have to start diving into her background and see if I can find out why this is happening. I feel sorry for her but at the same time, I feel very betrayed, and I was not too thrilled when she told me she works as an escort. She says it is only at parties to have old guys look good but I'm no fool, I know how the game is played. I always felt sorry for most of the prostitutes we arrested them, they had such shit lives as slaves to their pimps.

This is not exactly that but still the principle is the same. I must make up my mind how much Deidre means to me and if I can persuade her to stop. It makes my job tougher when there is an emotional twist because of my personal life. I wish with all my heart she had come to me, and I could have helped her before she had to give herself to Ali. Just then Finley's cell rings, it's the lab tech. "I have some news for you, he says I'm not sure you will be pleased."

"Go ahead and let me have it, it's been that kind of week and another punch in the gut won't matter."

[Chapter 46]

Several months later Max's case is in trial at full swing. Ali and Marlene are in the courtroom every day. He is going crazy because most of the evidence is circumstantial and to get a conviction Finley told him that he must go on the witness stand and tell why he was in the alley with Joe and saw Max murder Joe. Ali is pissed, he hates the thought of that because what would Marlene think? He would definitely have to make up a story and lie. Ali racked his brain trying to think of what a good reason for them to go in that alley.

Finally, he comes up with a story. Joe was drinking heavily when they went for a ride on the motorcycle, and he had to relieve himself urgently, so they went into the alley and that's when he was attacked by a crazed homeless man. That sounded ok but what if she asked why Ali didn't try and stop the crazed homeless man? Maybe because it was raining so heavily that Ali slipped on the wet pavement and hit his head and was unconscious and could not help Joe. That begs the question then why didn't the homeless man rob and kill him too? Ali hoped she wouldn't think of that. That would be his story and he would flim, flam the rest if he had to. Ali did not tell Finley that he was lying, he still hoped that he would not have to go on the stand.

Finley held back the evidence of the ring. As the trial moved forward Finley was pressed by Ali to do something so that he did not have to testify and say why he was in that alley that night. He wants Finley to find evidence that the street bum is really the serial killer and then focus on that and not on Joe's murder. But Finley does not have anything to prove Max is the serial killer and although Ali is insisting, he fake something he hesitates to do that because if he presents false evidence and it is ever proven he would lose his job.

Finley told Deidre he needed a break from the arduous grueling of the trial and they should have a quiet dinner and relax.

"Thank you for having dinner with me," Finley said to Deidre I needed to get away and relax and have time off but mostly to get away from Ali. He is literally driving me crazy with calls and texts every 5 minutes asking me how I plan to keep hm off the stand."

"I know he can be a pain in the ass and make life miserable," Deidre responded.

"Diedre, I want to ask you a question. It's not an easy one and I apologize for it in advance," Finley said.

"What is it," asked Deidre concerned.

"You know when I had your ring cleaned a few weeks ago?"

"Yes, so what?"

"Well, I really forgot to bring it with me when I went to the jeweler, and I was telling the lab tech about it and he suggested that he could do it at the police lab, so I let him take the ring. You will never guess what happened next."

"What happened?" Deidre asked with a dumbfounded look on her face.

"I'm going to put this right out there, the tech found blood under the crown of that ring. It has had me worried, and I was afraid to ask you about it, where did you get that ring?" John told her.

"Why I got it at a flea market like I told you before, so what does that matter?" Asked Deidre.

"Here is the thing the lab found that the blood on the ring matched the blood of the dead man they found in the alley, so you see it is a huge problem. I need to find out who gave the ring to the flea market merchant to sell. And until I know that I can't introduce it as evidence."

"Oh my God! You're kidding. I don't know who owned it before I bought it at the flea market," Deidre lied.

"I understand that and I'm not accusing you of anything but if I introduce the ring it will implicate you," Finley said.

"Oh, yes I see," said Diedre.

"No, you don't see because if I introduce the ring as evidence then they will begin a chain of custody and investigate you, and I don't think you want that to happen."

"That's right I don't want anyone investigating me," Diedre responded.

"Ok so then I must ask you if you know anything more about the ring, we will go to the flea market, and you can show me which booth you bought the ring from and then I'll take it from there."

"Oh John, I feel so bad that I have to tell you this," Deidre said as she began weeping, "You may not believe me, but I work at another job, and I got it from one of the men I know. Wait don't get the wrong impression he didn't really give it to me I took it from his apartment."

"Why were you at another man's apartment?" Finley asked although he already thought he knew. If she went to Ali's apartment, then maybe she would be with others too. It made him quite upset.

"He had been drinking and was tipsy and I didn't want him to fall. I put him to bed and saw the ring and thought I should have it for all my extra trouble. I intended to tell him about it the next time I saw him and give it back but then he never called."

"Finley said nothing his expression changed, and he looked as if he were in misery, he held his head in his hands and though them muffled, "tell me more, tell me all of it."

Diedre told Finley about her other job as escort and that she had been doing that for quite some time but added it's not what you think. Mostly they are older men who are not looking to have sex but just want to show up at a dinner party with pretty girl on their arm to show they are still in the game. It's not such a bad thing it restores confidence to older men who feel they have lost it. It doesn't mean that I have sex with them." Deidre insisted, "Please believe me."

"Do you need the money that badly for something?" asked Finley. "Why didn't you come to me?"

"Come to you and say what? Hey Honey, I hope you don't mind I go out with other men as their escort for money when I'm not dating you. Do you think I'm stupid?"

"No, but you don't have to do that I have enough money to take care of you and I would have expected you to trust me with any secrets you had," Finley declared.

"John, I appreciate that, but I have not felt I could do that with any man I met so far in life so why would I think that of you?" Asked Deidre.

"I guess I'm dense. I thought we had a thing going. Where does that leave us now?

"I, I'm not sure, I was beginning to think that you are different than the others but how can I ask you to accept what I have done?" Diedre spit out, her mood going from one of feeling guilty to anger.

"Let's just calm down for now and not talk about it anymore right," Finley suggested.

"Ok let's sleep on it and see if we come up with a solution," Diedre said, very upset and crying.

"Ok, ok, let's not talk about this anymore tonight. I'm sure I can come up with something to solve the problem," Finley murmured as he took her in his arms and held her tight while she cried.

The next day all Finley wanted to do was sit in his office and go over all that had happened. But his phone began signaling that Ali was calling him yet again and he became so intensely pissed at Ali he wanted to punch his face off. He knew he could hardly keep his cool when he talked to the man. He bugged him day and night about the murder case. Having a suspicious mind Finley began wondering why else Ali would be so pent up about this case besides taking the stand and having to face Marlene. Maybe he's not telling me all he really knows about what happened. Maybe he didn't hit his head and passed out. I have an idea; I will put a bug in that briefcase he takes everywhere he goes and see if I can find out what else is on his mind. No matter I know he is blackmailing Deidre just like he is me, but she is paying a much higher price and I understand why she would kowtow to his demands. She is trying to break into interior design and keeping the Green House job. She is not as tough as she lets on.

[Chapter 47]

Deidre was spooked. What in the Hell was she going to do now? John knew about her escort job, and she was sure that he was going to ask her to stop doing it. Did he really believe in his heart everything Deidre told him. That her escort job was just for fun? My other worry is, can I be sure that John believes my story about the ring. Surely, he knows in his gut what men would demand of me and that they pay to have sex with me. I haven't even thought of John's throwing cases to my brother and making him look good as if he were a successful lawyer. If he decides he doesn't want to see me anymore that will most certainly stop. I must not tell him anything else and just wait and see if he still wants to see me. I need him in so many ways.

The thing is I now know that Ali killed Joe that's why his blood was on the ring. He has no idea that I took the ring and it's a good thing I did it, now I can get him to stop blackmailing me and leave me alone. If he doesn't, I will tell Finley where I got the ring and how it got blood on it. I can't wait to see the look on his face when I tell Ali to shove it. Ali will have a fit.

Neither Finley nor Deidre were answering his calls or texts and he wanted to talk to them. He went out to the receptionist's desk to make sure he had no appointments and then he would go and find Deidre. As he approached the desk, he overheard the receptionist on the phone telling someone that today was the final day for the punch out list for the Green Street house and all the contractors would be doing their final walk through.

What good news now I know exactly where Deidre would be most of the day I will go to the house in the late afternoon and find Deidre and let her know who the boss is. When Ali called her, she needed to answer him and that was that. Deidre had a few final touches to add to the front parlor and the secret room and then she would just wait for Marlene's approval, and it would be a finished product. Deidre had received several messages from Ali but ignored them and decided she was going to distance herself from him. If he gave her any shit, she would ask John Finley to help her get him off her back.

The court had granted a two-week recess from the trial and Max was restless waiting in Thomas's apartment. Thomas was gone most of the day and many times well into the night and Max had nothing to do. Max decided to go to see Hog. As he was walking to the camp, he met Hog and asked him what he was up to.

"I'm headed to Green Street," Hog replied, "why don't ya come with me?"

"Why are you going there today?"

"Tomorrow is punch out day and anybody who worked at the house will be doing a final inspection before they sign off on their contract for the final payment. The paint guys asked me to come help," Hog explained, come hang with me?"

"Maybe I will after all this will probably be the last time, I will ever work on a project like that again, I might be in jail awaiting sentencing soon," Max replied sadly.

By late afternoon the painters left saying they needed one more day to do some patching upstairs and would be back. Hog and Max left too and made plans to meet at the diner a little later because Hog had to go see one of the other people, he did things for. Max was walking back from the house when he felt for his lucky coin and couldn't find it. He searched all his pockets and even his shoes but no coin. I must have dropped it in the house when we were checking out the floor upstairs. I have to go back and find it. Max went in the house and called out to see if anybody else was there. Deidre answered. She said she was in the kitchen and would be leaving in a few minutes. Max began looking everywhere to find the coin. He went upstairs and began surveying the floor. Almost at the same time he spotted his coin and heard voices downstairs. Not sure if Deidre left or maybe someone else came in, he listened. He recognized Deidre's voice and was surprised to hear Ali's voice as well.

As she opened the door to let Ali in, she said, "So you made it. I didn't think you would come."

"Why would I not come to see a beautiful woman who summoned me to a clandestine meeting?" Ali said and gave a shitty laugh.

"Well for one thing you need to know this is an important meeting and I expect you to be completely honest with me."

As they moved further into the parlor Max was able to hear their discussion.

"Honest with you? Why would I do that?" Ali answered.

"Because this has turned into more that the disgusting fact that you are blackmailing me it's all about sending someone to prison or being executed when they are innocent. "Deidre said dramatically.

"Whatever are you talking about?"

"I know that the homeless man in the alley did not kill Joe, you know that too don't you?" Deidre queried.

"What homeless man are you talking about?" Ali replied playing dumb.

"The one you're trying to frame with your lies and deceit." Deidre said sarcastically.

"What kind of nonsense are you talking about?" asked Ali.

"I know you think I'm a blond air-headed bitch that doesn't have a brain in her head, but that's just not the case, you stupid ass. I just went along with your little charade because it suited my goals at the time. Now it's different," Deidre snarked.

"Different how?" Ali asked.

"Because you are trying to put an innocent man in jail for a crime you committed, and I can't stand for that."

"What, what the Hell are you talking about are you nuts? Asked Ali. What innocent man? That street bum that killed Joe. He deserves to be punished for what he did to him, how he slashed him and left him to bleed to death. And since when did you become a savior of humanity?"

"I'm not a savior of humanity, far from it but I don't like to see anyone abused by another, and you want that man to take the fall for your murder. So now you are judge and jury and want to see this guy burn for something you did?"

"I don't know what you are talking about I would have tried to help but I was unconscious and didn't even realize what was happening," Ali said raising his voice and getting very angry.

"Right, right I forgot you are the innocent victim here not the killer." Deidre said and laughed sarcastically.

"What do you know about it anyway you weren't there."

"No, I wasn't there but Joe's ring was."

"What ring are you talking about?" Ali asked.

"The pinky ring Marlene gave Frazer that he had on when you killed him."

"I don't have that ring I don't know what happened to it the street guy stole it." Ali said haughtily.

"I went through some photos of the events you attended with Marlene and Joe, or should I say Snooky? And in several of them the ring was visible on Joe's hand when he had it around a glass of champagne that they were toasting with. The same one I got from your apartment."

"You little slut. You stole that ring from my apartment, you cheap whore."

"Sticks and stones and all that," Deidre said, "You are correct, I know you thought that my services were not worth much and you felt so contaminated that you had to take a cleansing shower after being with me as if I was dirty or trash. So, I took the ring because I thought I deserved something from you."

"What does that mean? Why did you take the ring?" Ali responded.

"Well for one thing it shows that you were not unconscious at the crime scene like you are saying, and for another your blood and Joe's blood were both found on the ring by the police lab. Put that in your pipe and smoke it," Deidre purred sarcastically.

"How did you find out that there was blood on the ring?" Ali asked.

"By a fluke, and if you weren't so fucking greedy and demanding and thought you had all the answers and could control everybody around you, you are wrong," Deidre said with a sardonic laugh. "Now all I have to do is tell John where I got the ring from, and he will know the truth too."

Max was listening and when he heard Ali and Deidre arguing he couldn't believe his ears. Ring what ring he didn't know anything about a ring. His lawyer didn't know about the ring, what was going on?

You're a real bitch. You stole that ring from my apartment and now you want to accuse me of murder? You are fucking crazy. You will never get away with that John Finley will never believe you when I tell him that I was fucking you and you loved it and you didn't want him to know it. What do you think about that?"

"I think that is just like you and your slimy body and your small dick," Deidre said and laughed, maybe you should get a pump-up dick and be like the big boys."

"I could easily snap your neck and leave you here no one would be the wiser. They would think that the homeless guy struck again and that he is the serial killer." Ali spit out angrily and started walking toward Deidre.

"Don't you come near me you worm." Deidre screamed.

Ali lunged forward with his hands outstretched as if to grab her by the neck. Deidre reached into her purse and pulled out her gun and shot him. He collapsed on the floor.

Max had been listening to the whole thing and when Deidre shot the gun, Max called out "No, don't kill him he is the only one who can save me."

Deidre was shocked where did that voice come from?" Max ran down the stairs as fast as he could, to see Deidre sitting in a chair calm as a cucumber.

"Max, what the Hell are you doing here? No matter, it's wonderful you're here. Please help me. Ali was going to rape me, and I got so scared I shot him, now what am I going to do?"

"Deidre, I heard everything and now I know there is evidence that can prove I didn't kill Joe. Where is the ring and can we get it to the cops ASAP?"

"You men are all alike. Ali needed to be killed because he was going to do great harm to you, and you don't even realize that. You need to help me put him up in the secret room and no one will find him for a long time just like they didn't find Lukas who was up there for a long time. Deidre stood up and said, "Max you have to help me now, we have to get rid of this body. With that she turned and walked outside to find a tarp and Max followed, trying to talk some sense into her. Searching in the trash pile she found an old blue tarp and said, "are you going to help me or not?"

Max followed her back into the living room where the body was and both gasped. The body was gone!

"Oh, Jesus here we go again, "Max screamed and ran to the front door to see Ali's car driving away.

[Chapter 48]

"What are we going to do now?" asked Deidre. "I don't know about you but I'm going to the police and tell them everything."

"No, no you can't do that they will turn it all around and you will go to prison or die," Deidre stated.

"Why do you say that you know I didn't shoot him or kill anybody I heard you tell him that. And you have proof, the ring. Where is the ring?"

"I can't let you call the police and tell them I shot someone. We have a wash here wouldn't you say?"

"What do you want to do?" asked Max.

"Let's get this place cleaned up and get out of here. We won't say anything to anybody. If Ali tells Finley what happened, I will say he tried to assault me, and I shot him in self-defense. He doesn't know you heard all about the ring and since it is in the police lab already you can use it as evidence to prove your innocence."

"Finley is in Ali's pocket he will make that ring evidence disappear fast and for sure, I will be convicted."

"Not if I can persuade him not to do that," Deidre said with a sly grin.

"What do you mean?" asked Max.

"I think Finley is ready to get rid of that bastard, Ali has been blackmailing both him and me and this is our chance. The ring evidence has his blood on it and shows he was there at the crime scene at least. I will testify that he told me he killed Joe, and you will describe to me how he did it. At the very least his reputation will be ruined, and Marlene will know he killed her Snooky and kick him to the curb."

Max was in a spin and didn't know what to do. He couldn't talk about an assault with no victim, what could he do? He decided he needed to talk to someone and that was Hog.

Max to Hog's tent. Hog immediately knew something was up.

"What gives Max?" asked Hog.

Max told Hog what happened, and Hog looked at him in disbelief.

"You mean to tell me the body took a powder?" Hog said trying to make the conversation light.

"I guess you could say that," Max said a slight grin and a sigh.

"It looks as if Deidre is holding all the cards right now, so we have to try and fix that. Tomorrow we will go back to the Green Street house and see if we can find the bullet. The painters had a final punch list when I was there earlier today and they need somebody to do a final walk through for trash, paint spots or and touch ups so they will be glad to see us," Hog declared.

The next morning Hog and Max went to the Green Street house. The painters were already there. They asked Max and Hog to pull any trash they saw and to look closely at all the walls and floor for any touch ups that needed to be done. The going was slow but finally they came to the living room. Max knew where he saw Ali lying on the floor and they had cleaned up the blood that was there but saw no bullet holes.

"What do we do now Hog?" asked Max.

"Hold on now let's think of this, the man had to be standing when she shot him not lying on the floor so that the bullet may be in the walls somewhere if it's not still stuck in him. Let's go over every square inch of that wall behind where the man fell to see if there is anything there."

Each took a section of the wall and moved over it with their hands to see if there were any holes. They found none. They were sitting on the steps when Stanley came down and asked if they found anything he needed to patch.

"No, we didn't see anything they almost said in unison."

"Well let me give a professional eyeballing to it and make sure since this is the main room of the house, boys."

Stanley stood back and took his time and stared at the walls.

Then they heard him say, "Whoops! Here is a small hole in the wainscoting, weird place don't know how we missed that."

Max and Hog got up and watched as Stanley first put caulk in the hole and then paint over it and they just looked at each other.

Later that evening when everybody was gone Hog and Max came back. They dug out the hole, shined the flashlight in it and saw something shiny. Hog had some needle nose pliers and put them in and pulled out a bullet casing. He looked at Max and said, "I think we just hit paydirt."

[Chapter 49]

When Thomas heard the story, he was bug eyed. "You are making this up aren't you, Max?"

"No, I wish I could say I was but all of it really happened. What do we do now?"

"First off, we call your lawyer and get him over here and I hope to God he knows what to do with all this." Thomas stated.

When Morris Lane the lawyer arrived, he listened carefully to the story. "I will say that this is a very unusual case and I have to give it some thought. However, what you tell me about the police detective and Ali and Deidre who all want to control people. We will have to be very smart with this. First, we need to send that bullet casing to an independent laboratory because we can't trust the police lab. Detective Finley might be able to keep it from our purview. I will come up with a plan.

Max's trial date came and now it was game on. The first part of the trail lasted a full day. The prosecution laid out its case and the defense theirs. The fact that fragments of Max's ID found at the scene proved he was there. The police were trying to make a case without having Ali testify if possible. But if Ali gave an eyewitness report of Max killing Joe that would make an airtight case. The second charge was more serious, it consisted of charges for the murder of all the victims of the serial killer. The prosecutor stated that they suspected Max of killing several other prominent people and that he may be the serial killer. Morris Lane protested vehemently, and the judge made them strike it out of the record, but it put a thought in the mind of the jury. The charge of the serial killings was dropped for now but could be pressed at another time.

The trial was not going well for Max and to make matters worse, in order to show his good character and name his lawyer revealed why he was posing as a homeless street person and Max felt his credibility with the people in camp went totally down the drain. He did not talk to Hog about any of it before the trial and when he looked over at Hog, he turned his head. Max felt very sad about that. As the trial went on it seemed that all the evidence, although mostly circumstantial, was against Max.

Morris asked that the police lab tech be brought in to testify and he questioned the tech about the ring. The prosecution was surprised as they were not going to present the ring as evidence, but Morris subpoenaed the police lab records, and they showed where the ring had been swabbed and the blood of both Ali and Joe were both on the ring. This put a different slant on the killer and the question of why Ali would have kept the ring if robbery had been the killer's motive. Further, why wasn't Max's blood not on the ring?

As Max looked around the courtroom, he saw Lenny and several others from the camp who came to cheer him on. He was happy to see that Ellie was there. Max was rather surprised to see Marlene and Deidre there also. Detective Finley was there and would be testifying to the evidence he had collected and the interviews he had conducted.

Several people Max knew from the Winning Circle were there not by choice but had been subpoenaed to testify. They called Ali to the stand, and he was very perturbed about that. He was not cooperative and would only answer with yes and no answers. Morris asked the judge if he could treat him as a hostile witness and the judge agreed. This gave Morris some leeway in what he could ask Ali. After several leading questions he asked, "Did you kill Joe?'

"No, I did not kill Joe."

With an innocent face and trying to look as sad as possible, he told his story of losing his best friend and of course they found blood from both he and Joe on the ring because after he awoke from his unconscious state, he tried to help Joe and cut his hand. The prosecuting lawyers made it seem as if Ali turned the ring over to the police as evidence, but Morris stated he had to subpoena the police lab to get the evidence.

Deidre was called to the stand next and testified that she took the ring from Ali's apartment. She also told the court that the reason she took the ring was because Ali was blackmailing her. Deidre said Ali told her he killed Joe because he got in the way of his and Marlene's relationship. When Deidre made that statement Ali jumped up and called her a lying whore. Deidre screamed curses at him from the stand. An uproar broke out and the judge banged his gravel for order. When she completed her testimony Deidre stepped down from the stand and walked to her seat.

Ali who was sitting behind Deidre began to heckle her.

"Hey, you lying tramp does John know you would screw anybody for money. Is he ok with that? You have no talent and will never make it as a decorator Marlene only kept you because I told her what a pathetic person you are. She really didn't like your work.

"Shut your face your disgusting bastard Ali."

"I'm going to tell John how you really liked it in bed, and you begged for more and more like a cheap street whore that you are, he'll like that, knowing that his girlfriend sleeps with anything that walks."

"I'm warning you Ali shut up right now."

"He should have seen right through you before; he will never make anything of himself with you as an anchor around his neck."

"I'm gonna tell you once more to stop it and if you don't you will be sorry."

"John's not a bad guy by himself but with you sucking off him he will never make it."

Deidre calmly got up and walked across the courtroom and got close to the guard, as if she was going to tell or ask him something, she then took his pistol and turned toward Ali and fired twice. She hit Ali once in the chest and one bullet hit Max.

Chaos broke out in the courtroom, and it was mass hysteria with people running every which way afraid of getting shot. The police grabbed Deidre and took her down. The EMTs arrived but they could not save Ali. They checked Max's wound and saw a small trickle of blood on his shirt. Then they took off his shirt and jacket. They saw a small wound on his chest. It looked like a small piece of metal stopped the bullet from penetrating deeper into his chest. Max looked down at the wound and remembered he had placed his lucky coin in his shirt pocket, and it had prevented the bullet from killing him. The EMT cleaned the wound and Max was ok to go home.

Later that week the case against Max was dismissed. Max talked with Thomas and his lawyer.and said, "I'm shocked at Deidre, what is going to happen to her?"

"She will be going away for a long time if not forever," Morris said.

"I know she shot Ali but is it possible she could get a manslaughter charge instead of murder?"

"That could happen," Morris said within uncertainty, but I'm pretty sure that's not how it's going to go for Deidre. I never had a chance to talk with you about this but remember the shell casing you gave me when she shot Ali the first time?"

"Yeah, what about it?" asked Max.

"It was a match to the body they found in the backyard at Green House, and we know she kill Ali. When they questioned her, she said she kept John Finley as her boyfriend for two reasons. One so she could keep her eye on the evidence the police had on the murder of the janitor and two because he was feeding her lawyer brother cases to keep him in business."

"Oh, Jesus, I can't believe it! That's the guy that secret room in the Green Street house?"

"That's the one. Oh yeah, Deidre spelled her guts about the old man to see if she can get off with a life sentence. It seems she lived around here when she was a little kid, and the old house was abandoned then. Across the street there was a building which has been torn down, it was an orphanage. The man in the secret room was the janitor who lived in the basement of the orphanage. He lured little girls into the basement and raped most of them and abused others, Deidre didn't live in the orphanage but played with the kids there. Deidre's best friend was one of those girls and she told her about the janitor. Deidre's best friend and the other kids played in the deserted house. She knew about the secret room and stashed the body there because she was afraid, they were on her trail, there was no other place to hide the body. When they started to remodel the house, she knew she had to get the body out of the secret room, or someone would find it.

"But the doors were all locked and the windows of the house all boarded up the painters told me that," Max informed them.

"Deidre and the other kids knew a way to get in through the basement door where the janitor used to get in and out without being seen," Morris said.

"I would have never suspected that. She was so concentrated on her career and getting the decorating right."

"She knew the victim that's why there was never a struggle. She felt that the janitor was an abuser and got away with it and she couldn't stand that since she knew so many of the girls at the orphanage or foster homes were abused. Her brother the lawyer confirmed her story. He said she talked about getting revenge for them for a long time."

[Chapter 50]

Max went back to the camp and talked to the people there and asked them for their forgiveness and permission to write their stories. He promised never to reveal their names or location and they agreed. He told them that if they ever needed or wanted his help, he would help them in any way he could.

Max, Morris, Thomas, Ellie, and Hog got together to have a meal and catch up on what they were all doing now. After they had brunch, they ordered coffee and dessert and Max suggested they make a toast to a job well done and a great life moving forward. As they toasted, they heard sirens in the background, and they looked at each other and laughed.

Max was so grateful to everyone who helped him. "My grandfather's prediction came true the coin saved my life. My next important job before I even begin my book was to go to camp and apologize to the people there and ask their forgiveness for deceiving them which I have done. Now I will begin to put all the material I collected and dear Ellie documented for me and move ahead with my book.

Ellie was sitting next to Max and gave him a kiss on the cheek and a hug. Ellie and Max had become very close in the last few months. Everybody clapped and they each began in turn to talk about the coming year and how all of the things that happened had brought them so close together.

The noise of the sirens grew closer, and two police cars pulled up beside the restaurant followed by several other cars. The two policemen got out and ran up into the restaurant and stopped at table the group was sitting at. They told Ellie to stand up and put her arms behind her. She did and they placed her in hand cuffs. She had a look of surprise and then sadness and hung her head but said nothing. The others began protesting asking why they were doing that to Ellie. Max tried to get to Ellie's side but was held back by several other officers.

They walked Ellie to the squad car, and they began reciting her rights to her. The others were astounded and tried to console Max and asked each other what could have happened. Why they were arresting Ellie. Another plain police car pulled up and Detective Finley stepped out. He went to their table and asked if he could talk with them for a minute. All of them began talking at once and Finley held up held up his hand for them to stop.

Finley had apologized to Max and the group for his part in Max's false arrest and was being sanctioned by the police department for his actions. Finley began by saying he was sorry for how they arrested Ellie and asked if he could explain.

"You see we have been watching Ellie for a few weeks. We know she worked at a soup kitchen twice a month. Two months ago, they shut down the building where the soup kitchen was housed. On the last day they served food, Ellie was there and forgot her briefcase. One of the regulars who was a woman Ellie befriended found the briefcase and knew it was Ellie's. She ran after Ellie to try and give it to her but couldn't catch her. So, she decided to open it and see if her home telephone or address was in it. When she opened the briefcase, she found a gun in there. She was surprised but thought maybe Ellie had it for protection when she came to this bad neighborhood. She didn't know what to do now so she told one of the men she knew, and he convinced her they should pawn it. They took the gun to the pawn shop, when the owner saw the gun, he said he couldn't take it and called the cops. The woman and her friend grabbed the briefcase and ran away. The cops came and tracked down the two people from the description the shop owner gave them and brought them in for questioning. They ran the gun through ballistics and lo behold the slugs from two of the serial killings matched the gun."

"No, I don't believe any of that," insisted Max. "Ellie is as straight as an arrow she wouldn't hurt a fly."

"I'm just telling you the facts because I know all of you have been through some tough times. You can come down to the station house to see her tomorrow after she has been processed, I will leave you to yourselves now," and Finley got up and left. The group was in disbelief.

The next day Max and Morris went to see Ellie, she refused to see Max but accepted Morris as her attorney. Morris talked with Ellie and Max waited. Max was physically fully recovered from his time living on the street, but this shook him up. He was shocked but certain that this was all a mistake, and it would all be alright as soon as Morris got the whole story and got everything straightened out.

When Morris came out, he told Max that he was going to try his best to help Ellie but that Ellie did not give him much information. "Max did Ellie seems different to you in the last few weeks?"

"No, I didn't see Ellie much the last few weeks. Her mother lives in Florida and she was sick, and Ellie was staying there to take care of her."

The trial had been postponed three times, once by the district attorney and twice. By Morris. When Ellie was first arrested Max asked Morris to defend her and he agreed, but Ellie had not been trying to help Morris to preparing her defense. He asked for a postponement because he did not have much evidence for a good defense.

Within a few weeks a lawyer named Jerry Comstock Jenkins called Morris and told him he had been hired to defend Ellie and he would like Morris to work on the case with him. Morris agreed and was happy to have the assistance especially because Jerry Comstock Jenkins was a well-known defense attorney and had gotten some big-name celebrities off criminal charges and a man for embezzlement of millions of dollars who ended up being sent to a "Gentleman's prison," for a few short months. He gained most of his fame when he got a cartel boss off on probation when he was accused of killing 6 people in front of witnesses.

When Morris asked Jerry how he heard about Ellie's case or if he knew her, he told him it was immaterial. Morris told Max about Jerry's notoriety and he was as surprised as Morris was. They talked about who hired Jerry, and Max suspected that Ed Donaldson the newspaper editor and part owner of a publishing company probably was footing the bill for Jerry but didn't want it to be public knowledge.

Max, Morris, Thomas, and Hog got together to discuss Ellie's case to see if there was any way they could help. The shock of them being there celebrating Max's freedom and then seeing Ellie get arrested right there at their table, before their very eyes, stuck with them, especially when Ellie refused to say anything to defend herself.

[Chapter 51]

Feeling very distraught about Ellie and needing help with editing and preparation to get his book published Max returned to his old office at the newspaper and began putting his story together. He was grateful to Ed for allowing him to return and helped by writing a story or column if they were shorthanded. The newspaper editor, Edward Donaldson known to everybody as Ed had spent many years as a reporter and was as tough as nails but had a good heart. He was as concerned about Ellie as anybody and asked how the groundwork for the case was going often. Max suspected that it was he who was paying Jerry to defend Ellie, but he never said a word. When Max asked him point out right, he denied he was paying him. Later he heard a rumor in the office that Ed and Ellie's mother were once lovers. Who cares, thought Max as long as he helps Ellie.

Ed told Max that he could work with Jo Ellen, who was an assistant photographer and copy editor, to work with him when she was not on assignment. She mostly checked on facts for the stories or did research to keep the facts straight when pictures were published for the newspaper. She knew Ellie and Max from office parties but did not work closely with them. After becoming familiar with Max's outlines for the book and felt she understood the story, she suggested that he use some photographs to illustrate his main points. Max did not like the idea and had promised not to reveal the names of the people he wrote about so he felt that would not work. He did not want to bring attention to them about where they lived. There was a staff meeting that afternoon and Ed asked Max to stay after the meeting for a few minutes.

"Max, I want to ask you to do something for Ellie," Ed told him.

"For Ellie? Sure, what is it I would do anything to help her."

"As her boss I got a call from the resident manager at her apartment building this morning and they want her things moved out of her apartment because they want to rent it out. I thought maybe you might want to do that yourself and store her things unless you know of someone else that would want to do it."

"I can do it. When did they say it had to be done by?" Max asked.

"They want everything out by the end of the month and since it is already the 27th so it should be done pronto," Ed stated emphatically.

"Ok I'll make sure it's done by the 31st," Max agreed.

Max decided to ask Hog to come with him to Ellie's apartment and help him sort out all her things after all they were good at that by now.

"Hey Hog, how are you doing?" Max asked after giving the man a bear hug and a slap on the back.

"I'm hangin in Max what brings you around?" Hog inquired.

"First, I miss you guy. I miss talking with you and our working together and just everything in general. But I did come with a purpose. I was wondering if you had any plans for the weekend?"

"Ya, I do, boy I do. Janey, my wife, asked me to come to her house and we're hav'in a barbeque. Ribs, chicken, the whole schemer, and she's gonna ask my son to come. She been jawin with him he might be coming around some if you know what I mean."

"Hog that is the best news I heard in ages, I hope it all works out for you, you deserve it," Max said smiling from ear to ear.

"What're you gonna do?"

"Ed at the paper asked me to clean out Ellie's apartment and I thought about sorting out stuff and I know you are great at that, but you're doing something way better than that."

"Cin, it wait. I would help but…… and Hog's voice trailed off.

"No way, no way should you change your plans. I'm going to get Thomas and he will help me but he's not as good at it as you," Max exclaimed.

"Now you're joshin me Max," ya know I would help you out, but Janey is prettier than you," Hog jived.

"You are definitely right about that," Max said, with a chuckle. Do you need any scratch Hog?"

"There's a Grant waiting at the pawn shop from some of the last stuff we sold and there may be more.

"I'm ok."

"Fifty bucks, that's not too bad, there must be a few more things still hanging around from the junk we got from the Green Street house right!" asked Max.

"Yeah, could be, I'll check it out when I go get the coin," Hog confirmed.

"Ok let me know how the barbecue goes I'm pulling for you," Max called as he walked off to go to his car.

[Chapter 52]

Max called Thomas and asked him to come with him to get Ellie's apartment cleaned out. There wasn't so much stuff that he couldn't have done it himself, but he wanted moral support.

Saturday morning, they went to Ellie's apartment. It felt kind of eerie with only a small light on, so they opened the curtains and put on all the lights. The one-bedroom apartment that was once cozy and well-kept was a total disaster. The cops did a very thorough search looking for more evidence. Ellie told Max once that she had most of her mother's old furniture when she moved to Florida because she was paying her way through school to get her masters. The bedroom was quite spacious with two small portable closets the contents of which had been pulled apart and thrown on the floor. The mattress was cut open and left with the stuffing hanging out.

Thomas began packing up the kitchen and Max went down to the storage area to get several suitcases that were stored there. He brought them up to the apartment and took them into Ellie's bedroom and began picking up the clothing and putting them in the suitcase. He had cleaned up the top of the pile when he gave a whoop of surprise.

Thomas called form the kitchen, "Max what's wrong?"

Max replied, "you need to come and see this, Thomas."

Thomas went to the bedroom and Max pointed at the clothes on the floor. He held up several low cut, short, sexy sequined dresses, halter tops and short skirts and shoes.

"Look at these shoes," Max invited, "they must be seven-inch-high heel with no backs."

"If I'm not mistaken, I think they call those fucking shoes Max." exclaimed Thomas with a look of wonder on his face.

There were all kinds of big dangling earrings and rhinestone necklaces and costume jewelry scattered all over the floor.

"Where do you think she wore this kind of stuff?" Asked Thomas I've never seen Ellie dress like that have you?"

"Never she always had on sweaters and collared blouses and clothes that were more business-like.

"No, I mean I don't know what to say, I had no idea, I never knew Ellie to wear anything this flashy, she must have had another life that I don't know about," Max intoned sadly. "I sure am glad you're here with me to see this because no one would believe I found this stuff."

"It looks like she had a wild side to her, I guess," Thomas said. Maybe she was a dancer or in a play or something," Thomas said grasping at straws to explain the gaudy, sexy looking garb and thinking some bad thoughts.

"That must be it, that must be it she must have had to take a drama course and been in a play or something," Max said, as his voice dropped off in disbelief.

"So, no big deal," Thomas threw out, "Just pack it all up and worry about it later there may be a very good explanation for this."

The last room left was the bathroom, there was a small chest of drawers against the wall with the drawers left open and Max could see there were G-strings and thongs hanging out of it and sex toys on the floor, he gasped.

After they had packed up all of Ellie's things, they took them down to the car and turned in the key. And as they drove to Max's place, he was very silent.

"What's eating you Max," asked Thomas.

"I was just thinking, what did the cops think when they found all this stuff I mean they probably took pictures to use as evidence of her character and all this stuff surely made her more suspicious. Maybe they would think that's how she lured them to wherever they were killed with those outfits. I feel so guilty saying that I don't know what to think I'm all mixed up," declared Max.

"It is all crazy, I agree," Thomas reflected, but we can't make any judgements because we can't ask Ellie about it so we will have to keep it all to ourselves and just forget about it."

"I'm embarrassed for her," Max confessed, "and to think I was going to bring Hog here to help me clean that mess up."

"Max he must have seen this kind of thing before living on the street and being a biker don't you think?"

"Yeah, probably but not when it's somebody you know and somebody who is not like that in life. He always thought she was someone special who stood by me like that, he thinks she is a sweet girl."

"She is and this should not change that perception she still has a good heart and was willing to help you when it could have been dangerous for her. We can't forget that."

"You're right we can't forget that if only she would let me see her and talk to her, I would feel so much better.

[Chapter 53]

Jerry Comstock Jenkins was cock sure of himself and let everybody he came in contact with know it. His stance with his head held high made you think he thought he was better than anybody else. He came from a prominent family in Boston and their claim to fame was that their family came over on the Mayflower. Jerry was first in his class at boarding school and then went to Harvard undergraduate and law school. He also spent two years at Oxford in England before coming back to join his father's law firm, Jenkins, Kennedy and Smith. His retainer to represent clients was $50,000 and any additional billable hours needed for research.

Jerry was married to a socialite Betty Brownstone of the Brownstone Building Industry and was educated at Harvard in world literature and the Arts. They had a boy and a girl and seemed like a model family.

Both Thomas and Max started doing research on Jerry's background as soon as they heard he would be representing Ellie. They stopped guessing who was paying Jerry's bill and instead wanted to make sure he was going to give her his best. Neither Thomas nor Max had gone to college at Harvard, but Thomas had several friends that did. The main guy, Luther, who could probably help was out of the country at the moment, but

Thomas called his buddy Michael Goshen, to ask about Jerry since he went to Harvard too.

When Michael heard what Thomas wanted, he was more than willing to help, in fact he was overjoyed. It seemed that Jerry and Michael have a few acquaintances in common and though Michael did not say what happened he wanted a piece of Jerry's ass for some reason. Michael met Thomas and Max one evening and told them all he knew about Jerry.

Michael told Thomas and Max that Jerry was not all he seemed, yes, he won some big cases, but he was not really a nice fellow. Michael and his friends had gone to several parties with Jerry, and he had a way of wanting what other men had including their wives. What was known only in some very private circles was that Jerry and Betty had what is called an open marriage. In public they were about as loving and respectable a couple one could meet, but in private they each went their own way. There was a rumor that Jerry was AC/DC, but no one really knew for sure. Anyway, one thing Jerry was hooked on was watching dirty dancing and strippers and he would go to the raunchiest club he could find, disguised because he didn't want anyone to know who he was. Sometimes he would have his front man go backstage and hire two or three of the girls for the night after the show. It was even rumored that he went to drag queen shows and did the same.

"I can't stand the man for what he did to my friend, Kevin. Kevin was a good friend of mine, and he was in business. He worked so hard to get it started he was not rich like the other guys, but he was doing quite well with 4 retail stores and two more on the way. He sold only toys that were made in American. When the first big waves of electronic toys from overseas were introduced and were so cheap his business began to bottom out. Michael knew this was coming and was trying to steer his business in another direction to become a specialty store with personalized toys something like the Build a bear line, but he was not fast enough and didn't have enough liquid capitol. His stores started going under one at a time. Jerry always had plenty of big money and he approached Kevin knowing he was having a bad time of it. He gave him a proposal if Kevin would give him his wife for one weekend Jerry would bail him out and make sure his new business would be a success.

"Oh my God," both Thomas and Max almost said at the same time, "What happened?"

"Now you need to know that Kevin and his wife Tiffany had a great marriage. They were like two peas in a pod and had been that way since they met in college. One evening when Michael and his wife were drinking and pondering what they were going to do, Kevin told Tiffany about Jerry's proposal and was taken by surprise that she knew about Jerry's offer because Jerry had already approached on his own and persuaded her to go to lunch with him. He told her how enamored he was with her and told her about the proposal he made to Kevin," Michael was shocked.

"I'm on pin and needles wanting to know what happened," Thomas anxiously let out, "What happened next what did Kevin's wife do?"

She talked with Kevin and wanted to know what he thought about the idea. Remember they were desperate and were about to lose everything they owned plus be in debt maybe for the rest of their lives, and here is this guy throwing them a lifeline so to speak. Kevin was violently opposed. He told her he would rather die than have her sacrifice herself like that because that's what it amounted to. Kevin wanted her to promise she would not even entertain the thought and forget about the whole thing. For a few months they continued to work hard and never spoke of it again. Then one day there was a knock on the door, and they were served papers telling them that they had 30days to vacate the property because the house was going up for foreclosure. They had already sent their kids to her sisters and closed all the stores so there was nowhere for them to go. Kevin began to drink heavily and was out of it most days. One day Tiffany, in her desperation, contacted Jerry and spent the weekend with him. When she got back, she found Kevin passed out in the back yard with several bottles of booze around him. He was a mess. When he came to his senses, they packed up the things and put their last money into a mobile home and hit the road.

Now they had the money Jerry promised but Kevin refused to use any of it. Kevin got off the booze and they both found jobs and after 6 months began to put their lives together again. Although they lived together, they did not share much. After a few months went by Kevin decided it was time they got together again and after a good meal and a pleasant evening they went to bed together for the first time and had sex for the first time since the Jerry thing. All seemed to be well they have great sex and the next morning Kevin suggested they shower together the way they used to do in the past. When they got in the shower Kevin saw it for the first time.

"What was it what did he see," asked Thomas.

It was a tattoo just about her pubic area, it said, "she's not yours anymore with a little arrow pointing down."

"Oh, brother, that would be the last straw for me," Max declared, "but what did Kevin do?"

Kevin got out of the shower dressed and broke into the last store that they had. He tied himself to the supporting beam and set the place on fire. They found a note he left that said, "At least you will have the insurance money from the fire, instead of Jerry's blood money to get clean. I loved you more than money, Kevin."

Tiffany went to Jerry and asked him what she should do. He told her he kept his part of the bargain, and she had enough money now to do whatever she wanted, "Just be smarter and don't pick out somebody like Kevin again."

"Holy shit that certainly gives us a true picture of what Jerry is about," said Max, "And it makes me nervous."

Michael stood up, "I hope I gave you what you needed. Myself I hate the guy for some of the other stuff he pulled that I know about but that's not what you needed to hear." I got to go, keep in touch Thomas."

"Max, you need to settle down. What we heard is about Jerry's private life not what he is capable of. I hate to say this, but I don't care if he is a monster, we only care about getting get Ellie off."

"Yeah, I guess you're right it's just that we don't know how he got here and what are his real costs if he does get her off?" Max said worriedly. "What if she got mixed up with Jerry's crowd and will have to pay back with more than she can afford, and I don't mean in money."

[Chapter 54]

Hog had a wonderful time over the weekend with Janey. They had a barbeque and Janey had invited a few of her friends and they all seemed to like Hog. She was living in a trailer park and most of the people knew each other. Some of them retired and took their RV on trips all around the country and would return to home base to rest. It was mostly adults with few little children so the time the group got together often.

Janey had invited Marcus their son, and he showed up and was not as friendly as Hog would like but he at least shook Hog's hand and asked how he was. He didn't stay long, and Janey was disappointed, but Hog told her they needed to give him some space and he would come around in his own good time.

Anthony, who had the double wide a few spaces down from Janey worked in a mechanics shop. He and Hog had a lot to talk about and he told Hog about all the computer information that was available now and how people really paid for advice about what was wrong with their bikes or cars. He told Hog about how the computer was used to diagnosis what the problems were and that it was much easier these days than when you had to trouble shoot everything in the car before you could get an answer to the problem. Hog enjoyed talking to him and before the evening was up, he invited Hog to come to see where he worked. Hog wondered if Janey put him up to entertaining Hog knowing he would be among strangers.

Janey had not lost her touch when it came to cooking and others brought side dishes and there was more than enough for all that came. Janey ended up giving out doggie bags to most of the guests as her refrigerator was small and would not how many leftovers.

After everybody left, Hog and Janey sat close to the firepit and talked about old times. They were both wrapped in a blanket, and they hugged and kissed but were not intimate. That didn't matter to Hog, he was just as content to be sitting with Janey and able to put his arms around her.

It was getting late, and Hog had ridden the old bike that Max had restored and he wanted to make sure he could still ride it back. He got up to go and Janey told him it was too dark out to ride the bike.

"Why don't you stay I have the other bedroom all fixed up and it would be better if I didn't have to worry about you getting home safe," Janey suggested. Sound like a winner to me," Hog agreed.

The next day Hog got up and Janey made him breakfast and they went for a walk down by the pond and they enjoyed each other's company. As they sat on the bench at the pond Janey asked Hog if he ever thought about them being together again.

"I wish I could tell you all the times I dreamed of us and how we were, and I often wondered if it were possible for us to get together again. For sure I know it wouldn't be the same as so much time has passed and we live in different worlds now," Hog said sadly.

"I dig it Hog. I really do. The thing is we are not getting any younger now and time is passing. I know how important and emotional it is for you to make up with Marcus, your son, but that will take time too. I have had nothing but a struggle after what happened, and I was able to move forward but I'm not where I want to be in life. Are you?"

"I never give it a thought like that. I don't plan on what is going to happen day today because mostly they are all the same. That is until Max came along. That guy is something. He thinks I saved his life, but that ain't so, it is really the other way around. He is so funny and is willing to take a chance on anything. We worked together, cried together, laughed together, and got drunk together. And the thing about it is that he never tried to coax me into leaving the camp or starting a new life, although he offered me a chance, but he wanted me to do my own thing, to do what made me happy."

"Are you happy now with what you have?' asked Janey.

"I don't know nobody has ever asked me that." Hog said.

"Max took me at what I was, he never asked me about my past I told him about it when I was ready. That says a lot about a person who could have left me to fend for myself when I snatched by the cops, but he stuck by me and saved my ass.

"Hog," Janey said, "I'm asking you to come back to me and start a new life like the one we had before. I know it can't be the same, but I love you, I have never stopped loving you even though I was a hateful bitch, deep within my heart I never stopped loving you."

"I know exactly what you mean Janey," Max said teary eyed. "I never stopped loving you either, but the life I live now is so different. I live on the street because I thought there was no one who cared for me and that was all I had. Do you think we could start again?"

"Do you remember what you used to tell our sons when they couldn't tie their shoes and they would beg for you to do it, "Nothin beats a failure like a try."

"Yeah, yeah, I remember. I guess I'm just nervous that it would fail and then what would I do?"

"Let's do this we will start spending weekends together and see how that goes. If we agree, then we will progress to more time together. I'm not gonna push you into doing something you are not comfortable with," Janey said sincerely.

"I'm buyin that, Hog said with a smile on his face."

[Chapter 55]

Max sat back in his soft leather chair with his feet on the desk. It had been a long day because the newspaper was short staffed, and he had worked with them to get some stories ready for print. He was relaxing before doing some work on his book when his phone rang.

Hey Thomas, how are you? What's new?"

I'm just checking up on you. I wanted to see how you were doing and maybe we should get together for dinner this evening."

"That sounds great. I heard Marlene moved into her mansion and it is party time for the elite

"Yeah, that's what I heard too. I was wondering how Hog and Janey were doing?"

They seem to be making progress with getting their lives back together again. I'm so happy about that., Max replied. How did your story go over with the editor, you certainly scooped every other newspaper in town."

"Ed couldn't be more pleased it will be on the front page in tomorrow's edition," Thomas said proudly.

"That's great Thomas I'm looking forward to seeing you. I was just sitting here in my office in my soft chair with my feet on the desk thinking about you, Hog and Morris and how much you all mean to me and of course I worry so much about Ellie. Sometimes I feel she is in trouble because of me somehow and I'm hoping that Jerry is as good as his reputation, no matter what his own personal flaws are, and he can get her off.

When I decided right here in this office to write about homeless people, I was so full of myself at the success of my book and now after my experience of being homeless I feel humbled by these unfortunate souls. I never thought it would change my thinking about other human beings. I wanted to write another book, and I decided I had to become homeless to see how it really felt. You have heard me say this before, I expected to find the nastiest, foulest human beings ever put on this earth among those living on the street, and some of the people I met were mean, nasty and cruel. But mostly they were sad, wretched, forlorn, individuals who lost hope because of life events, problems they were not able to fight off, or addictions. They couldn't escape the demons that chase them, and their lives have been shattered due to a situation they could not control, mental illness or because their emotions got in the way.If I have learned nothing else, I know now that we should have compassion for these broken people because as John Bradford said in the 1500s "There, but for the Grace of God go I.

The End